KNOW YOUR OWN DARKNESS

Howard Robinson

Published by Inspired Quill: November 2020

First Edition

This is a work of fiction. Names, characters and incidents are the product of the author's imagination. Any resemblance to actual events or persons, living or dead, is entirely coincidental. The publisher has no control over, and is not responsible for, any third-party websites or their contents.

This book contains references to depression, trauma, kidnapping and murder.

Contact the author through their website: www.howard-robinson.com

Chief Editor: Sara-Jayne Slack
Cover Design: Venetia Jackson

Typeset in Minion Pro

Paperback ISBN: 978-1-908600-83-7
eBook ISBN: 978-1-908600-84-4
Print Edition

Printed in the United Kingdom
1 2 3 4 5 6 7 8 9 10

Inspired Quill Publishing, UK
Business Reg. No. 7592847
www.inspired-quill.com

Praise for Howard

Micah Seven Five leans much more towards Morse or Midsommer than towards the bleak, melancholy of Nordic noir or the urban grit of The Sweeney. There's considerable detail, following the police investigation while intimately reporting everyday reality. [...] At the end, it's satisfying to be surprised by the final page.

– R. Hoseason,
Murder, Mayhem and More

[Micah] is a very readable, extremely accessible police investigative novel. I enjoyed the way that the narrative flowed, picking up pace as it went along and keeping you engaged right through to the conclusion. The language is modern and there is good humour in the dialogue. I recommend this novel very highly. It should be excellent as a holiday page turner.

– S. Johnson,
reviewer

Howard's use of language [in the Sixth Republic] is both emotive and enticing. Drawing the reader into a world that is only just removed from the one we inhabit. A big thumbs up and 5 very well deserved gold stars for a beatifically crafted story. Highly topical, a little scary in its plausibility, and riveting.

– AC,
reviewer

In respectful memory of AJB,
1963-1973

PROLOGUE

IT WAS 1975, on a Sunday in early June and the sun, which beat down on a group of families relaxing by the outdoor swimming pool, gave this little corner of south east England a Mediterranean feel it scarcely deserved. Its powerful brightness played tricks with Matthew's eyes and made things he knew to be one colour appear to be another. He was sat, cross-legged, at the foot of his mother's sunbed, a sky-blue towel draped across his shoulders, eating an apple and feeling cool with a new pair of sunglasses resting on the top of his head.

The black transistor radio that had been entertaining their mothers all morning played *Never Can Say Goodbye.* Kevin's mum was doing her best Gloria Gaynor, much to her son's obvious discomfort. Despite the heat that warmed Matthew's skin, the temperature of the pool from which he'd only just emerged – at his mother's insistence – had provoked a shiver or two as his body adjusted, goose pimples appearing across his hairless torso. He traced them with his fingernail like a join-the-dot puzzle.

At ten years old Matt revelled in the freedom of the swimming pool; running, jumping and dive-bombing people, most of whom didn't want to be bombed but went along with it anyway. He and three friends from school – Danny Carter and his twin brother Simon, and Kevin Simpson – had reluctantly given into the pleas of their parents and were eating a picnic on the grass alongside the sunbeds on which their mothers cultivated unlikely tans. Other children, only some of whom they knew, occupied themselves in a similar manner with their own families at different points around the pool's perimeter. Matthew, Danny, Simon and Kevin – and the twins' older brother Mark – played a game of Cluedo as they waited impatiently for their mothers to decree that their food had been properly digested. Occasionally the board, which was perched on the end of one of the beds, would topple off, scattering dice and pieces round and about. Despite the inconvenience, within an hour the boys had finally found Reverend Green guilty of the heinous crime, perpetrated with some lead piping in the library. Satisfied with their work, they placed everything back into the box and, parental approval given, returned to the pool.

MATTHEW WOULD COME to remember the morning as one of blithe independence and fun; in fact, the last of its kind. He would recall the afternoon, with hindsight, as the first black milestone in a hitherto bright young life and one that would cast a cool shadow over all of them in different ways as they transitioned from boys into men. Matthew's recollection of the exact sequence of events that followed would become a little shadier with the passage of time, but he would always remember with clarity the piercing scream of Kevin's mother. Not even Gloria Gaynor could have hit a high note like that. The discordant sound would become embedded in his mind, in much the same way that it shattered the tranquillity of the late summer afternoon.

"Oh my God, it's Danny."

In the decades that followed, Matthew had re-heard it countless times in his quietest moments and revisited it himself when his eyes were shut and his head rested on a pillow. His mind's eye would show him three men, two of them fully clothed and the third in swimming shorts, dive in to retrieve the young boy's lifeless body from the bottom of pool. He could recall how it felt to be transfixed with horror as he watched them scoop Danny out of the water and lay him on the concrete beside the pool.

His heart rate always stepped up when he thought about it; tightness closed in across his chest. He could still see how the body of his young friend had taken on a bluish hue and could taste again the tension and the all-pervading terror in the back of his throat. So many years on, he experienced anew the panic of that once calm and carefree afternoon. He could remember the disbelief etched onto every face, recalled how his mother had turned him away so that he wouldn't watch the futile attempts to breathe life into one that was now lifeless.

Danny was dead at eleven years old.

Suddenly and brutally the fun was over in the most profound and awful way. And that was as much as Matthew knew; then and now. But that was the moment when it all began.

He could barely recall the car journey home. He had witnessed death up close for the first time and it had been somebody he'd been playing with until moments before, somebody who had been vibrant and alive in every sense of the word; yet nobody had asked him then or since if he was okay. He felt selfish even thinking about it. There had been no offer of counselling. Nobody enquired if he wanted to talk or had questions to ask. Nobody recognised his grief or his confusion. And yet at home and at school it enveloped him.

Now, more than thirty years on, Matthew knew that Danny's death had touched and disturbed him in a most profound way. Why had he survived and Danny not? How would people have reacted if it had been him instead of Danny? Why hadn't he been saved – he could only have been at the bottom of the pool for a matter of seconds; there had been plenty of people present. Surely, somebody should and could have been able to do something. In the years following, that day had eaten away at Matthew's sense of self; the damage had become not only irreversible but had also compounded every setback, little and large, that he had endured since. It had contributed to what he had come to consider a cancer of his soul.

CHAPTER ONE

JACK MUNDAY ROLLED a little to his right and in the half-light of the early morning studied the face of the woman lying next to him. To Jack, its soft youthfulness had a depth that reflected authentic life experience. It encapsulated everything that was beautiful about his world, or had been, once. It had been longer than he was proud of since he'd had sex so passionate, so unexpected and conducted with such abandon as last night. But that wasn't, ultimately, what had made it such a wonderful experience. The thrashing and the grinding and the moaning had been great, but it was the simple touch of skin against skin with somebody you loved, had always loved and cared so deeply for that shocked him a little.

Elaine slowly opened her eyes and smiled. It almost felt as if they had been estranged as long as they'd been married. Each day without her had felt like being forced to sit on the periphery of their world – hers and their son Connor's – being only able to observe it from a distance, like a stalker looking through a window into their lives. Each day without her was a reminder of the moment he had lost his mind and hit her. Until last night he'd always thought there might be no coming back.

"Good morning," he whispered.

She smiled. "That was nice. Unexpected but really nice."

They'd been for dinner to talk about Connor. Jack was buoyed by having put another murderer behind bars and for finally securing his promotion to DCI, even though there was no DCI job for him to move into. He hoped that putting on hold a promotion that required him to move away from them had been the right thing to do and that she would see it as his commitment towards rebuilding their family. He wanted it to be the last piece in the reconciliation jigsaw. Sure, he was frustrated that a new superintendent was being brought in above him, but his family was his priority so he would just suck it up for a while. After leaving the restaurant the previous night, they had found themselves in a hotel bar, drinking Bombay Sapphire and then tequila shots as if they were still in their twenties. On the cab journey home one thing had led to another and, well, suffice to say it's how they came to be naked in bed together as dawn broke on a new day. All it needed now, Jack thought, was Barry White playing on the radio and the moment would be complete; cheesy but complete.

Elaine rolled onto her back, her left breast appearing

above the top line of the duvet as she did so, and looked at the clock on her bedside table.

"Shit," she screeched in a half shout, half whisper. "It's six in the morning. You've got to go."

"Calm down, it's Saturday. I don't need to be up for work. I thought I'd have a shower, make you breakfast in bed and then maybe we could go out for the day… or stay in… whichever takes your fancy."

Elaine was already half out of bed, wrapping a bath robe around her body.

"Neither takes my fancy, Jack. You need to be up and out. Connor could be up soon, and he can't see you here. You can shower at your place."

Jack propped himself up in bed. "Slow down. What's the problem? Why does it matter if Connor sees me here?"

"If Connor sees you, he'll get the wrong idea. He'll think we're back together."

"We were pretty together last night."

"Don't joke about this. Come on, get up and get dressed and do it quietly."

Jack leant out of the side of the bed and tried to hook his boxer shorts off the floor with his middle finger. "So what was last night all about?"

"Last night was a shag, Jack. Don't get me wrong it was a good one, not that your ego really needs a boost, but you don't rebuild a relationship like ours on the back of drunken sex."

"It seems a pretty good place to start to me."

"That's what makes us different. I don't want to be a bitch about it but I was off my face. We both were. That's not how this is going to happen, if it's going to happen at all."

Jack was up, boxers on, shirt on but unbuttoned, his trousers discarded in a heap near the bedroom door.

"Even taking that on board, why can't I see Connor?"

"You know the answer to that. If he sees you in a bathrobe, sitting at the breakfast table playing happy families, he'll get his hopes up that we're getting back together and I don't want to do that to him just now."

"Because you don't want us to get back together?"

"Because I don't know what I want."

Jack was dressed.

"I'm not saying last night wasn't fun, I'm just saying I need time."

"Can I grab a coffee before I get thrown out of my own home?"

"Get one from Starbucks on your way."

Given the intimacy of the night they had just spent together, Jack thought Elaine's goodbye peck on the cheek as she opened the door more than a little impersonal.

As he walked away from the house towards the high street and a much-needed caffeine injection, his phone bleeped twice to signify an incoming text. He pulled the phone from the inside pocket of his black leather jacket, its battery level almost requiring intensive care, and opened the message. It was from his colleague Lesley Hilton;

beautiful, curvaceous, flirty, sexy Lesley.

"It's Saturday morning and I'm lying in alone. Want to come round and lie in with me?"

Jack read the message twice. Any other day, he thought, *any* other day and he probably would. He deleted the text and ordered a flat white instead.

CHAPTER TWO

TEN-YEAR-OLD CHARLIE CARTER had run home from school even more enthusiastically than usual, resisting the increasingly loud and frustrated protestations of his mother, Esther, to be careful of the road and to stay where she could see him. He had been waiting outside the front door, panting, for a full five minutes before Esther arrived hand in hand with his younger brother Joe.

Her blonde hair billowed back in the breeze, school bags lodged halfway up her left arm, two Transformers lunch boxes in her right hand as well as her door keys, which were beginning to cut into both her and Joe's wrists. He screamed to alert her just in case she hadn't noticed.

The urgency to get back from work in time to collect the boys from school had been even more of an effort than usual because she knew how excited Charlie was to be home in time to decorate the house for his Dad's birthday dinner. That meant not only having to negotiate the early rush-hour traffic, but also finding the time to stop and buy the cake and candles that Charlie had decreed as mandatory birthday accompaniments. She knew Simon didn't like birthdays, particularly his own, but she wasn't prepared to dampen her little boy's enthusiasm; she didn't want him to take on the prejudices of his father, no matter how understandable they might be.

And so, once in the kitchen, and having been forced to go into the downstairs shower room and wash his hands – not once, but twice, to ensure they were clean enough to pass muster at Esther's inspection – Charlie was allowed to see the items that she had bought. He squealed in eardrum-splitting delight as each item was revealed with melodramatic effect from the confines of a plastic carrier bag: first the candles – blue with a hint of glitter in the stripe; a badge the size of a saucer that screamed out "I'm the Birthday Boy" and, best of all from Charlie's perspective, a Lightning McQueen birthday cake, white icing topped with a picture of the *Cars* star himself, wrapped tightly round the outside with a matching red ribbon. This, Charlie thought to himself, would be perfect.

All Esther had to do was keep Charlie and Joe awake long enough for Simon to get home, for him to be in enough of a good mood to indulge them and for them to administer their 'surprise' quickly. None of which, she knew, was necessarily guaranteed.

To ensure she was as prepared as possible, she fed the boys with individual pepperoni pizza fingers and oven chips. Okay, she thought to herself as she watched them, it wasn't exactly healthy eating but at least they were eating it rather than playing with it on the plate. It gave her as much satisfaction as any mother sticking her middle finger up at the food Nazis who were all over the media. By six thirty both boys were fed, bathed, in their pyjamas and sitting on the bottom stair near the front door of their recently built 'executive' house awaiting their father's return.

Within fifteen minutes Charlie noticed the lights of Simon's car as it pulled onto the drive and began running in excited circles around the hall, mimicked by Joe. Monty, their jet-black cocker spaniel, sat and watched them in some kind of canine disbelief.

They waited as a key turned in the lock, Simon's worry-worn face cracking into a smile as the two little ones ran enthusiastically towards him. Esther knew the tell-tale signs of stress by now: a slight flickering of his left eye and a flaring of the eczema evident just beneath the shirt cuff on his right hand. He dropped onto his knees and both boys wrapped themselves around him, clinging on tightly as he climbed back to his feet with both still gripping like molluscs to a rock as water swirls around it. For a moment, Esther thought she detected just a hint of happiness in his eyes.

"Good day?"

He nodded. "The usual."

"The boys have something for you."

"Oh yes?"

"Yes!" shouted Charlie, repeated almost immediately by Joe, as they continued to cleave tightly to their father's torso, at one point threatening to rip his shirt until Simon rearranged them both mid-stride. They entered the kitchen and the boys escorted Simon to a seat at the table and made him promise to close his eyes and keep them shut. He nodded, though Esther thought she could detect early signs of frustration. The boys, checking frequently that their father wasn't peeking, helped Esther carry the cake bearing four lit candles to the table and began singing happy birthday when they were within a pace or two of their father. When given permission to do so, Simon opened his eyes, beamed as wide a smile as he could muster, pinned the badge that Charlie had given him onto his shirt and then, encouraging the boys to join him, blew the candles out with one deep gasp of breath. He hugged both boys as close to him as he could before kissing each of them once on the tops of their heads and ushering them up to bed in their mother's arms.

When Esther came back downstairs ten or so minutes later Simon had poured two glasses of red wine, a New World Syrah he had brought back on his last business trip abroad, and was slumped back on the sofa, his tie loosened, the top two buttons on his shirt undone. The television was on but he wasn't watching. Behind him on the corner of their coffee table stood a wooden frame bearing a picture of a small boy a little older than Charlie was now; today of all days Danny was front and centre of

Simon's mind.

"So," said Esther, letting the red wine warm the back of her throat, "someone's now firmly in their forties. You're a confirmed cradle snatcher."

"You're not that much younger." Simon swilled the wine around his glass, watching it coat the surface as close to the top as he could risk getting it without it spilling.

"The boys were really excited for today."

"They were very sweet."

They sat in silence a moment longer as Esther fetched some pretzels from the kitchen and lay the bowl down between them. Simon scratched a red rash on his wrist. Esther reached out to stop him.

"Have you spoken to your mum today?"

Simon shook his head.

"Don't you think you should? I'm sure she would want to wish you happy birthday."

"You know as well as I do that today doesn't have the happy feelings for her that it should. It just reminds her of Danny."

"Sure, I know that. But everything reminds her of Danny; what about *you*?"

"I'm just the constant reminder that he's not here."

"No, but you *are*. Surely she can take some pleasure in that fact without always thinking about Danny. It's not as if it happened yesterday."

"To her, I think, it's exactly as if it happened yesterday."

"And what about you?"

"I think about him every day, too. I wonder what he'd be doing; would he be married? Would he have kids? Would we still be close?" Simon shrugged his shoulders and sipped again from the glass in his hand.

"And what about Mark?"

"Mark?"

"Have you spoken to him? Has he wished you a happy birthday? He's still your older brother. It wouldn't kill him to remember either."

"You say that like you genuinely think he's forgotten. Besides, who speaks to Mark?"

"So today will always be a non-day?"

"I guess so."

"Don't you think it's sad?"

"It is… but not as sad as losing your son or your brother when he's only eleven years old."

"Okay. I hear you. None of you can move on but please don't let something that damaged your childhood damage our own kids' childhood."

Simon nodded again. "I promise."

"Good," replied Esther, "then top up my wine and come into the kitchen, I'll dish up dinner and then you can have a bath and we can have an early night."

CHAPTER THREE

ADELE CARTER HAD been sitting in the same armchair since four in the afternoon; on the small table next to her a telephone rested, waiting in vain to ring. She had started to dial Simon's number on at least three separate occasions but had stopped short each time, unsure what she would say if she followed through and made the call. Thirty-four years may have passed but it might as well have been thirty-four minutes. The feelings remained as vivid, the pain as raw, her sense of loss and helplessness still as palpable.

She looked at the grainy photograph of her lost son – the same image Simon had in the frame by his sofa – and wondered about the fairness in the fact that she had reached her seventy-fifth birthday when Danny hadn't even reached his twelfth?

Earlier in the day she had made her fortnightly pilgrimage to Danny's grave, to tidy up the surroundings and talk to him as if she expected him to reply, before making her way back home on the bus alone. In the early days people would know what today was; some would phone, some would call round, but with the passage of time, people forgot and now, as her contemporaries began to die off, she knew it would be a day she would have to navigate alone. She had hoped that Simon might call, today of all days, but perhaps he was too busy celebrating… or just too busy. They probably should have talked years ago about all this, but now so much time had passed, she wouldn't know how to start such a conversation. She wondered if Simon would spare a moment for Danny today.

She knew that Danny's death had changed forever her relationship with her other sons; it had changed her relationship with most people. Certainly, her marriage to Lenny had never really recovered and in the years since he'd died, she had heard friends whispering to each other behind the palms of their hands that surely it was time for her to move on. The truth wasn't that she didn't *want* to move on necessarily, it was that she *couldn't*; that feeling of missing Danny had never gone away. A piece had been ripped from her that afternoon. Of course, no matter what she thought, the pain now was not as intense as it had been when she'd taken the phone call that sunny afternoon; when it was as if the person at the other end of the phone had been speaking a foreign language. The words had sounded familiar but nothing made any sense. But in the time since, there remained a gaping wound that simply wouldn't heal and nobody, least of all Simon, could do anything to close it. She knew it was unfair on him but nothing had been as unfair as losing Danny.

There was also guilt, of course. This wasn't the inevitable consequence of a tragic illness but something that was avoidable and shouldn't have been allowed to happen. If she had been there, she had convinced herself, it wouldn't have happened. She had turned that anger in on herself. *She* was to blame, and the subsequent isolation came when everyone around her remained at a loss as to what to say to help her move forward.

For some while after Danny's death, the mental effort that was needed to function even at the most basic level was more than Adele had at her disposal. She resented the fact that Lenny had returned to work; how could he think about such mundane things? How could they afford for him not to, he would argue back. Despite the fact she would say truly hurtful things simply because he seemed better able to function through his grief, he remained committed to trying to help her through. They were both experiencing extraordinary stress, the doctor had told them; their normal coping mechanisms were simply not going to be sufficient. It would be a process accompanied by disruption and pain until they each found ways to cope with the intense grief and begin to move on.

Some of us, though, do not. The grief becomes incapacitating. Their reactions had been different. Lenny's response had been active; he needed to do something, *anything* that would bring something positive from such a terrible situation; Simon's response had been to just give in and live with the guilt of having been the twin that survived. Mark's response had been anger. Adele had experienced all of these and more but was unable to see that the depth of her powerlessness was abnormal. Those who managed their grief differently were in some way less respectful of Danny's memory.

Then there were those who, perhaps with all good intentions, simply made things worse. She just resolved never to see or speak to these people again. One friend told her that she should never forget that those who were left behind needed her every bit as much as Danny did. She liked this because it acknowledged that Danny still needed her, but she couldn't move beyond it. It merely increased her sense of isolation.

THE TELEPHONE RANG, splitting the silence and startling her.

"Mum."

"Simon."

And then they both wept.

CHAPTER FOUR

"TELL ME ABOUT Danny," Esther said, without warning, as she and Simon lay in bed. Monty lay curled up on the floor at the foot of the bed and had begun to snore. It seemed safer to ask the question in the pitch darkness of the night than across the breakfast table or over a glass of wine on the sofa. "You've told me often enough what happened. You've never really told me about him."

Simon remained quiet, the silence lying across them like an additional duvet.

"What do you want to know?"

"I want to know what he was like. I want to try and get to know him rather than have him defined by the way he died. I don't want him to be a tragic figure anymore. I want us to be able to introduce him to the boys without everything having to be about his death. We should be able to talk about him. *You* should be able to talk about him."

Simon rolled to face her. Their relationship had always been open – they prided themselves on it – but when it came to Danny, this had always been the one place where Esther couldn't reach Simon. She lifted her hand and ran it down his cheek as if to reassure him that this was a time and place in which he could safely cast off the shackles of his brother's passing. In the darkness she could hear Simon's breathing and feel the rise and fall of his chest against her breasts.

"He was my best friend, even though we bickered; you know, the way brothers do," he began slowly and quietly. "He was always more confident than me, sportier than me, funnier than me."

"I think you're funny," she replied, her head sinking into the feather pillow.

"I don't know. We were alike in lots of ways, I guess. He had a mad sense of humour, as if he didn't know when to stop, but then he had this disarming manner which meant no matter how far he took it, everyone just forgave him anyway."

"I bet you were a real pair together."

Simon sniggered to himself. "Danny was the mischief-maker. He always wanted us to pretend to be each other but we were never alike enough to be able to pull it off. Occasionally he would try it with my grandmother and actually convince her after a while that he was me and I was him but then when he was bored of the joke, he wouldn't be able to persuade her back again."

"I can imagine the two of you being a nightmare for your mum."

"I think we were a bit of a nightmare for Mark, too. The older brother's meant to be the king but it's tough when you've got *two* little brothers snapping at your heels."

"You cramped his style."

"Not sure Mark ever had any style to cramp, but kind of."

Simon reached over and ran his hands through Esther's hair before leaning forward and kissing her just long enough for their tongues to touch. She pushed him gently away, the fingers on her outstretched hand momentarily playing with the dark hair on Simon's chest.

"What do you think he'd be doing if he were still alive?"

It was a question Simon had often considered, but had never found an answer for. Danny had forever been confined to his eleven-year-old self.

"Jeez, I have no idea and what does it matter anyway?"

"It doesn't, I guess, but the more we talk about him the more it keeps him alive in our minds, I suppose."

Simon went quiet again. Esther rolled onto her back and stared upwards towards the ceiling. After a few moments Simon spoke again.

"I think he would've winged his way through life and have been successful on the back of his personality. I'd like to think that we would still be as close as we were, that he'd have a family and that our kids would be best friends. Daft really."

"Why is that daft? Sounds great to me. I wish I'd known him if only so I could tell him that, as much as I loved him, I preferred his better-looking twin brother."

Simon laughed, imagining what Danny's response would have been.

"And what about Mark?" asked Esther.

"In many ways Mark took it hardest of all. He was there that day and for years he blamed himself for not being able to do anything to protect Danny, him being the older brother and all that. I think he thought we all blamed him, which of course we didn't, and he was never really the same person again. I still worry about him. He told me once that at Danny's funeral he thought everyone was talking about him behind his back."

"How old was he then?"

"I don't know, nearly fourteen, I guess."

"Still a kid himself."

"Exactly. We told him that it was just an accident, a horrible and tragic accident but an accident nonetheless, but he never believed us. To this day he still says somebody must have caused it. He needs somebody to blame because if there *is* then perhaps, in his mind, it wasn't his fault."

"And your mum?"

"I can't even start to imagine what it's been like for her, you know, to have to bury your child and live with the guilt that you weren't there to protect him. I don't know if she gets comfort from visiting his grave every couple of weeks but I just can't do it without thinking that it could have been me laying there. I think half the problem between us is that I don't visit his grave that often and somehow she thinks I've either forgotten or it doesn't hurt me anymore. I've just never felt I need to be there to be close to him."

"You need to talk to your mum, you know. You have to ask her the questions you need answers to while you still can."

In the stillness, Simon seemed to process the weight of the comment.

"So, what would you and Danny have been doing for your birthday today?"

"What, if he was still alive?"

Esther nodded into the darkness.

"I don't know. I guess I'd be the one saying keep it simple, it's just another birthday and he'd be the one getting excited, making plans, wanting to celebrate."

"Sounds like Charlie," said Esther.

Simon smiled. He had to admit that it did. Tears formed in his eyes, and as he cried himself to sleep, Esther's arms wrapped protectively around him.

CHAPTER FIVE

A year earlier

MATTHEW WOKE WITH a start. Next to him, Susie slept, her breathing barely audible; no sound came from the children's rooms. Even the road outside was silent. The pillow on which his head lay was cold and wet from his perspiration. His chest, his head and his arms felt damp and heavy, but tremors still rippled through him. The clock on the bedside table showed it to be nearly three in the morning.

The dream had been the same for decades; his body being carried gently by the sometimes warm, sometimes cool water. The sounds he could hear were the distorted resonances of happiness, of innocence, of children playing, of families talking, but each muffled by the water. He could feel himself floating, the absence of gravity making it seem as if he were suspended on air, laying back, relaxing, watching through squinted eyes as the strength of the sun played tricks with the colours of the world around him.

But the dream always ended in the same shocking manner with a single, piercing scream that time and again would wrench him pitilessly from his sleep. He would lay awake in the darkness for the rest of the night, listening to the racing beat of his heart and feeling alone.

LATER THAT MORNING, after the shower's hot water had refreshed him, Matt stood with his back to the kitchen worktop, drinking a mug of hot, black coffee and grasping a slice of granary toast. On the television, Breakfast News presenters tried to combine both solemnity and affability from the edge of a sofa whilst discussing the "global shock" surrounding the previous day's collapse of the investment bank Lehman Brothers. Matt didn't need to be a financial expert to know this was serious. It was the worst day for the markets since the 9/11 terror attacks in 2001 and, although it had been swilling around for a number of weeks, it was, with hindsight, the first time that the term 'credit crunch' had properly entered Matt's consciousness.

He picked up the remote and flipped the channel to CNN, where a young, attractive Asian woman with an East Coast American accent was declaring that the turmoil at Lehman's and another giant, Merrill Lynch, would mean job losses in the already hard-hit financial services sector. So far though, she reported, neither company had indicated how many jobs would be cut.

"This crisis is clearly deeper than anybody had

imagined only a short time ago," a hired talking head from the Wall Street Journal in Asia was telling her on screen.

"Remember the date," he said directly into the camera. "September fifteenth is when the recession got ugly."

And yet still any impact seemed far off; this was all taking place in a different city, in a different country on a different continent. But there had been signs closer to home. So, yes, people were nervous, but somehow nothing more than that. Until now. He clung to the naïve hope that Lehman's issues wouldn't impact too heavily on his own little design business in London. By the end of the day, though, the London Evening Standard would be reporting the looks of shock and horror on the faces of Lehman's traders. They had been forced to leave their offices carrying their personal belongings in cardboard boxes. Head-hunters had set up shop in local bars and cafes to meet people to try and find them new positions in a market that was contracting by the hour.

He folded back the pages of the newspaper and read about a woman with a dog-walking business in West London. Her company had collapsed overnight as bankers decided they no longer needed a professional to look after their dogs. Some, he read, had even decided to have their dogs re-homed to save money. Matt sensed that life for everyone was spiralling downwards and that, soon, there would be little anyone could do to arrest the slide.

It didn't take long for vulnerability to feed into the anxiety which frequently rose within him. Within days, clients that had previously paid him on time were telling him they would now be taking additional weeks and, in some cases, even months to pay. Some took his calls and fed him lies; others simply never took the calls nor returned them either; a few were honest enough to say they simply couldn't afford to pay. As the money coming into the business tightened, it meant less money for food, less money for bills and, critically, less money to meet the mortgage repayments.

The world may have been in the throes of a global recession, but already this was beginning to feel extremely personal. If you take away a person's ability to provide for his family, Matt reasoned, what else does he have to fall back on? Neither he nor Susie had talked about the increasing distance in their relationship; it was the great elephant in their particular room. He dreaded that sense of feeling diminished in the eyes of his family and the looks of pity on the faces of others should their circumstances become obvious. And then there would be the unspoken messages of sympathy for Susie for stoically standing by him.

The exhaustion affected him most; the kind of fatigue that seemed to make every joint hurt and every simple decision much more difficult than it needed to be. It drove him to sleep as much as he could because it was the only place he felt safe and secure. And the more time he had on his hands, the more he wanted to sleep. The more he slept, the more he felt Susie's revulsion.

It had been nearly three years since he and Susie had last made love and, even at that point, it had been both irregular and mundane. There had been no electricity between them. Dare he say it, no sense of love. She would recoil if he even tried to cuddle her and so he'd given up trying. Now they slept back to back, Matt clutching hard to the side of the bed to avoid rolling across in the night and making contact with her, no matter how much he would have liked to. The situation was what it was. Even though he doubted anyone else would want to sleep with him, it was *Susie* who he wanted, nobody else.

The first time somebody had suggested that he might be suffering from depression he had listened with disbelief. At first, he dismissed the notion as preposterous. What did *he* have to be depressed about? Here he was, married, healthy, with two great children, his own home, in work, a wide social circle of friends and outwardly confident, funny; the person that others gravitated towards for reassurance or simply for company. And yet he knew – and soon others would surely guess – that this was all just a mask that he wore; the performance he had perfected. Inside he had none of the energy or the confidence attributed to him and, in truth, he had forgotten what it *really* felt like to be Matt. He'd forgotten what it *really* was to be happy or content or at ease. The energy required to maintain the facade and keep the mask from slipping merely fed the spiral of exhaustion.

Although it was barely autumn, he knew that Susie's

mind was already turning towards Christmas. He had always felt pressure at Christmas; pressure to join in, to be good-humoured, to have fun, to not be the disappointment he felt he'd been for the rest of the year.

He knew Susie hated the way he felt. He could tell by the way that she looked at him. He knew he was no longer the same person she had married. Over the years, her loving looks had moved to disinterest, to pity and now to complete disdain. Their conversation had all but stopped; monosyllabic answers to monosyllabic questions, they spoke rarely about anything other than the functional necessities of life, most of which seemed to revolve around the one thing he could no longer provide; money. He knew she deserved better and, more to the point, *she* knew she did, too.

CHAPTER SIX

JACK MUNDAY'S LIFE *surely* couldn't get much messier. As he lay next to his colleague Lesley Hilton in her bed, the early morning sunlight more effective than any alarm clock, he contented himself that this was about nothing more than the pure physical act of sex. Lesley had told him on more than one occasion that she didn't do relationships, but he had asked himself how true this really was, given that they were now spending at least four nights together each week. Surely that in itself constituted a relationship. Nobody at the station knew about them, or at least he didn't *think* anybody knew, and Lesley had become visibly angry when he'd mentioned it to her, asking him whether he really felt she was the type of person to broadcast such news. He suspected that his sergeant, Harry Duggan, had probably worked them out but, so far, if he had, he'd been decent enough to say nothing. Harry might be the fount of all knowledge; the station's all-seeing eye but, thankfully, he also remained its soul of discretion.

Jack checked the time on his watch, which sat beside him on the bedside table. He had another ten minutes before he needed to get up. Beside him, Lesley began to stir. She lay with her back towards him, a naked shoulder inches from his face. Her sandy blonde hair, always so immaculate when she was on duty, was dishevelled from sleep, making her look all the more attractive. He looked at the contours of her tanned skin and had to stop himself from leaning forward to kiss the nape of her neck as he knew where that was likely to lead. She rolled over, taking care to lock the duvet into place under each arm. She looked up at Jack and smiled as he returned her gaze.

"Sleep well?" she asked.

"Yeah, you?"

She leant forward and kissed him on the lips, placing her hands on both of his cheeks as she did so. He tried to probe her lips with his tongue but as soon as she realised what was on his mind, she pulled away.

"Coffee?"

He nodded.

"You shower first and I'll put the coffee on."

Jack lay back and watched as Lesley climbed out of bed; her taut bottom momentarily at his eye level before it disappeared beneath her robe. He desperately wanted to lean forward and run his hands across it but thought better of it and lay back into the pillows instead.

On some level, he worried that he might be falling in

love with his colleague. At first he thought the sex had been so satisfying because it was illicit and dangerous, but he sensed his feelings towards both women in his life were changing. He still loved Elaine, but the longer she kept him at arm's length the more he began to imagine a future with Lesley. That would be complicated and not only from a work point of view; Jack was pretty sure that Lesley didn't share his feelings. She had no interest in what was going on in other aspects of his life. She never mentioned Elaine or Connor and once, in the midst of a drunken row, had told him she never wanted *him* to mention them either.

Jack showered, shaved and dressed in a black suit and an open-necked white shirt; it could have done with an iron being passed over it, but he really didn't have time this morning. The fact that on the days when he woke up at Lesley's he arrived at the station looking clean rather than untidy was the biggest clue anybody needed to know that something was going on in his private life. He tied the laces on his black brogues and followed the scent of fresh coffee and toasting bread towards the kitchen; talk radio providing a low hum in the background. He ate, he drank and, giving Lesley a kiss on the lips, he left a full ten minutes before she did to ensure they arrived separately at the station.

CHAPTER SEVEN

THE YOUNG WOMAN switched on the bright white light and studied her face in the bathroom mirror before mixing the cheap facial scrub with warm water from the tap. Its ingredients roughed her skin as she rolled the liquid between her fingers and applied it in a circular motion first to her cheeks and then to her forehead, taking away the top tier of dead skin cells and exposing the new emergent layer beneath. She hadn't been in London long but already she felt like she needed to do this often to rid her skin of the city's pollution. She hadn't known what to expect when she'd said her farewells to family and friends and left Ukraine in search of a new life. She knew London would be big but she had no idea *how* big. When she had called her parents to let them know how she was settling in, she had tried to give them an indication; that she thought her hometown of Lutsk would probably fit into one small suburb of this breathtakingly enormous metropolis with room to spare, but she knew that without seeing it for themselves they couldn't possibly appreciate the difference. Her only point of reference for a city had been Kiev and she'd only been there once and that had been to catch the plane to London. The scale, complexity and noise of her new surroundings intimidated and excited her in equal measure. She needed to work hard to fit in, to feel at home, to not be daunted by the underground or overawed by a whole range of things that those around her took for granted: from the rush hour crush, which meant she had to allow more time than she had ever imagined she would need to actually get anywhere, to more mundane things like tea with milk or beans in a sweet, tomato sauce for breakfast.

She banished from her mind all thoughts of Lutsk; of Lubart's Castle, the splendour of Saint Peter's and Paul's Cathedral, and her parents' small but comfortable apartment that she had always called home. Nothing could distract her from forging this new life that she'd promised herself.

Her first task had been to move out of the hostel and find herself a proper place to live. She needed a job to support her while she tried to study in the evenings, perhaps waitressing or cleaning; she didn't really mind what she did as long as it enabled her to pay her way and ideally have enough spare to send home to her parents.

Soon after arrival, one of the Romanian girls staying in the hostel had introduced her to the thriving market among wealthy men in London looking for sex with girls from the East. She had been reticent at first but this wasn't prostitution as she had first envisaged it; this was not about walking streets or standing on corners, but involved smart men and even smarter hotels. And it paid well. She wasn't prudish about sex – not that she would want to tell her parents that this was how she spent her time – and believed what the Romanian girl had told her: that it was merely providing a service, a case of being the supply to meet the demand. She wasn't in a relationship herself (maybe that would change things) and, in some bizarre way, meeting the men had satisfied both her own temporary need for intimacy and company as much as it had for money. Those she had met had mostly been nice enough, gentle, generous even and, as she was scrupulous in ensuring that precautions were always taken, she didn't really see a problem. It was well organised, as safe as it could be and all she had to do was wait for an email or a text to arrive telling her where to go, at what time, and who to meet. Some of the girls would disguise themselves with wigs or heavy makeup, but to her it seemed tawdry and would bring her face to face with the reality of what she was involved with. So instead she always made sure she was clean, smartly dressed and wearing lingerie that enhanced her figure and contrasted with her porcelain skin but not in a way that lived up to the stereotype. She removed any jewellery that meant anything to her and replaced it with some that she had bought purely for the job. Her hair would always be washed and fragrant, her nails neatly and conservatively painted and her face would carry only minimal makeup. She would dab a little perfume on the sides of her neck.

Perhaps naively, she wanted the men she met to see her as a real person; she wanted to talk to them, to find out more about them and it was true that some didn't mind, but in the final analysis their paths only ever crossed for one reason. Some wanted to be mothered, some wanted to be seduced, and some wanted nothing but the interaction for which they were paying. She had quickly become used to identifying the different types and giving them what they wanted in the hope of attracting repeat custom. Her father, who owned a small hardware shop in Lutsk, had always told her it was important to keep the customer satisfied. She pushed to the back of her mind how horrified he would be to know how she was now applying his lesson.

She suspected the men that she met never used their real names and so she had decided that on these visits, Irina would never attend... but Nataliya would. It was more important to her than could be imagined that her two lives be kept completely separate.

CHAPTER EIGHT

THE AUTUMNAL GLOW from the streetlamps washed colour across the sitting room of the small bedsit that Mark Carter had taken on a short term let. The narrow street of Victorian terraces lay quiet as he sat, unshaven and shaking a little from a chill in the air that was more imaginary than real. His arms emerged like sparrows' legs from the fraying sleeves of a stained, white tee shirt and, even with a belt, his trousers hung loose around his waist. In front of him a pack of roll-up papers and a pouch of tobacco were his constant companions. His hands shook as he tried to lay an even line of tobacco across the paper and then roll and seal it ready to be smoked. In the past he'd dabbled with something more 'herbal' but he couldn't afford it anymore so he was back on the conventional stuff, which was expensive enough. In his wallet sat three creased and fading photographs – one, a picture of himself, his eyes wide with expectation, his teeth as bright as the ivory on a piano keyboard and his hair, immaculately side-parted. Looking down at it was like an out of body experience for Mark. He tried to stare into the small boy's eyes and imagine how different everything might have been. But that was just too much of a stretch. Now his eyes were hollow, his skin pasty beige, almost jaundiced, a five o'clock shadow defining his sharp jaw line and cheekbones.

He laid the three photographs on the tabletop in front of him. The second showed Danny in school uniform, a slightly quizzical look on his face where he'd finished smiling moments before the photographer had clicked the shutter. The third was a family photograph taken, Mark estimated, probably six months before Danny's death. He felt like he was looking at a different family, at a different time on the other side of the world. There was a simplicity, a lightness about the image that seemed alien to him; his mother's smile was natural, unforced. Try as he might, he couldn't remember her ever appearing like that and certainly not since. They looked at ease, comfortable, even carefree both as individuals and as a group in a way they'd never been after the day that would define their family for a generation.

They'd told Mark it'd been an accident; a tragic, awful, horrible accident that nobody could have foreseen. He had heard the words a thousand times but there were questions that nobody seemed inclined to answer. Why couldn't it have been prevented? Why didn't any of the adults there *do* something? Why wasn't there a lifeguard on hand, watching, ready and able to jump in and save him? Why Danny? And then, just why? Nobody, it seemed, wanted to talk to Mark and fewer wanted to listen.

They had told him that nobody blamed him; he was only a child himself. These things happen, they had said. That in time, things would slowly hurt less and the pain would begin to subside. But the pain had never subsided and there were days like today when it still felt as raw as it had that bright June afternoon.

He had once mentioned the rumours to Simon but he was still struck dumb with shock, bereft of his other self, the way only a twin denied his twin could understand.

Looking back, everyone had wanted or maybe needed to put the whole incident behind them as soon as the funeral was over; yet the rumours persisted and Mark had always felt unable to ignore them, whilst still at school and then as he moved through adolescence into adulthood. His parents had always waved them away and Simon, on the few occasions they had spoken about it, had pleaded with him to leave well alone and let everything lie. But if the rumours were true and it hadn't been an accident then somebody owed it to Danny to find out what really happened that afternoon. It had become Mark's life's mission and he wouldn't rest until it was complete.

CHAPTER NINE

"WHAT A DUMP," the woman muttered under her breath as she steered her black Volkswagen Passat into the police station car park, bringing it to a stop just before its front bumper made contact with a badly maintained brick wall. She wasn't feeling her best, if truth was told, and the sight of the Victorian building before her did little to lift her spirits. This wasn't the kind of place in which she had expected to be working at this stage in her career. It reminded her of a Dickensian workhouse.

She leaned down beneath the rear-view mirror to get a clearer view of the building, "I must have seriously pissed off somebody in a former life to deserve to be sent here."

She sat back in the driving seat for a few minutes, squeezed a penny-sized swirl of transparent gel into her palms before rubbing her hands together. The antiseptic smell overpowered the enclosed space as a knock on the driver's side window caused her to start. She pressed the button on the door to lower the window and leaned away as a young man with bad breath leant his head through the window, displaying no respect for her personal space.

"I'm sorry love, you can't park here," he started. "This is staff only. There's a pay and display round the corner."

She turned her body as much as the space allowed so that she faced the young uniformed officer square on.

"I'm sorry, I didn't catch your name?"

"PC Pemberton, but I really need you to move your car, love. We have a new detective superintendent starting today and I've been told I need to keep a space free for him."

She nodded. "Well, PC Pemberton, there are a couple of things you need to know."

Realisation began to dawn and colour started to drain from the young officer's complexion.

"The first is that I'm *not* your love. The second is that I *am* your new detective superintendent and, thirdly, if you don't stop staring at my tits, I'll have you on school crossing duty for the rest of your career. I'm old enough to be your mother."

The constable reared back, narrowly avoiding hitting his head on the doorframe.

"With respect, that can't be right," he glanced down at his notebook. "I've been told to expect a DS Johnny Jacobs."

She reached into the open handbag, the contents of which had already spilt across the passenger seat and produced her warrant card.

"Detective Superintendent Jenny Jacobs," she spoke wearily. "Spelling's obviously not one of your stronger points, PC Pemberton. Let's both hope we find the ones that are."

She began to open the driver's door from the inside but, in an act of chivalry far too late in the day; Pemberton continued to open it from the outside and offered his arm to help her out.

"Put your arm away sonny. This isn't *Strictly Come Dancing* and you're certainly not my dream partner. I don't need a welcome party, so while you point me in the right direction for CID, I need you to go and find DI Munday and tell him I'm here. Then – and most important of all – I need you to bring me a decent cup of coffee. And I warn you, PC Pemberton, I can detect vending machine shit a mile off so don't try and fob me off with any old crap. Get a move on."

Harry Duggan watched the scenario in the car park play out from his vantage point of an open second floor window, listening to the raised voices below and enjoying the young policeman's evident discomfort. He had told Jack time and again that he wouldn't step in and rescue him anymore and yet he couldn't bring himself to turn his back on a friend, even one as flaky as Jack Munday. He took a mobile phone from his inside jacket pocket and punched out a text.

Wherever you are, whoever you're with, get here now. The new DS has arrived and will want to see you and SHE doesn't look like she suffers fools gladly – which means you're probably fucked.

He pressed send and waited less than a minute for a reply.

Shit. Cover me. Am less than ten minutes away.

Harry doubted that very much, but he knew he'd do it anyway.

Duggan watched through the glass panelled door as Jenny Jacobs bustled down the corridor, trying to balance a handbag, a briefcase and a plastic bottle of water that seemed to have taken on a will of its own. Twice she dropped the bottle; twice she bent down to pick it up, feeling her back once she had done so. She edged towards him and he smiled and held out a hand. She didn't have a spare hand to offer in return.

"DS Jacobs?"

"And you are?"

"I'm Detective Sergeant Duggan, ma'am. Harry."

Jacobs stood and eyed Duggan from ginger top to scuffed-shoes bottom.

"Well, look, Harry. I've only been here five minutes and you're already the second person I've had to tell that I'm not the Queen, so cut the ma'am crap. Call me boss or any derivative thereof but just don't call me ma'am. Stick to that and we'll get on just fine. Now where's DI Munday?"

"He's on his way in, boss, just stuck in a bit of traffic. He should be here in a few minutes."

Jacobs put her bags down on the floor beside her, exhaled heavily, took a swig from the water bottle, and smiled at Duggan.

"Is he bollocks! If I can get here for the start of the working day and you can get here for the start of the working day, sure as hell Detective Inspector Munday can do it too. It's good of you to cover for him and I admire that, but I suspect the Detective Inspector and I are going to have to have a coming together of minds over the way we are going to work, otherwise it's just going to get messy. As the saying goes, DS Duggan, 'a dame who knows the ropes isn't likely to get tied up'."

"Boss?"

"Mae West, Duggan. It's one of hers. Now, point me in the direction of my office, tell Mr Munday to come and see me when he finally gets here and find that scrawny PC from the car park and remind him he was meant to be getting me a decent coffee."

And with that she clenched the water bottle under her fleshy right arm, bent both knees to pick up her bags, the way a weightlifter might prepare for a clean and jerk, and pushed forward past Duggan and through the double doors towards her new office. Heads turned and the rest of the team suddenly adjusted to give the impression they were actually working. Jacobs ignored them all.

JACK MUNDAY ARRIVED a little over twenty minutes later, still knotting his tie as he jogged down the corridor towards a smirking Duggan. To Harry's obvious amusement and Jack's consequent displeasure, Duggan shook his head, glanced down at his watch and then pointed his friend towards the new detective superintendent's office. He ran straight past. No words were exchanged.

Jenny Jacobs lifted her eyes from her desk as Jack Munday collided with the doorframe of her glass-encased office in the corner of the main CID room. The noise shook her.

"The coffee's shit and I'm sitting in a goldfish bowl but at least the prodigal son has arrived at last, albeit very fucking late. Assuming that is, that you are Detective Inspector Munday?"

Jack nodded.

"Come in and close the door behind you, if possible without knocking it off its hinges."

With the comment made and noted, Jack closed the door far more carefully than was strictly required, pulled a seat from the desk, and sat down, crossing his left leg over his right knee.

"You have to go out to get decent coffee or you need to keep a little stash of your own where nobody knows about it. That's the only way. You're not going to get anything that looks or tastes like real coffee in here."

"And do you have a little stash of your own, DI

Munday?"

"I've got a little pot of ground Arabica and a cafetiere locked away but I'm happy to share if it gets us off on the right foot."

Jenny leant back in her seat, which startled her as it swivelled without warning, and smiled.

"You obviously know how to treat a woman, Jack."

"I'll drop some round to you in a bit."

For a moment Jacobs studied the man in the seat in front of her. For somebody whose file said that he exuded supreme confidence, he seemed more than a little unsure of himself.

"So on a scale of one to ten just how pissed off were you when you found out I was being brought in above you?"

Jack laughed. He wasn't used to having a superior officer with quite so much front.

"I was never in the running for a superintendent's job."

"No, but your file tells me you passed up a DCI's job to stay here. The last thing you would want is somebody else coming in above you."

"I'm sure I'll cope with the disappointment. It's just that it's more important for me to stay here as a DI than move on as a DCI at the moment."

"Your wife and kid?"

"My file?"

Jenny nodded.

"Well, look, Jack, I like my teams to work *with* me rather than *for* me, if you know what I mean, so we'll get on just fine as long as you don't try to bullshit me. I need to be able to rely on you more than anybody. So, as long as we both know where we stand?"

Jack pushed back the seat and stood.

"Understood."

Jacobs smiled.

"Louis, I think this is the beginning of a beautiful friendship," she replied, in a strangely deep and twisted voice.

He looked at her inquisitively. She sighed in frustration.

"Are you all complete heathens when it comes to film? Humphrey Bogart says it in *Casablanca*."

He nodded. "I'll fetch that coffee."

CHAPTER TEN

ESTHER HAD NEVER felt close to her mother-in-law. It wasn't that she didn't want to be; far from it. In fact, she had always thought that being closer to Adele might bring her even closer to Simon. But now, Esther had decided, the time had come to bring everything out in the open. Esther had had to do more than simply invite her to join them for lunch, she had had to *insist* that she join them, and in such a way that afforded Simon little option but to comply. So he had set off on a bright, cold Sunday morning to bring his mother to their home. The boys were excited to see their grandmother who, despite everything, had always been attentive on the occasions when they actually saw each other, and no birthdays or Christmas passed without a gift. Yet Esther never really felt that her boys had enjoyed true affection from her or had had the opportunity to get to know their grandmother properly – or her them. She remained a simultaneously ever-present and yet somewhat distant figure in their lives.

Once, at a family wedding three or four years previously, one of Simon's cousins had casually remarked to the group just how much Charlie resembled Danny at much the same age. Esther had spent the entire time at the reception observing from a distance as Adele watched Charlie ruefully as he played. She thought then that maybe Adele saw Charlie as some kind of surrogate for Danny and the thought made her shudder.

The sound of the boys coming hurtling down the stairs told her that Simon was home. She joined them at the door to help them welcome their grandmother. The boys rushed out onto the driveway towards Adele as she climbed out of the passenger seat and locked their arms around her midriff in an embrace. She hugged them awkwardly and bent down to kiss both on the tops of their heads. She looked towards the front door and smiled at Esther who called out to the boys to release their grandmother at least long enough for her to come into the house.

Adele carried a small supermarket spray of carnations, which Esther accepted and admired as if it were a display five times its size. She knew that Simon had probably been made to stop and buy them on the journey over. Once inside she fetched a chilled sparkling water and then listened from the kitchen as the old lady attempted small talk with the boys. It was a stilted, rather one-way conversation as they sought to engage her in their latest video games. Her responses revealed that, not only was this unsurprisingly an area in which her knowledge had gaps, but also that she had generally long been out of practice in the art of conversation.

"Now come on boys," Esther said re-entering the room, "stop badgering Grandma about your games and expecting her to be up to date on Mario Kart or whatever else it is you're playing. Why don't you go upstairs and I'll call you down once lunch is ready?"

With permission granted to return to their console and play, the boys didn't hang around long enough for the invitation to be withdrawn. With them gone and just Esther in the room, Adele immediately seemed less comfortable, somehow more exposed and on edge. Perhaps she was as fearful as Esther and Simon about having this long-overdue conversation.

"I'm so pleased you could come today," Esther started, slumping back into an armchair that was big enough to swallow her whole. "I've been telling Simon for ages that we don't see enough of you. We'll do lunch as soon as he's changed. How are you keeping?"

"I'm still here, sometimes I wonder why, but I'm still here."

"Well we're pleased you're still here. I know the boys certainly are."

"They're growing up. Charlie seems to get bigger every time I see him."

"Yes, I think eventually he'll end up being taller than Simon."

There was a moment's silence. This was more uncomfortable than Esther had been anticipating.

"How are things generally, Adele? How are you spending your time? Are you going out with friends?"

"Is that what all this is about?"

"What do you mean?"

"Simon wants you to get me to start going out? Because if it is, I'm telling you I'm happy as I am."

"Actually, it's not about that and Simon hasn't asked me to do anything, but one thing you have to admit, Adele, is that you're clearly *not* happy as you are."

Adele cringed in the new bout of silence; so loud and intense she almost needed earplugs.

"We found some photographs of Danny and Simon when they were kids the other day. Would you like to see them?"

Adele nodded. Esther left the room and returned from the kitchen with a small, well-thumbed white envelope. She moved next to the older woman and pulled out half a dozen small photographs. The square format of two revealed they had been taken with one of those once revolutionary Polaroid cameras. Adele reached into her handbag and retrieved her glasses from their case. Esther wondered what could possibly inhabit that handbag that made it so crucial to keep it no further than six inches from her side at all times. The old lady studied each image intently and, as Simon entered the room quietly and almost unseen, Esther could see that tears were beginning to trickle from the sides of her mother in law's eyes.

"Don't cry, Adele. I didn't mean to upset you. You shouldn't cry every time you see a picture of Danny."

"And what do you know about it? You still have your boys. You have no idea what it feels like, even now."

"Mum, I won't have you talking to Esther like that," Simon interjected forcefully, stepping forward into the centre of the room. "You can't resent everybody else who still has their children just because of what happened to Danny. Nobody's saying you shouldn't think about him or talk about him. We want nothing more than to talk about Danny without it causing so much sadness, but I'm still here and so is Mark, though God knows where, and you have two grandsons who want to have a relationship with their grandmother. We have to talk about this, we should have done it years ago; but it seems as if none of us can move on until you say it's okay for us to do so."

"Is that so? Well *I* can't move on. So you'll either have to move on without me or actually honour your brother's memory properly."

"What's that supposed to mean? You really think that me wanting to live my life whilst also remembering Danny is somehow dishonouring his memory? Danny died, mum. It was terrible... horrible and I would do anything to go back and change that, but I was eleven years old as well. You may not realise it, but Mark and I didn't only lose our brother that day, we lost our mother as well. And I – no, we – think that, as painful as it all is, it's about time you started to be a mother to the two sons you *still* have."

Detecting the tension in the air, Monty, who had been curled up on the sofa next to Esther, jumped down in search of peace and quiet in another room. Adele turned her face away, twisted a tissue tightly around her middle finger and inhaled short, sharp breaths. Simon had never spoken so forcefully to her before and she hadn't expected him to do so now. Slowly and calmly she removed her glasses, returned them to their case and, in turn, placed the case back inside her handbag. She returned the photographs to the envelope and rested it carefully on the arm of the chair. She then shuffled her body forward in the seat, which was too soft to give her the leverage that her ample frame required to stand, and looked up at her son.

"Simon, I'd like you to take me home and, if you won't, I'd like you to call me a taxi. This was a very big mistake."

Simon stood above his mother and looked down on her. It felt like one of those rites of passage moments when the child takes on the parental role and the parent becomes the child.

"No, I'm not taking you home and you're not getting a taxi. Esther has cooked. The boys have been excited to see you and we have things we need to discuss. And then we're going to have lunch."

Adele, looking suitably admonished, pushed herself back into the seat and turned her head away again in a kind of petulant disgust, looking out towards the garden.

"I'm sorry I said those things just now." An element of calm had returned to Simon's voice. "Well, actually, I'm sorry they had to be said in such a way but, no, I'm not sorry I said them."

"So, you've started, you have me captive. You might as well carry on and get it all off your chest."

"This isn't about getting anything off my chest; this is about being able to have a normal relationship with each other and being able to talk about Danny without feeling like we all need to walk on eggshells around you. We want to tell the boys about Danny. I want them to know who he was and what he was really like. I don't want them to see him as the kind of tragic, mythical figure that you try and pretend him to be."

"You're lucky Simon. You have two lovely boys. You don't know what it's like to lose a child. Let me tell you. When you lose a parent, it's as if the child in you dies with them. But when you lose a child, it's like being condemned to stay here when all you would have wanted was to have been taken with them. Or, at least, that's how I felt."

Simon inhaled deeply. He knew it had taken a lot for her to open up like that, but he still needed her to see things from his point of view too.

"And you don't know what it's like to lose your twin brother when you're only eleven years old and to never be allowed to grieve properly for him because you've always been made to feel guilty for being the one who lived."

Esther wanted to fist pump her husband, or at the very

least rush over to hug him, but instead she took herself into the kitchen to finish preparing the lunch. She could still hear from in there and she felt less like she was intruding into a private conversation between mother and son, albeit one that should have taken place many years previously.

"What happened that day?" she heard Simon ask.

"You were there. I wasn't. You tell me."

"You know what I mean. You would have been told things after it happened. You'll know things that you never shared with us. I want to know. I *need* to know now, from you, what happened to Danny. I need to hear it from you."

A silent moment. Esther pictured Adele shaking her head, frustrating Simon.

"Jesus, mother. We're all you have left and you're going to lose us unless you help us understand what you've been going through and start seeing things through our eyes as well as just your own."

Simon crouched down on his haunches in front of his mother and took her bony hands into his own.

"Please mum, I need you to do this."

Adele sighed and wiped her nose with the scrunched-up tissue that she held tightly between her fingers. She spoke slowly and fitfully.

"We were invited to go swimming for the day, but I had to work that morning. You were both so excited – Danny especially – that you badgered me until I agreed to let you go. Kevin's mum said that you could go with her and that she would look after you."

"Kevin Simpson?"

She tried to confirm but her voice faltered. Simon remained resolute, his hand around his mother's, offering continued encouragement. He couldn't quite believe that, for the first time in over three decades, he would hear in his mother's words what had happened that day.

"From what we were told and from what I understand, your brother dived into the pool and hit his head on the bottom or the side as he went in. They told us at the hospital that this probably knocked him out and before anybody noticed what had happened, he had already taken in too much water. They told us he probably knew little or nothing about it. The first I knew that something was wrong was when Marion telephoned. I knew something was wrong as soon as I heard the phone ring, but when I heard her voice cracking as she said my name, I knew something terrible had happened. She told me that Danny was being taken by ambulance to the hospital and that we should get there as quickly as we could. She told us she would bring you and Mark home with her. I don't know if she already knew that Danny was dead but, if she did, she didn't say. I suppose she thought it would be best for us to hear that from the doctors. I don't know how I would begin to say that to somebody else either. And so now you know all that I know."

"Have you ever talked about it with her?"

"What is there to say? Honestly, Simon, what is there

to say? Danny is dead. What good would come from talking about it with her now? She has always felt terrible because Danny was in her care and she probably thinks that somewhere deep down, I blame her for what happened."

"And do you?"

"Not now. I think part of me did at the time; part of me felt that I had to have somebody to blame, but despite the rumours that were doing the rounds at the time, I've always felt it was just a cruel accident."

"What rumours?"

"There were people who said it wasn't just a straightforward accident, that somebody tripped Danny as he ran to dive and that caused him to enter the water at an odd angle. Some people pointed fingers but, honestly, you must believe I wasn't one of them."

Simon sighed, placing his head in his hands before lifting his eyes, from which tears were beginning to emerge, to speak to his mother.

"I've tried so many times to relive that day and to remember exactly what happened, but I just can't. I can recall the good bits of the day and then everything else is just blocked out. I'm not even sure I know who was there. I remember Kevin and Matthew Baines being there, but something has always told me there were others."

"There were others, there was a whole group of you: the Swain boy, little Paul Cherry and Christopher Blakemore and his sister Karen. There were probably others too. I don't remember much about the days that followed; it was all so much of a blur. Your Dad told me later that all of the parents came to the funeral, but I wasn't really functioning that day. I was there in body but not much else of me was. Your Dad talked to most of them, and he would tell me in the evenings how badly it had affected so many people."

"And you've never had a conversation about it with any of them since?"

"I became the woman you crossed the road to avoid speaking to. Not because people didn't care or because they were being nasty, but because what can anyone say in that situation? Nothing would have done. Even now, nothing would. So I gradually just stopped going out. Perhaps it wasn't the right thing to do, for me, for Dad, for you or for Mark, but you have to understand that it was for self-preservation. I didn't want to live, and I certainly didn't want to get out of bed and continue my life as if nothing had happened. I'm sorry if that hurt you but... but I don't know what else to say."

"Do you still visit Danny's grave?"

"I try to go as often as I can. For a while it gave me some comfort, it made me feel close to him again. Now, I think it's just routine. I don't know how I would feel if I didn't go. I tidy it up and put fresh flowers down each time. It's the only thing I'm able to do for him now."

"You need to speak to Mark, you know. He's always taken it particularly badly."

"I've never been able to find a way to get to Mark. I've never known how to start that conversation; where to begin."

"That's doesn't mean you can't try now. He's always felt responsible for Danny's death."

"Why should he feel responsible?"

"Because he was the older brother and he feels like you feel: that he should have been able to protect Danny. That's a hell of a burden to carry for so many years."

Adele sighed once more. Simon thought she looked less hunched, as if a burden, however small, had been removed from her shoulders. He passed her another glass of water.

She sipped and looked again out of the window towards the garden, where a climbing frame stood in a far corner.

"I remember you and Danny playing on the climbing frame in the park."

"I do too," Simon replied. "Danny was always a bit more adventurous than me."

"He was adventurous enough for both of you."

"I'd like to go and visit Danny."

Adele looked directly at him and Simon could have sworn he saw just the hint of a smile.

"I could come with you."

"If you don't mind, I think I'd like to go on my own first time. But then we can go together."

"I'd like that."

"I'd also like to take the boys at some point."

"I think that would be nice too, when they're a little older, perhaps."

Simon nodded. Out of the corner of his eye, he could see Esther gesturing that lunch was almost ready. The sound of the boys careering down the stairs would shortly break this moment of solitude, but there was still something Simon needed to ask. He held an index finger up towards Esther to ask her to wait for just a second.

"You mentioned there were rumours, Mum?"

Adele, watching the breeze blow through a blue potted hydrangea on the patio outside, finally turned her head back towards him, slightly distracted.

"You remember Matthew Baines?"

Simon nodded.

"Soon after Danny's accident his family moved away. They took Matthew and his sister out of the school and moved out of the area. It seemed quite sudden and unexpected. I think his father's job was relocated."

"So why should that produce any rumours?"

"Because it came as a surprise to most people. I don't think anyone knew they were leaving because I don't think they had a lot of notice either."

"But the rumours?"

"Well, you know what people are like."

"I do, but why don't you tell me anyway?"

Adele looked at her son, clearly unhappy about being pushed to spread a rumour, however old, that she didn't want to see creep further.

"They said that Matthew tripped Danny. Kids can be very cruel. At school, children were saying that Matthew killed Danny. It's not true, of course, but when the family moved away some people said it was because the rumours were true."

Simon felt sick and, despite the years that had passed, he wondered if Matthew had known of the rumours and, if so, how he had coped with the whispering campaign against him. Had he thought about that day since or had he pushed it to the far reaches of his mind? But all of that would have to wait.

"Charlie, Joe," Esther called out. "Come down now, we're going to have lunch."

CHAPTER ELEVEN

THE MAN GLANCED out of his leaded office window and studied the scene before him as sideways rain lashed across Lincoln's Inn Fields, the largest public square in London. He had long since lost count of the number of times he'd looked out of the same window, each occasion feeling like the first regardless of whether the scene was drenched in sunshine, being buffeted by a storm like today or occasionally dressed in freshly fallen snow. For almost half of his adult life his eyes had been drawn to and his anxiety soothed by this green oasis in the middle of the city. Today, though, he'd caught a momentary sight of his reflection in the glass. He looked older than he imagined, more tired, heavier and, despite all the accomplishment and the esteem in which he knew he was held, his life seemed vacant; he wished he had somebody with whom to share the rewards of this successful career but he sensed that ship had long since sailed. At least he could use those rewards to buy the company he couldn't seem to find any other way.

It still surprised him how much money could talk. Those girls always indulged him, they listened to him, and they never questioned what he wanted nor seemed reluctant to help him explore the deepest, darkest corners of his sexual imagination. But that couldn't be just because of the money. They were happy to see him more than once, so they must have felt a connection. It *had* to be that.

It had been a punishing few weeks at work but now that the intensity was over, he deserved something of a release. While colleagues would go back to their families and indulge them with designer shoes, Michelin-starred dinners and expensive weekend breaks, he would book a hotel room and order in one of his girls; perhaps the elfin-like Ukrainian, who had seemed the most willing to experiment with his more extravagant fantasies. He knew that it was not without its risks but he took precautions, and not just the obvious ones. He never used his real name, never shared a photograph of his face and rarely, if ever, booked the same hotel with the same girl twice. He knew that if it were to come out, there would be no shortage of people willing to report it, exploit it and see him brought down from his elevated position. *Plus ça change, plus c'est la même chose*, he thought to himself. Really, who were they to judge him? So perhaps it wasn't strictly legal and, given who he was, he acknowledged that could be a problem, but it was consensual on both sides and nobody had been hurt. It wasn't the first time he had wrestled with a crisis of conscience over this – in fact, he would worry himself almost to the point of illness after each meeting – but, so far, his physical desire had always won out over his rational thought. He had become inebriated by the transient but liberating feelings of freedom that these liaisons gave him; a kind of sexual junkie always looking for his next fix, nothing else mattered. Temptation would always win out over common sense.

He moved across his office towards the laptop on his leather-topped desk and brought up the website that he used to book his girls. There was still time to close the browser but he knew what he wanted. He sat so that he was at eye level with the screen and began to type his username, Christopher Sinclair.

CHAPTER TWELVE

WHAT HAD STARTED out as a recession, a credit crunch, a minor stumbling block on the route to growth was now being likened to the Great Depression. Matt had laid off his pitifully small team, and closed his studio in fashionable Hoxton Square, smack in the middle of London's unfashionable East End. Everyone was talking about the area's regeneration from an Olympic Games still nearly four years away, though more and more people seemed to feel it was something the city could ill afford.

The sombre news poured from almost every direction. In America, more workers had lost their jobs than in any year since the Second World War, so when the Bank of England cut interest rates to the lowest levels in its history and the government unveiled a plan to guarantee up to £20 billion of loans to small and medium-sized businesses, Matt hardly paid any attention. It all seemed too little, too late; certainly for him.

Within two weeks of leaving Hoxton Square and

taking his Mac back home, the credit crunch bit. Projects cancelled and late payments by others – some now more than six months overdue – meant the mortgage had gone unpaid for three months and the credit and store cards that Susie had relied upon to get by whilst Matt built up the business were now calling in their debt. Credit card balances, unlike businesses, don't come crashing down. The anxiety at home was fast becoming a blame that nobody would articulate, so it was left to fester.

"I need money to buy food," Susie would ask, breaking the silence.

"I don't have any."

"What do you expect the kids to eat?"

"I don't know. I'm trying to find work but nothing's coming off."

"Then ask yourself if you're trying hard enough."

Failure, the voice would whisper, with a chuckle.

Matt began the tedious and humiliating job of speaking to the bank and each of the credit card companies, or their appointed debt recovery agents. He explained his lack of work and his inability to provide even the basics for his family to a person at the end of a telephone line who, in each case without exception, he knew was thinking what a loser he was. Sometimes he had to fax them or email them a complete breakdown of incomings and outgoings and then listen as they gave him patronising advice on how to manage his budget more effectively.

"I would be managing fine if there was any fucking money coming in," he would want to say. But instead he simply gritted his teeth and agreed with whatever they asked. They made him feel as small as his bank balance, and just as empty inside. One even picked on a payment for a takeaway pizza as an example of the kind of extravagant living he could ill afford. But agreeing repayment schedules was just about better than living in fear of answering his mobile phone lest it should be somebody else calling to demand money. He knew it certainly wouldn't be anybody calling to offer him work.

"Your brother rang," Susie said one evening. "He's angry you missed your nephew's birthday. Not so much as a card, he said."

"What did you tell him?"

"I said you'd probably forgotten. I said you had a lot on your mind. He said *he* has a lot on his mind too, but he still remembers birthdays."

"I didn't forget, but I had less than two pounds on me in total. Not enough to buy a card and post it, let alone send a present."

"Like I said, I told him you had a lot on your mind."

Susie walked out of the kitchen, into the hallway and called upstairs.

"It's beans on toast for dinner, kids. Again."

Matt heard the groans of disappointment from where he was sitting at the kitchen table. He knew it wouldn't be long before the incessant questions began again about why this friend's family or another could afford food, cinema trips and even holidays when they couldn't.

He sat at the kitchen table and tapped out text messages to any name in his contact book who he thought might be able to give him some paying work; however little. Most replied with sympathetic notes of support, some said "if only" they had spare work to hand around, they would; others didn't reply. Matt made a mental note of exactly who they were.

The text that interested him most, though, arrived shortly before midnight. Matt sat alone, lit by one small table lamp, looking for inspiration on the black television screen. This could be the chance to turn a corner, to show Susie he was worth it and to stick one solid middle finger up to the credit crunch and those who had caused it.

Anderson James, the sender of the message, was a young, self-made entrepreneur, probably in his early thirties but difficult to age precisely. He'd broken free from humble estate roots in Stockwell, South London to develop a successful media business: a magazine, a radio station, and a fashion line all of which tapped into London's growing urban culture. Matt had first met him in connection with a music project that had promised much but delivered little. But those were different days. Now, Matthew Baines was a beggar who could ill afford to be a chooser.

"Great to hear from you," the message read. "Sorry things are tough. Meet me at Villandry on Wednesday at

11. Have a project you'll love."

Okay, so it wasn't a job. There had been no mention of payment, but it was an opening and Matt wasn't about to turn his back on it.

WHEN MATT ARRIVED at the Villandry café two days later, Anderson James was sitting at a corner table, a Kir Royale and an almond croissant in front of him. Although his eyes watched the busy traffic travelling south on Great Portland Street towards Oxford Circus, his concentration was focused on the individual at the other end of his mobile phone. He barely noticed Matt until he was standing before him at the table. Anderson gestured for him to sit, ushered a waiter, and continued the call all at once. What little Matt knew of Anderson James, he admired. Slick, smart and successful, he had triumphed over a tough, poor upbringing to become one of the poster boys of London's Afro-Caribbean community; a role model for a generation of young Black men who felt disenfranchised, without hope or opportunity.

He certainly exuded success. Dressed in a smart, Air Force blue Hugo Boss suit, brown Loake brogues, he wore a silver identity bracelet that made occasional appearances on his left wrist from beneath his white double-cuffed shirt sleeve. A trademark Paul Smith striped tie, bearing a silver 'A' tie pin, was fastened neatly at his collar. His lapel bore the badge of The Prince's Trust, for which he'd recently been appointed an ambassador. His hair was neatly styled into distinctive cornrows; the nails on his hands unquestionably manicured and a single diamond stud nestled comfortably in his left earlobe.

"Listen, I have to go. I'm about to start a meeting. But whatever you need to make it happen, you do. Understand? We have to have the new line ready for Easter. It's all sound, whatever it takes. Okay, I'll call later."

Matt had sat down and now turned to face Anderson as he ended the call and placed his phone on the table. He sipped from the Kir Royale and then dabbed either side of his mouth with a white linen napkin.

"You want one of these?" he gestured, tipping the champagne flute towards Matt before resting it upright on the tabletop.

"Too early for me. A coffee would be great."

"Too early for me too, to be honest, but I find it hard to resist and they know me in here. Have you eaten?"

"Yes, I'm fine," replied Matt. He hadn't and he was hungry but he was nervous of who would have to pick up the tab.

"Times are tough?" asked Anderson.

"Tough, yes, but no tougher than for most, I guess."

"I'm sorry to hear that, brother. Plenty of good people are going to be struggling and I fear it's going to get worse before it gets better."

Matt nodded.

"We're busy, though, thank God. We've launched the

magazine and the radio station in the Caribbean and in the US and both are going well. Now we have this new fashion line we're launching, championing young designers who can't get noticed through the usual routes. We're going to bring out our first collection, well, you heard, at Easter, and we're trying to tie up some retailers to making them high street available."

"Exciting times."

"Very."

A black-shirted waiter brought over two white cups of steaming black coffee, a bowl of mixed white and brown boulder-like sugar lumps and a small plate of miniature macaroons. Matt dropped two of the brown ones into his cup and stirred. Anderson finished the last of the Kir Royale before lifting his coffee cup to his lips.

"So what are you working on at the moment?"

"To be honest, not too much; hence the text. I'm in the market for anything I can get my hands on, really."

"You're advertising, aren't you?"

Matt was anxious not to be pigeonholed.

"Mainly, but to be honest in the current market, I can do general design and marketing as well."

"Cool, cool," replied Anderson, summoning some iced water from the black-shirted waiter.

"You mentioned a project?"

Anderson adjusted his position, leaning forward and clasping his hands together on the tabletop as if in prayer.

"Yes, sure, the project."

He reached into his Mulberry messenger bag, which sat on the bench seat to his left, and produced a piece of paper in a plastic folder.

"Do you mind signing an NDA?"

Matt was pretty sure that any non-disclosure agreement wouldn't be worth the paper it had been printed on. Coupled with the fact that he wasn't in a position to do anything else, he signed at the bottom where Anderson indicated.

"Okay, so," said Anderson, pouring two glasses of iced water. "This project is a new business I started under the radar about eight months ago but not under my usual banner. It's going to stand-alone; it's started okay but I really want to ramp it up. I have business interests in media and now in fashion, and I'm planning something new in music but this one will square the circle. This is a dating business."

Matt nodded inquisitively.

"But not just any dating business. That's a crowded market and we all know that the money is in the niche. I have a very clear exit strategy for this one, hopefully for both of us, if you come on board. The premise is very simple. A large number of young women come to London because they still believe the streets are paved with gold and are looking for any route to the lifestyle they want. And there are plenty of wealthy guys who are willing to help, if you catch my drift?"

Matt nodded.

"So that's it in a nutshell: mymillionaireboy friend.com. We have spent the last few months quietly putting together the girls and the guys and taking a cut from the guy's subscription to the site. Now, I want to really go for it. Get more girls and we can command a hell of a fee and the rest we leave to nature. It should be a piece of piss."

"And the exit strategy?"

"Simple, we build the business as quickly as we possibly can, get it up towards the top of its business curve, because let's be honest it's going to have a finite lifetime, and then we sell it to one of the really big dating companies for a few million and get the hell out. Two years, three at a push."

"I like the idea."

"I was hoping you would."

"So what role do you see for me?"

"I want you on board. You'll be a proper director of the business, with an equity stake, say twenty five per cent, and you can look after all of the marketing, the look and feel of the new site, all of the kind of things that are right up your street anyway."

"And money?"

"No, I'm not looking for you to put any money in and you'll get dividends as soon as the business can pay them."

"But what about payment now?"

"You need to see the bigger picture, Matt. This thing is going to be massive and you're going to have a great big chunk of it."

Matt swallowed some water.

"All that's great and I'm really interested in coming on board. But I can't tell my wife and kids and my bank manager, or the credit card companies to see the bigger picture. They don't want jam tomorrow; they want it today and I'm not talking figuratively."

Anderson nodded.

"Okay, here's the deal. If you can do some design work for the new fashion range alongside building up My Millionaire Boyfriend, I can put you on the payroll. It won't be much, say a thousand a month, but it'll help you along while you look for other projects."

Matt thought about it. His bargaining position was weak and at least what money he could prise from Anderson would be put to good use. Plus, if this project did go as big as Anderson suggested, then within two to three years, his problems could be a thing of the past.

"Let's do it," he heard himself say. Anderson stood and held his hand out to shake.

"Great stuff, brother. We're going to do great things together. Let's speak tomorrow and, in the meantime, I'll get the paperwork sorted."

Matt, unsure as to what had just exactly happened, smiled as the waiter arrived bearing the bill. There were an awkward few seconds as the bill was offered to Matt, only for Anderson to reach across and take it himself.

"This one's on me. You can buy lunch the day we sell out."

CHAPTER THIRTEEN

"MARK, IT'S SIMON again. Call me. It's been a while since any of us have heard from you and, frankly, we're all a bit worried."

Simon let out a deep, frustrated sigh.

"That's the third message I've left him," he told Esther, who was only half listening as she stacked dirty plates into the dishwasher. "I'm beginning to get concerned."

"You know what Mark's like. He's probably not charged his phone in days. All you can do is keep trying."

It had been less than four hours since Simon had returned from visiting Danny's grave for the first time in years. The decision to go had been a spur-of-the-moment thing and, as he had said he would, he had gone alone. He'd put a meeting for himself in the office diary and told his secretary that he was contactable only if absolutely necessary.

A maelstrom of conflicting emotions swirled: anger, frustration and a deep unremitting sadness but most of all, even after so many years, just an emptiness borne out of the knowledge that someone who should have been there, was not. In many ways, Simon wished that he was a man of faith; it might have made everything so much easier if he'd been able to believe, as others did, that taking Danny had been a necessary part of some greater plan, but he thought that was both shallow and disrespectful to his brother's memory. So many times he had wanted to ask how a supposedly merciful and compassionate God could simply rip a young boy away from his family, but he'd never seen the benefit from such an argument, especially as his mother had found some crumb of comfort in the church.

Whilst Simon's anger had substantially subsided over the years, Mark's had not. They had spoken about it only rarely, but Simon knew that Mark was consumed by resentment for what had happened and an almost evangelical need for what he referred to as justice for Danny, but which Simon had always thought of as misplaced vengeance.

The last time they had seen each other, they'd not parted on the best of terms. Simon had pleaded with Mark to speak to somebody about the anger he carried.

"You're not the only one who's suffered," he'd told him. "We all have those dark places we retreat to every now and then, but none of us, not even mum, stays there; except you. It's not healthy. You can't make Danny's death your life's work. You can't put it right no matter how much you might want to. It just can't be done."

IT HAD TAKEN Simon more than an hour to drive out to the cemetery. As the car moved eastbound towards the Essex coast, the blue sky that had watched over him on the journey from the office had become edged with grey. The wind grew stronger and droplets of rain formed on the windscreen, but the wipers swatted them away like flies almost as fast as they had come. He glanced across at the silenced sat-nav. The display indicated that he needed to turn left at the upcoming set of traffic lights. Almost as soon as he had done so, he squeezed through a scuffed width restriction and turned off the James Morrison CD that was playing. It made no rational sense to do so, but as he closed in on his destination, it felt appropriate to spend some quiet time with his own thoughts.

The surroundings had become more rural until he saw the red brick wall that marked the boundary of the cemetery and, just the other side of yet another width restriction, the dramatic stone entrance and wrought iron gates. He turned in; gravestones, in differing shades of white, grey and black, lay ordered to his left and in front of him, some upright and standing proud, others leaning under the weight of sadness and distress. Some people dressed predominantly in black had gathered at the far end of the otherwise sparsely occupied car park in a huddle in front of a low, wide red brick building.

Simon took a piece of lined notepaper from his pocket

to check the grave number that signified his brother's resting place for all eternity.

It didn't take long to locate him: he was the third grave along in that particular row. Simon moved between the graves until he stood directly in front of the headstone, which was styled as an open book, with a marble ribbon laying down the centre of the page.

"In tender and loving memory of Daniel Michael Carter. Died June 8th, 1975. Aged 11. Deeply mourned by his heartbroken mum, dad, brother Mark, twin brother Simon, other relatives and friends. Forever in our thoughts and hearts."

It said everything and yet it said nothing at all. It couldn't possibly convey the anguish that his parents must have experienced when they brought him here to lay him to rest. Simon felt as if he could hear their cries being carried on the otherwise silent wind as it swirled around him and feel their tears on his shoulder as it began to lightly rain again.

He wasn't sure what he was meant to do next. He hated the fact that Danny had been here alone for all these years, surrounded by people who he never knew. He allowed himself to wonder how, if that day had been different, it might have been his name on the headstone in front of him. Simon lowered to his haunches and pulled a clean tissue from his jacket pocket. He spat onto the tissue and used it to clean a mark from base of the grave. He whispered to Danny. He didn't know why.

"I'm sorry it's taken me so long. I should have come earlier."

Did he expect a reply?

"I've never forgotten. I've always thought about you... about that day. I've often wondered what would have happened if... well, let's just say, I've always wondered."

Simon had played out this moment so many times in his mind and yet had never known how he was supposed to feel when he stood at Danny's grave. He didn't have a sense of his brother being there, and simply standing alone talking to a marble headstone made him feel strangely self-conscious. Yet here he was, drawn by... something, working hard to say the things he wanted to say, but not out loud. He found it hard to formulate the words, but when it came down to it, all he really wanted to say was sorry; sorry that it had happened, that nobody – it didn't matter who – had been able to save him. Sorry that their relationship had come to be defined by that day. He resolved in that moment that Danny would once again be the brother he was rather than just the memory he had been left to become.

Simon looked up to the sky, raindrops coating his face, and thought about who made the decisions on who would live and who would die. He didn't believe in a God, but wanted to know who had decided it should be Danny. Why him? Was it truly random and, if not, what had he done or not done that marked him out? Why should somebody who hadn't even started living yet have that opportunity taken away, and more to the point, why should Simon have been allowed to go on? And for those who lived on, what was the purpose of making them all carry this profound sense of sadness for the rest of their lives? The rain came down stronger and began to form little pools in the mud around the base of Danny's grave, where moss had begun to attach itself.

"Now I know where to find you, I'll be back more often."

He backed away from the grave, gulped fresh air deep into his lungs, pulled the collar on his jacket up and jogged back to the car. He opened the door, sat inside, turned the heater on and, for a minute or two, wept uncontrollably. He called Esther first and then Adele from the car. As he drove, Simon began to feel a sense of peace that he couldn't remember experiencing before. He would play with the boys when he got home and then sit and reflect with Esther over a glass of wine.

"It would be fascinating to know what goes through Mark's mind," Esther repeated later.

"I don't know what to think. It frightens me that he's so obsessed with revenge."

"Well, look, there's not much he can actually do. I mean, even if he does think that 'somebody did it', none of you who were there that day have seen each other for years. You don't know where they all live and neither does he."

CHAPTER FOURTEEN

"DON'T YOU THINK this is overkill, sending the two of us to somebody who's received a couple of dodgy text messages?"

Jack Munday was irritable. Not only had he been finding it difficult to sleep – and nobody craved sleep more than Jack – Lesley had been away on a course. He had begun to realise that he missed her; her laugh, her conversation, her just being there. He missed having somebody to care about and to care for him. Lesley had told him he could stay at her place on his own but it didn't feel right so he had spent three nights instead in his cramped and untidy bedsit. He was not in the best humour and now, here he was, being sent to do a job a uniformed officer with half his experience, twice his amount of patience and four times his level of sympathy should be doing. Harry responded by turning the radio up. That new Take That song played loud. Jack leant forward and turned the volume back down.

"And I hate that song. You can't even go for a piss without hearing it coming out of a speaker somewhere."

"You're a regular little ray of sunshine this morning, aren't you? This poor woman is going to be made up when you walk in to help free her from the terror of her stalker. She'll probably prefer to take her chances with him rather than you."

"Why are you so sure it's a him, the stalker? It could be a woman."

"Figure of speech but at least you're thinking like a copper again rather than a spoilt kid who's had his favourite toy taken away."

"What's that supposed to mean?"

Duggan drove on without answering. He had no interest in getting involved in a conversation on the conflict between Jack trying to win back Elaine from the comfort of Lesley's bed. There would be no point in him telling Jack that there could only ever be losers.

"You know it's a test," Harry said, as they sat in traffic in the one-way system that had supposedly been created to ease traffic flow around the town centre. Jack grunted in reply.

"This job is a test. The new Super, it's her way of finding out if you're going to be a good little Detective Inspector and play nicely as part of her team."

"You reckon?"

Duggan nodded.

"We catch murderers, Harry. We don't do house calls

because somebody's lost their shit over some iffy messages."

"Well today we do, so best get with the programme."

Silence again. Jack began to alternate between drumming his fingers on his right knee and checking his phone for non-existent messages.

"This is all – well, mostly – bloody school traffic," Duggan observed. "In my day we walked to school; none of this 'driving your little darling all the way into the classroom' nonsense."

"I used to walk Connor to school. I miss that."

Duggan threw him a despairing glance. "Snap out of it, man. Stop being so maudlin."

Jack laughed, not a snigger but the type of full-on laugh that, had he been drinking at the time, would have resulted in the whole inside windscreen being coated with skinny latte.

"You crack me up, sometimes, Harry. How old are you?"

"You know how old I am."

"You'd never believe it. I mean, you're the only person under eighty-five I know who would use a word like 'maudlin'. And, for your information, I was just saying that I miss walking Connor to school."

"You should listen to yourself sometimes. If I'd have said something about stopping for breakfast, you'd have gone into one about missing breakfast with Connor. If I'd have said I needed a shit, you'd have talked about wiping his bum as a baby…"

"Okay, I get it. I won't mention him again."

"Now you're just being stupid. You can talk about him all you like but you need to find something *else* to talk about for your own sanity as much as everybody else's."

Jack lowered the window and rested his arm on the door, momentarily enjoying the cool air coming into the car. He turned the radio back up now the Take That track had finished to be replaced by Amy Winehouse.

"Man, I love listening to her when I'm stuck in the car. Much better than the shit you normally listen to."

The traffic eased and Harry moved the car into second gear with aspirations for third.

"So, what's happening with you and Elaine anyway?"

"I wish I could answer that. No idea. I thought things were beginning to happen, but now I'm not so sure."

"Still playing the long game?"

"Not completely sure I'm still *in* the game."

"And with Lesley… what's going on there?"

Jack turned to face his friend and let a slight smile play across his face.

"Even for a copper, you ask too many questions. Just drive."

Eventually Duggan turned the car into a neat suburban side street of mostly semi-detached houses, with well-ordered front gardens and an assortment of SUVs parked tidily on driveways. Baskets trailing ivy, which would have burst with bright pink and white petunias over the summer, hung from almost every door as if decreed by some unwritten by-law. Across the street from where Duggan brought the car to a stop was a small park, a children's playground evident some way from the border, a few dog walkers using hand-held ball launchers to exercise their hounds.

They exited the car and Duggan looked down at his notebook and nodded in the direction of a house three down from where they were standing. It lacked character, Jack thought, not that he was in any position to make judgements on the living conditions of others. The driveway looked as if it had been newly laid within the last couple of years. Small evergreens in coloured ceramic tubs framed the doorway as they walked forward and rang the bell.

The woman who answered was as prim as the house in which she lived. Standing in the doorway made her appear taller than she was. She smiled the smile of somebody who had mistaken her visitors for unwanted double-glazing salesmen or similar.

"Mrs Westcott? I'm Detective Inspector Munday and this is my colleague Detective Sergeant Duggan. We wanted to have a word with you about these intimidating messages you've been receiving."

Both men produced their warrant cards, which were only afforded cursory glances. She continued to look startled.

"Well, you had better come in. I must admit I wasn't

expecting CID to turn up for this."

"You and me both," Munday muttered under his breath but still loud enough for Duggan to hear and dig him sharply in the back of the ribs.

Karen Westcott ushered them into a show house-clean lounge, with a carpet so deep Jack felt his shoes sinking into it. A display of dried flowers filled a fireplace with an extravagant white stone surround, suggesting that it had never been used for the purpose intended. On top of the fireplace sat framed photographs of a happy family, at least one shot in the formality of a studio, a small carriage clock showing the incorrect time and an evidently expensive fragrance diffuser with sticks rising from the neck of a squat, square bottle to spread the aroma of vanilla around the room. The men remained standing until Karen Westcott returned with a tray bearing three dainty mugs of tea.

"You have a lovely home, Mrs Westcott. Now, how can we help you? These messages?"

Karen steadied herself with a sip of English Breakfast and then looked up from her armchair at Jack, who had remained standing. Harry Duggan had rested his petite mug on the edge of the fire surround and had taken a small notebook from his inside jacket pocket.

"There have been three or four, the first two via Facebook, the third by email and then the last one by text message."

"And what did they say?"

"Well, saying it out loud, they don't sound all that bad."

"Why don't you let us be the judge of that?" reassured Jack, cursing Jenny Jacobs for sending him to question an apparently flaky middle-aged housewife.

She sipped again from her thimble of tea. Jack did likewise, resisting the urge to down it in one.

"The first one was a message asking me if I thought it was time that we all got together for a reunion."

"That doesn't sound too intimidating. What about the others?"

"The second one asked if I thought about him often and whether I remembered the last time we saw each other."

"That's still doesn't sound threatening, though, does it?"

"The email was sent with a picture of this house attached to it and said that maybe we would see each other soon. The last one, the text message, was sent with a picture of my children, saying that they looked to be about the same age as the last time we saw each other."

"And you said that you knew this guy?"

"The Facebook message and the email came from handles with Danny Carter's name."

"Okay, so we need to track this Danny Carter down and get him to stop. Should be simple enough. Who is he to you and when was the last time you saw him?"

"There's the problem, Inspector. I last saw Danny

Carter in nineteen seventy-five, on the day that he drowned. I was there when it happened."

Jack choked back a little of the tea.

"And you've had no contact with his family since?"

She shook her head.

"I was very young when it happened, we all were. There was a whole group of us from school and I'm a bit ashamed to say that until these messages arrived, I hadn't really thought much about Danny or that day for years. You know, life just goes on."

"And you haven't replied to any of these messages?"

She shook her head unconvincingly.

"Are you in contact with anyone else who was there on the day that Danny Carter died?"

"My brother, obviously. His name is Chris. Chris Blakemore, but he's lived in Toronto for over fifteen years now and another, Kevin Simpson, is a Facebook friend of mine, not that we've seen each other since we left school."

"And do you know if either Chris or Kevin have received similar messages?"

"I know Chris hasn't but I haven't asked Kevin."

"And you say Kevin is a Facebook friend of yours?"

She nodded.

"Is Chris?"

"No, Chris isn't on Facebook. He thinks social media is all one big waste of time."

"I have to say I'm inclined to agree with him. What about the others who were there that day? Are any of them on Facebook as well?"

"I really don't know. I can't honestly say I've looked."

"And the pictures that were attached, of the house or your kids, are they pictures that you've posted on your Facebook profile or elsewhere, or do you think they're new pictures that this person has taken?"

"I don't recognise them and that's..."

"And that's what's got you worried?"

Karen Westcott nodded, her body tensing as she did so.

"As I said, Inspector, the messages themselves don't sound threatening, I accept that. But if somebody is out there taking pictures of this house and, even worse, of my kids then that scares me. I keep looking out the windows but, of course, I have no idea who I'm looking for. They could have been watching you come up the driveway and knock on the door, for all I know."

"How old are your children?"

"Max is fifteen, Sophie is twelve."

"And do you know if either of them have been approached by a stranger in the last few weeks or noticed anyone following them?"

She shook her head.

"We'll need copies of the messages that you've been sent as well as the pictures. Can you do that for us?"

Karen Westcott rose from her seat, crossed to the highly polished dining room table and picked up a brown envelope.

"My husband printed them out at work. They're all in here."

"Well, at the moment, whoever is sending these messages hasn't made any explicit threat against anybody but we'll certainly still look into it. If you receive any more of them or if your children notice anything that worries them, give us a call immediately."

Munday and Duggan took their leave, advising Karen Westcott that their tech colleagues – people who Munday described as 'geeks who don't get a lot of natural daylight' – would be round to look at the messages on her computer and mobile phone in order to try and track their source. He also mentioned that a uniformed officer would come and gather as much information as she could remember about this boy Danny Carter and the circumstances around his death.

"Now that's a bit of a conundrum," Jack mused once they were back in the car. "How does a boy who died all those years ago send messages from beyond the grave?"

"Well, clearly it's not him."

As soon as he heard the words coming from his mouth, Duggan realised he was answering a rhetorical question and yet he felt the need to finish the thought anyway. "It has to be somebody doing it in his name?"

Munday looked at his sergeant with a kind of benign despair.

"Is that what you think, Watson?"

"I think we might just have something we can get our

teeth into."

"Well, maybe, except no threat has been made. The messages are a bit creepy, I'll give you that, but you have to ask yourself what could we charge anybody with?"

"And she hasn't actually asked him – whoever it is, him or her – to stop contacting her."

"Let's go back to the nick and ask the new DS how she wants this handled."

Duggan nodded, turned the key in the ignition and listened appreciatively to the roar of the Mondeo's engine.

From his vantage point on a park bench some yards away, a man in his early forties, shivering, observed them as they departed, spotting Karen Westcott looking after them from an upstairs window. He smiled a little. It warmed his heart. *It's good to see old friends.*

CHAPTER FIFTEEN

"SO LET ME get this straight. The woman has been receiving messages from a school friend who died thirty-odd years ago?"

"Well, not from him boss, obviously somebody purporting to be him."

"No shit, Sergeant Duggan. Thanks for clarifying the bleeding obvious."

Superintendent Jenny Jacobs looked each of them in the eye in turn.

"You're very quiet Jack, what does your gut tell you?"

"Aside from it needing a bacon sandwich?"

Jacobs glared at him. Munday didn't have that kind of relationship with her yet.

"Aside from that, it's telling me to pass it across to uniform and the geeks. There's nothing for us to investigate."

Jacobs nodded.

"Get them involved but I still want you to keep tabs on

it. Ask uniform just to run a check to make sure that nobody else has reported similar messages. I don't like that it concerns children. And if she *is* the only one to get the messages, tell them to find out why her. She said there was a whole group of them there that day. So who's trying to shit her up particularly and why?"

Munday nodded.

"And then, Detective Inspector, meet me in the car pound at one. I think you and I should go grab some lunch."

CHAPTER SIXTEEN

JACK MUNDAY PICKED up on the frisson as soon as he and Duggan walked into the shadowy open-plan office. Colleagues who would ordinarily be pretending to be making calls when they were really checking Facebook were *actually* making calls.

"What's the buzz?" Jack asked Mike Sheridan, a young detective high on enthusiasm but a little lower on common sense.

"They've had a body called in," he replied, without looking up from his screen, "in a hotel up west."

"So why am I the last to know?"

Jack had directed his comment to Duggan but realised almost as soon as the words came out that he had spoken loud enough for most of the office to hear. Jenny Jacobs looked up from her position leaning over Lesley Hilton's desk, placed the palm of her hand on the small of her back and smiled in Jack's general direction. She raised her right hand to indicate that she wanted him to wait where he was.

"Don't forget, you're not in charge," Harry cautioned. "So don't go off on one whatever she says to you."

Duggan finished making his point at just the moment that Jacobs joined them. She stood looking up at Jack, hands on her hips, feet planted slightly apart, waiting for him to screw up with his first comment.

"Sullivan tells me you've got a body."

"Indeed we have. A young woman in a hotel room."

"I'm a bit surprised you didn't call."

"Is your detective's nose a little out of joint?"

"Not really, but after you I *am* the most senior officer."

"You were busy and it may have escaped your notice, but outstanding though you are, you're not the only detective we have at our disposal."

The gritting of his teeth made Munday's displeasure plain without having to say anything at all.

"Frank Salazar is down there now getting the basic details together. I'm going shortly. Come with me, Jack, if I've ruffled your feathers that much."

"My feathers aren't ruffled, boss, but as the DI on the team, I think it's my place—"

Jenny sighed, irritated.

"Spare me the sanctimonious bruised ego business. I'm trying to run a team here, not one officer plus a few others. How much has Sullivan told you?"

"Woman's body in a hotel room."

Jacobs nodded as Duggan followed her into her office.

"Young woman, possibly as young as eighteen, naked on the king size bed, looks likely that she's been strangled. Somebody pre-ordered a room service breakfast the night before and when they got no reply this morning, they left it outside. A half hour later they passed the door again and nothing had been moved, so they knocked again. The waiter had a hunch that something wasn't quite right, so he called the front desk and the manager let himself in and found the woman."

"So presumably we're looking for whoever she spent the night with?"

"Well, that's a start, but it doesn't mean that person is necessarily the only suspect. After all, when the fox hears the rabbit scream, he comes a runnin'," muttered Jacobs, "but not usually to help."

"Boss?"

"*Silence of the Lambs*, Jack. Sometimes Hannibal Lecter speaks a lot of sense."

A police superintendent who quoted Hannibal Lecter; Jack desperately tried to ensure that his face gave no indication of what was going through his mind.

"So you think the room service guy might be a suspect?"

"I'm saying that, until we hear what Frank has uncovered, everyone's a suspect."

Salazar had at least ten years' service on Munday and general consensus had it that he resented having the younger man as a more senior officer. He had once asked

Harry Duggan, as a fellow sergeant, how he could possibly work as closely with Jack Munday as he did. Harry had simply answered that all he wanted was to do his job and then go home at the end of the day. It wasn't strictly true, but Harry had absolutely no interest in office politics.

Jacobs picked up her black leather bag from the side of her office chair and scattered some papers across her desktop to find the car keys that had become hidden beneath them. Grasping them at the second attempt, she tossed the keys to Munday, who caught them one-handed. She ushered him out of the office, the glass in the door rattling as she pulled it shut behind her.

"THIS FEELS A bit odd," he said, as he adjusted the driver's seat further away from the pedals. "I'm used to Harry doing the driving."

"A change is as good as a rest, Jack."

"Just tell me where we're headed."

Like most car journeys into Central London the distance actually being travelled was far shorter than it felt, with short traffic hold-ups punctuating the journey. If he'd been on his own or with Duggan then Jack may well have switched on the sirens and placed a flashing blue light on display to ease his way through the congestion, but he didn't yet have the measure of Jenny Jacobs so opted instead to play the situation with a dead straight bat.

"What made you want to become a copper?" Jacobs asked as they sat waiting for what seemed like an eternity for a red light to turn green.

"I was a massive Batman fan as a kid. I loved the idea of running around the city righting wrongs. Because I wasn't a superhero and my then girlfriend didn't think a Lycra outfit would suit me, it seemed that the force was probably a better way to do what I wanted."

Jacobs laughed.

"Does that amuse you?"

"I've just got this image of my Detective Inspector driving around my patch in a Batman costume. Guess that probably makes Duggan the Boy Wonder and Lesley Hilton Cat Woman?"

The reference to Lesley was not lost on Jack but he had no intention of rising to the bait.

"I think the least said about that the better."

The lights changed and they rolled forward a few more yards before a van turning right caused the traffic to bank up again.

"Is it all you thought it would be, this being a policeman lark?"

Jack thought about his answer. He hadn't yet shaken the feeling that every question was a test.

"Most of the time. Of course in Batman they never showed Commissioner Gordon having to deal with all the paperwork that we have to do but, you know, when you get a result and you get to put a real wrongun' away, I still think we're doing a pretty important job. How about you?"

Jacobs sighed deeply and rearranged herself in the passenger seat as if preparing for a serious conversation. Jack didn't want that. He had only asked the question to pass the time more easily and to appear polite.

"A lot of my decision was about proving my father wrong," she began. "He had this archaic view that women became secretaries or hairdressers. Don't misunderstand me, there's nothing wrong with being a secretary or a hairdresser, but the more he implied I couldn't be anything else, the more determined it made me to do it."

"So you broke through the glass ceiling?"

"It depends what you mean by that. I've never been any kind of suffragette if that's what you're implying. I worked hard to get here for myself, and any positive repercussions are just a bonus."

"I wasn't implying anything. I bet your Dad was proud in the end."

"I think he was, not that he would ever have told me to my face. That would've been like admitting he'd been wrong all along and he was too proud a man to do that. He died not long after I made sergeant so he didn't see me move into CID, but he kept a picture of me in uniform in his living room."

"I can't imagine you in uniform, boss."

Jenny laughed. "What about your folks? Are they proud to have a policeman in the family?"

Jack had found, over the years, that giving a bland answer to a personal question was the best way of not inviting a second one.

"Oh yeah, they're properly proud."

The traffic had begun moving again and Jack steered the car to the left of Great Portland Street station and down towards the cut-through that his sat-nav had proposed, crossing Portland Place towards Marylebone High Street.

The hotel itself was of the type that would once have been called "small" but was now billed as "boutique", which enabled it to charge even higher rates than some of its larger competitors. It stood anonymously on a quiet side street to the north of Oxford Street, close to Marble Arch. From the front, the building was unremarkable. Only a small brass plaque and a few discreet window stickers gave any suggestion as to the nature of its business. Jack parked the car in a permit holders-only bay and called a traffic warden over from the other side of the road as he shut the driver's door behind him. The young man came across, wearing a dark green coat and a white and green peaked cap, both of which seemed at least two sizes too big for him.

"I'm sorry sir," he began, before Jack even had a chance to say hello, "these bays are for permit holders only. You're not going to be able to leave your car here."

It was clearly a rehearsed speech he'd given a thousand times before, delivered with the kind of supercilious arrogance inherent in someone who believes he has real authority but is about to be put straight.

There were moments when Jack really did love his job and situations like this were among them. He reached into his inside jacket pocket and retrieved his warrant card.

"I'm Detective Inspector Munday and this is Detective Superintendent Jacobs. We're here to investigate what could be a murder, not that I want you blabbing that to your mates. So we're going to leave our car here regardless of what you say while we go inside and begin our investigation. While we do that, you're going to make sure that neither you nor any of your colleagues does anything to our car that I might interpret as impeding our investigation because if they do, it will be you that I will be holding responsible for it. Are you with me?"

The young man nodded and, if his coat hadn't been so large, Jack might have been able to see him shaking a little, too. Jenny smiled and they both pushed past the traffic warden to enter the hotel.

THE BODY WAS in a small but smartly furnished room on the third floor, the whole of which had been sealed off at Frank Salazar's request. Jacobs insisted they took the stairs rather than the lift and Jack was already wheezing before they reached the second floor.

"You're out of condition," Jenny smirked. "I might have to get you some fitness training to get you back up to scratch."

"You're all heart, boss." Jack paused, bent in half, hands on his hips, gulping in air.

If there were question marks about whether Jack was in a state of peak physical condition, no such questions could be asked of Frank Salazar. As they entered the bedroom at the corridor's far corner, Jack could see him standing over the large unmade bed, his back towards them, the material of his shirt stretched to the limit across his bulky torso, sweat patches evident across his back and under both arms. He heard Jenny Jacobs speak and turned towards them and where each shirt button had been done up under duress, the fabric threatened to burst open to reveal an unwelcome glimpse of his fleshy, hairy stomach. Moments earlier Jack had heard him bellowing instructions to the scene of crime team, all of whom were clad in white hooded jumpsuits, their hands encased in blue latex gloves.

"Boss," he greeted her with a smile, but only a cursory nod in Jack's general direction. *I'm still a superior officer,* Jack thought to himself, *a little bit of respect wouldn't go amiss.* He kept his thoughts to himself. Picking a fight wouldn't gain him anything, not yet anyway. Salazar stood back to allow Jacobs and Munday closer proximity to the bed. Pillows were scattered across it; two had landed on the floor. The duvet in its floral cover was diagonally strewn across the mattress, as if it had been carried that way in the throes of passion. Two glasses of what looked like half-drunk champagne sat on the right-hand bedside table. A pile of woman's clothes was folded neatly on a chair away to the left. The focus of everyone's attention was a young woman's naked body, splayed across the width of the bed, her eyes closed, her reddish hair trailing behind her, purple bruising just evident on the porcelain skin of her long, elegant neck.

"What do we know, Frank?" Jenny asked.

"Well, aside from what you see and from what we've found on a very cursory search of the room and her belongings, we think her name is Irina Kostyshyn."

"Polish? Russian? Ukranian?"

"Can't be sure yet. We're running some checks."

"Who booked the room?" Jack interjected.

"That would be a Mr Christopher Sinclair," Frank replied, reading from his notebook.

"Almost certainly a false identity. She could be an expensive pro. The type of blokes who book into hotel rooms with high class call girls rarely do it using their real names."

"Is that you speaking from experience, Jack?"

"If only I earned that much, boss."

Jack looked around the cramped, unremarkable room. Not great value for the two hundred pounds or more per night that the rate card suggested the hotel tried to charge for it. He wondered if they offered a rate per-hour for people like Christopher Sinclair. The kettle on a tray near the door had been left untouched and there were no clothes hanging in the pitifully narrow wardrobe. The curtains were still closed but a quick glance through the bathroom door revealed towels discarded on the floor.

Perhaps a shower had been taken as a precursor to a night of passion gone wrong. The SOCO officers would scoop those up and have them checked for DNA as a matter of routine.

"Please tell me they have some kind of CCTV?"

Salazar shook his head.

"Can the manager describe what this Mr Sinclair looks like?"

"He can but I doubt it's going to help us that much. It's all very generic. He says he was about five feet ten tall, slim build, well dressed, short dark hair, greying at the temples, do you want me to go on?"

"Pretty much like every other middle-aged bloke in London?"

"That's about the long and short of it."

"Was he English?"

Salazar flicked through the pages in his notebook, already knowing he had failed to ask the basic question. He ran a finger around the inside of his shirt collar, which had begun to feel a little tight. Jack tried not to revel in his minor triumph.

"I didn't ask that – what with everything else that's been going on. I'll ask him shortly."

"Please do, Frank," smiled Jack, trying not to appear as patronising as he was being. "It's important that we get as complete a picture as we can of the man we're trying to find."

Salazar threw Jack a look that, at best, could have

caused serious injury. Jacobs knew exactly what was going on.

"Boys, play nicely. Try and remember we're all on the same team. Okay, Frank, get as much information as you can and be prepared to brief the team in the morning. Jack, when we get back put together a group to work on this with Frank, reporting into you."

Jack nodded.

"What does your gut tell you, Frank?" Jenny asked.

It should tell him a heck of a lot given the size of it, Jack thought to himself.

"It all points to what Jack was saying, boss. An expensive call girl comes to the hotel to meet a client. Something here goes wrong with the transaction and either somebody disturbs them, kills the girl and removes the client, or the client isn't that impressed with the service being given and does her in himself."

"Let's keep an open mind for the moment. Get SOCO to take plenty of photographs and catalogue everything in this room. I want to know if they took a shower, made a coffee, even ate one of those complimentary packs of stale shortbread. If they took a shit while they were here, we need to know about it. Every towel needs to be removed for possible DNA evidence. Understand me, Frank? *Everything.* No slip ups on this one."

Salazar nodded. Jenny Jacobs turned to leave the room, nudging Munday as a way of beckoning him to follow.

"What's your problem with Salazar?" she asked as they climbed into the uncomfortably small elevator.

"I have no problem with him."

"Bullshit," she laughed. "You have no problem with him and I'm Beyoncé. 'Fess up, Jack, what's your problem?"

Jack scratched the top of his right ear, looked at her and smiled. He had to admit that he was already growing to like her, but he hated having a boss that had so obviously got the measure of him in such a short space of time.

"Let's just say we do things differently."

"We all have to get on and manage colleagues who don't do things exactly the way we would. It doesn't necessarily mean he's wrong."

"I didn't say he was. Frank Salazar is a good copper, but I like working with guys I know I can trust."

"Like Harry Duggan?"

"Like Harry Duggan."

"What about Lesley Hilton, DI Munday. Is she 'one of the guys you know you can trust'?"

Jacobs had barely finished the sentence when the elevator shuddered to a halt on the ground floor, a bell ringing to indicate its arrival and the doors slowly opening to allow them to disembark. As they walked along the corridor, a bar and lounge off to the left, reception to the right, Jack turned to Jacobs for a moment.

"I'm going to have a drink in the bar for a few

minutes. Care to join me?"

"I thought you'd never ask."

Jack helped Jenny up onto one of the bar stools that was just a touch higher than she could reach in one attempt before settling himself at the bar. The young, dark haired barman in a white shirt and a stained black waistcoat waited for their order. A tarnished gold badge revealed his name to be Andre.

"Seeing as you are both buying and driving, I'll have a white wine spritzer," she said to Jack as Andre, without waiting for his confirmation, reached below the counter for a large wine glass.

"And for you, sir?"

Jack desperately wanted to ask for a Peroni but recognised it wasn't really an option in present company.

"I'll have a sparkling water."

The drinks arrived with a small saucer of peanuts, which Jack had no intention of eating given all the rumours he'd heard about other people's hands on bar snacks. Either Jenny had never heard the stories or wasn't as bothered as her DI because she took a handful and pushed them into her mouth in one hit.

"I guess you know why we're here, Andre," Jack began.

The barman busied himself preparing the drinks, ignoring Munday's comment for as long as he could, before sighing, placing the drinks and then his palms on the bar in front of him and leaning in closer to the detective.

"Of course, I heard what happened. It's a bit of a shock. You don't expect it in a place like this."

"Where *would* you expect it?"

"What I mean is, nobody expects something like this to happen at a place where they work. It's the kind of thing that always happens somewhere else."

"Did you know the young lady who died? See her? Serve her?"

Andre shook his head.

"So you wouldn't know the man who was with her, the man who booked the room? Christopher Sinclair?"

Another shake of the head.

"And the name's not familiar to you?"

A third shake.

"Andre, where are you from? Originally, I mean."

The barman considered his answer.

"Algeria, sir. Why?"

"And do you have the requisite permits to be working in the UK?"

Jenny Jacobs had heard enough. She downed the spritzer.

"Thank you for your help, Andre. Sup up Jack, we'd better be making tracks."

"What was that all about?" Jack asked as they exited the building to find the traffic warden still standing guard over the car. "I was just applying a little pressure."

"Yes, but if the guy says he doesn't know something,

it's quite possible that he's telling the truth. Just because he can't or didn't give you the answers you're looking for isn't a reason to threaten him with deportation."

Jack responded like a sullen schoolboy, unlocking the car and steering it back into traffic without uttering a word. Jenny had no time for petulance.

"So, come on Jack, if you're going to lead this investigation as well, what's the first thing we need the team to do?"

"As well?"

"As well as checking on those threatening messages."

"Ah, those." Jack had already dismissed them as a sideshow compared with the main event of a murder enquiry.

"Surely you're capable of multi-tasking? I need you to run both enquiries. Use Salazar as your point man on this one and Duggan as your point man on the other and keep me in the loop constantly. Do you think you can do that?"

He nodded as he drove.

"So, what's the first priority?"

"Well, obviously, confirm the woman's identity and get some background on her. Finding friends and family will help us with that. We need to get a post-mortem sorted to confirm cause and time of death and then we need to start making some enquires about Christopher Sinclair."

"Agreed. Chances are if Christopher Sinclair isn't his real name, it won't be the first time that he's used it. If any of your guys have connections with the classier prostitutes, get them to hawk her picture around and see if any of them know anything. She may not be the first one to meet with Mr Sinclair and seeing her dead on a bed might freak them out enough to talk."

"I'm still not convinced the hotel manager is telling Frank everything he knows. If he *is* running an establishment that rents rooms by the hour to an upmarket clientele, then he'll want to brush as much of this as he can underneath his expensive shag pile in case it starts to have an effect on business. I mean, who wants to meet their favourite hooker at a hotel that's crawling with police?"

"So?"

"So we'll go through all their paperwork and emails with an inconveniently fine-toothed comb and see what we can uncover. We can see which cameras have the hotel entrance in shot and, if any of them are working, we might pick up either Sinclair or Irina."

"Of course, there's always the possibility that Sinclair didn't kill her. He could have left the hotel with her still alive."

"Cameras should tell us that based on time of death, but I'll have the guys interview every member of hotel staff."

"Sounds like a plan. Now, are you hungry?"

"I'm always hungry, boss."

"Me too. I'll tell you where to go and when we get

there lunch is on me."

Jack was intrigued. He felt like he was being played but couldn't do anything about it. Instead he drove north towards Kentish Town before turning right past the station into a narrow street with a small parade of shops, each of which looked like its most successful days were behind it.

"Park up where you can," Jenny instructed.

"Here?" Jack replied with incredulity.

"Here."

By the time Jack had climbed out of the car and locked it behind him Jenny Jacobs had already crossed the street and was striding purposefully towards the far end of the parade of shops. He called after her just as she entered the last shop, his view of which was partially obscured by a badly parked van. But the smell, as much as anything, told Jack what it was before he entered to find Jenny in animated conversation with a man of Mediterranean appearance, unshaven, in a stained white tee shirt and almost as wide as he was tall.

"Kebabs?"

Jack wasn't sure whether he had intended his exclamation of surprise to have been said out loud but there was no putting it back in its box now.

"Yes, kebabs," Jenny replied. "I told you I'd buy you some lunch and here we are. This is Edip and he makes the best kebabs in North London. Please don't tell me you have a problem with kebabs? You're not a vegan or anything are you? I'm not sure I could have a vegan as my DI."

Jack shook his head and tried to stifle a smirk as Jenny instructed Edip to produce two of his specials. He duly turned and began carving lamb for their doner kebabs. Edip stuffed the two pita parcels with salad and Jack gasped a little when Jenny asked him to pour extra chilli sauce across the top of both. He liked spicy food as much as the next man but double chilli sauce on a kebab at lunchtime was going above and beyond the call of duty.

Jenny bit into the pita, a little of the chilli oozing out to the side of her lip.

"I had you down as more of a niçoise salad kind of girl."

"And I thought you were a detective, Jack. Don't you think it's all a bit eighties to think women are only interested in salads?"

Munday had to admit it was a damn fine kebab, as kebabs go. All the same he still needed to drink two half-litre bottles of ice-cold water to numb the stinging in his mouth from the heat of the sauce. Jenny sipped hers as he necked his back.

"Why do I get the feeling I'm being tested," he asked her as they wandered back to the car.

"Because you are."

"And have I passed?"

She waited by the passenger door for him to unlock the car, staring directly at him across the roof.

"Jack, I've heard and read some great things about you but I'm still waiting to see if they're true. Mind you I've heard some pretty dodgy stuff too."

"So is all this a game to get me to impress the boss?"

Jenny sighed as if she couldn't quite believe that his naïveté was genuine.

"I may not be here for long, Jack, and when I go, I'd rather tell them upstairs that they don't need to appoint another new Super but that a new DCI will do. I just need to be convinced. *You* need to convince *me*. Now do you get why you're being tested?"

Jack smiled as he slipped the keys into the ignition.

"So don't fuck up. Make sure you pass."

CHAPTER SEVENTEEN

THE LIGHT OF the full moon and the childlike excitement of what he was doing made it difficult for him to sleep. Not that he minded too much; there would plenty of time to sleep later. For now, he had work to do.

He stood beside the few cupboards that passed for a kitchen and waited next to the dirty, food-encrusted microwave as he waited for the kettle to boil so he could stir himself a pot noodle. He wrapped a tea towel around the steaming plastic tub and carried it, fork rising up from the noodles, across to the table where his laptop sat. There were two tabs open on the browser, one on Facebook and one on the email account he had set up in Danny's name.

He had heard it ping earlier, indicating the arrival of a new message, but had resisted the temptation so far to see who it was from. He had to admit he hadn't been a particular fan of social media until now but he had found it such an easy way to trace the people and then observe so much of their lives remotely, particularly as hardly any of them had set their profile to private. He could see almost everything he needed; pictures of how they looked now, their contact details, where they worked, where they lived, their children and their pets. Some even had their mobile phone numbers listed. They were practically *inviting* him to get in touch. It would be rude not to.

He'd even looked at Simon's profile. Such a lovely family, such handsome kids, such a beautiful wife: a true example of suburban bliss and yet no mention, not even a cursory one as far as he could see, of the brother he had lost. They'd all be thinking about Danny again soon enough.

One profile interested him more than the others. Little Matthew Baines wasn't little anymore. He was all grown up with little Baineses of his own. He had always been the misfit, the one that all the others tolerated because their parents asked them to, and how had he repaid them? He knew his mother had always said that they were just malicious rumours and that he shouldn't listen to them. He was bored of hearing that it had just been an accident, that nobody could have done anything to save Danny. Maybe not – not now that history had repeated – but he knew there had to be *some* truth in the rumours. Why uproot your whole family at what had seemed like a moment's notice unless you had good reason to do so? Maybe nobody could have saved Danny, but if he hadn't been tripped in the first place nobody would have needed to try. It was time for all of them to have to stop and think about that day rather than their own precious little lives.

He checked the email inbox.

"Well, well," he said out loud, "an email from Karen Westcott."

He read it.

She wrote about how she remembered that day, how she thought about Danny and that day often, but she missed the point completely. This wasn't just about remembering Danny; this was about getting *justice* for Danny. This was about making the people who'd stood by reflect on their actions, on their little share of the blame. It didn't matter that they had been children then, they were adults now.

He loved the silence. The noise and the clamour of the day were too convenient an excuse for people who simply couldn't be bothered to remember. But against the backdrop of pure quiet with only thoughts for company, that was the time for recollection. It was his mission, his responsibility. Maybe if he had done so earlier, recent events wouldn't have happened and none of this would have been necessary. That had been *his* punishment for years of inaction.

It was time to reconnect with Matthew Baines. The fool had pasted his email address and his mobile number into the contact section of his Facebook profile. A little part of him despised Matthew even more for making his task so easy. He typed the address into a new, blank email and simply typed "remember me?"

He was enjoying himself now.

CHAPTER EIGHTEEN

THE FOLLOWING MORNING the team gathered in anticipation to see how Salazar and Jack could possibly work closely together. It was an open secret that they saw eye to eye on almost nothing.

Jenny Jacobs sat in her glass-fronted office eating a sausage sandwich and skimming the pages of an old copy of Empire magazine. A drop of brown sauce fell from the sandwich and landed squarely on the face of some minor star. She kept her door ajar and her hearing attuned so she could pick up what others thought they were saying out of earshot. As she glanced out she could see Salazar pinning multiple pieces of paper, some of them photographs, on a large wall-mounted board. Across the far side of the room Lesley Hilton was taking a call on her mobile phone; Danny Thorne, whose talent and aptitude didn't quite match his self-confidence, was pondering changes to his Fantasy Football team whilst the station's double act, Rob Shaw and Paul Price brought in vending machine coffees for everyone, even though, likely as not, they would all remain undrunk.

Jack entered through the double doors just to the right of Jenny's office with Duggan in tow. He looked cleaner, smarter than when she'd first encountered him, albeit in a cheap, washable suit, but his hair had been cut and he took the time to say good morning to each of his colleagues.

This could be one of two things, Jenny thought: either the influence of Lesley Hilton, if the rumours were true, or him making a genuine effort to rise to the challenge she had set him. She suspected the latter but had no idea how long the 'new, improved Jack Munday' would be with them. Jenny pulled herself out from behind her desk, walked into the main room, and positioned herself on the corner of Sheridan's desk, partly because that was where the biscuit tin was located and partly because she wanted him to be aware of her presence.

"Listen up lovely people," Jack shouted so brightly that Jenny almost thought he was about to burst into song. She noticed more than one quizzical glance being exchanged among the group. "We have important things to talk about."

"Like who dared you to wear that suit?" shouted Thorne.

Jenny tried not to choke on a chocolate digestive.

"You," Jack smiled, pointing directly at him, "can shut up or I'll have you doing traffic."

The comment, Jenny suspected, was made only half in

jest.

"Now as you all know we were called to a boutique hotel in Marble Arch yesterday morning where one of the guests, a young woman aged twenty-three who we now know to be of Ukrainian nationality, failed to take advantage of the breakfast buffet on account of having been strangled and left naked on the bed. We believe she was using the name Nataliya but from items in her possession we know that her real name was Irina Kostyshyn."

Salazar pointed to the scene of crime photographs on the board.

"The room was booked in the name of Christopher Sinclair. Frank has a loose description, which he will circulate, but we need more on him. He may or may not be the killer, but he is certainly somebody we need to be speaking to. There's a distinct possibility that Christopher Sinclair is not his real name. It is also possible that Irina was a pro but again we don't know anything for sure. Lesley, find out all you can about Irina; Rob, Paul, you work with Frank on finding out everything there is to know about Mr Sinclair and Dan, go to the hotel and ruffle a few feathers because they're not exactly breaking their backs to offer us information."

Salazar coughed. Jack's temptation was to ignore him but with Jenny still helping herself to biscuits at the back of the room, he thought better of it. He stood back and invited Salazar to speak.

"The DI mentioned that Irina was strangled and the bruising to her neck supports that," he pointed to photographs of the corpse on the hotel bed. "But until we get the post-mortem and the toxicology report we can't be certain of anything."

Jack couldn't see Harry Duggan from where he was standing but he could feel him enjoying his sense of discomfort.

"Thanks Frank," muttered Jack insincerely. "But we also have a second investigation on the go that DS Duggan and I will be looking into with Mike's assistance. This relates to a series of text messages, emails and social media messages that are bordering on harassment."

"Specific threats?" asked Sheridan.

Jack swallowed hard. He didn't want to admit he still felt all this was a bit beneath his area of responsibility now that he understood it to all be part of the test set for him by Jacobs.

"No specific threats as yet," he replied.

"Isn't this more a job for uniform?"

Jack could see Jenny chuckling to herself.

"It's a job for us because our esteemed Detective Superintendent over there wants it to be. DS Duggan will bring you up to speed, Mike, and together we will attack it with relish."

CHAPTER NINETEEN

THE MOOD IN the country had darkened palpably. Commentators and other experts on television seemed revel in the national sense of gloom. The headlines in the newspapers and on the rolling news channels gloried in screaming out the bad news. After reading in *The Times* that spending cuts would inevitably be followed by "a decade of pain", Matthew folded the newspaper neatly and dropped it into the recycling bin.

His decade of pain had long since started and he suspected many others' had too. But hardly any reports explored the impact of these statistics on real lives and real people like him. Nobody seemed to be talking about the anxiety of falling income and rising bills. Nobody talked about what would happen when you couldn't afford to feed or clothe yourself anymore, or keep a roof over your family's heads.

Matt wanted to scream at every credit card company pursuing him for money that his lifestyle was neither lavish nor extravagant, in spite of what they were trying to imply. He drove a ten-year-old car, the family drove to Cornwall to grab a break, rather than fly to the Caribbean sun, and he couldn't remember the last time that he and Susie had gone out for dinner or taken in a show. He had started buying supermarket clothes, had cancelled all of his TV subscriptions and would drive just a little bit further to save a few pence off a litre of fuel, as counterproductive as that sounded. He had begun to think twice about buying a sandwich if he was out during the day. He was even becoming used to the cash machine telling him that he had "insufficient funds" to give him a ten or a twenty when he asked for one.

In those moments after the children had gone to bed, and the house was quiet, Susie would catch him staring at the television, though in reality he was consumed by his own thoughts. She would try and encourage him to share them with her, telling him the situation couldn't go on forever and that he couldn't let it get him down.

"I spoke to Donna today," she mentioned. "I'm going to meet her for a coffee."

"Oh yeah? Gloating, was she? Has Ricky suddenly fallen into more money through no intelligence of his own?"

"No, actually. I was telling her how tough things are at the moment. She reminded me that there are more important things in life than money."

Matt laughed.

"Really? She said that? That's the type of garbage only ever said by people who actually *have* money."

Susie brought a cafetiere, steam creeping out from where the silver lid failed to fit tightly, and two mugs to the kitchen table. She placed it in front of Matt for him to plunge and pour. It was then that she noticed Leo trying to conceal himself in the doorway to the room.

"What are you doing down here?"

"I couldn't sleep."

Matt looked at him. Leo looked somehow so grown up despite only being twelve; this must have happened when Matt had been busy doing other things. He stood next to Susie, tucking his head against her shoulder, his slender frame enveloped by the pyjamas he had received from her parents for his last birthday and which were still at least one size too big. Every now and again Matt noticed him hitch up the trousers to prevent them from sliding down around his ankles.

"You can have a warm drink but then it's straight back to bed." Susie spoke with a kind of faux sternness.

Leo smiled and sidled up to Matthew, holding tightly but secretively onto something down by his side.

"What were you two talking about?"

"Grown up stuff, boring stuff."

"Money?"

"Money."

"What's boring about money? I don't think it's boring when I get money for my birthday or for Christmas. I love it."

Matt turned towards Susie, who was already stirring a small mug of lukewarm hot chocolate.

"I think we've reared a capitalist."

"Well, let's hope he's a successful one."

Susie placed the mug in front of her son, who ran his right hand wearily through his amber-blond hair. Leo picked up a Hob Nob biscuit and dipped it casually into the foaming chocolate drink.

"What's a capitalist?"

"Someone who is good at making money."

"Are you a capitalist?"

Matt chuckled to himself. "If I am, I'm not a very good one."

Leo processed the information and took another biscuit. "I heard you arguing about money."

Matt and Susie looked directly at each other and both instantly felt ashamed.

"We weren't arguing, we were talking."

"You were talking very loud then."

"Maybe, but sometimes that's what we do. It doesn't necessarily mean anything."

"If it doesn't mean anything, then why do it? That's just stupid."

Leo took a third biscuit just at the point when Susie was going to tell him that he couldn't. She moved the plate out of his reach. He threw her a disgruntled glance.

"You told mum we didn't have any money and she

told you, you would just have to work harder."

"Did she?"

"Did I? I don't think I did."

Leo nodded in the affirmative.

"So do we have any money or don't we?"

"Of course we have money. How else do you think we buy things?"

"So why did mum say we didn't have any?

Matt shifted uncomfortably in his seat and not just because of his son's unexpectedly heavy weight resting against his hip.

"Mum just meant that we don't have quite as much money as we would like at the moment. But then nobody does. Isn't that right, mum?"

Matt looked to Susie for confirmation, who duly nodded her head and placed her hand over Leo's.

"She said she didn't even know how you were going to put food on the table. That doesn't sound good."

"There's food on the table," said Matt, frustrated, as he lifted the plate of biscuits for emphasis. "And not only is there food on the table, you, young man, are eating it."

Susie stood up, sensing Matt's anxiety, put her arm around her son's shoulder and moved him away from her husband's side.

"In any case, money or no money, it's high time that you should be in bed."

As Leo turned his body towards the door he placed on the table the object he had been concealing down by his side: a shiny ceramic money box in the style of an old fashioned safe.

"What's that doing down here?" Susie enquired.

"It's my money box."

"I know what it is. I asked you what it was doing down here."

"It has thirty-four pounds and sixty-six pence in there. I thought that if we didn't have any money, you could use this for a while."

Susie made eye contact with Matthew. He kissed Leo's head, which was now resting in against his mother's side and passed the money box back to Susie to return upstairs to his bedroom.

Matthew sat back down at the table as his wife and son made their way back upstairs, rested his head in his hands, and felt sick to the pit of his stomach. At that moment his iPhone bleeped again. He didn't recognise the number from which the text message had been sent. But the message sent a shiver down his spine.

"Your son's a good-looking boy. A bit like you in 1975."

CHAPTER TWENTY

MY MILLIONAIRE BOYFRIEND had given Matt a focus. He rediscovered an energy that had been absent for months if not years, a drive that had parked itself. He even joked with Susie that perhaps he was trying to find a millionaire boyfriend for her; and it *had* been a joke, a moment between them of real humour, not a sideswipe or a chippy comment. They had shared a moment.

He had submitted three sets of visual concepts to Anderson for how the refreshed website might look. All had been well received, but one particularly so: the look and feel had been based on a traditional bachelor's pad, all black, burgundy, gold and luxurious. The theme had been carried through into various forms of lower level advertising concepts. All had been ushered through faster than had ever been the case with any of his paying client work, but then as Anderson had told him, this was his business too. Matt felt empowered. He constantly asked Anderson for the contact data of potential millionaires that he had promised him for the marketing activity.

"Let's do it by stealth," Anderson had told him. "Let people find it for themselves without alerting the big boys if at all possible. Let's fly a little under the radar." It seemed to make sense.

The site populated in short order, as Anderson's vision for My Millionaire Boyfriend began to become a reality almost hour by hour. Girls looking for a life of untold luxury began posting themselves on the site in their tens, and Matt noticed how subscriptions from anonymous wealthy men were following at a similar rate.

Anderson called irregularly but, when he did, his enthusiasm seemed more infectious than usual; his optimism more overt or, maybe, it was just that the deep contrast with the way Matt usually felt made it seem so. My Millionaire Boyfriend was declared a success. In the two months since he and Anderson had first met, more than two dozen dates had taken place and the site was gaining further interest.

Revenue in the following six weeks exceeded £20,000, comprising both the subscription fees paid by the millionaires and individual fees payable for each of the dates; 'arrangement fees' Anderson called them. It was still early, but the business trajectory was good; good enough for Anderson to pass Matt a cheque for £3,000 and to be talking about targeting other territories around the world with the same business model. Matt wasn't that bothered by the who, how and why, he was just glad to accept the money and to feel that he had something on which to build.

"It's going even bigger than I thought it would," confirmed Anderson speaking on a crackly mobile from one airport departure terminal or another. "It's all sweet. You're doing an amazing job. I want you to start thinking of what additional functionality we could add and how we might be able to attract more men to the site. Leave the girls to me; you just focus on the guys."

CHAPTER TWENTY-ONE

Irina Kostyshyn had only been in the UK for a little over eight months. Lesley imparted this information to Munday and Salazar as they sat in a cafe just around the corner from the station. Jack had a mug of frothy coffee, Lesley a tea whilst Frank was using a can of Coke to wash down a jam doughnut that looked at least twice as big as the mouth he was trying to force it into. The look on Lesley's face screamed disapproval. Even Jack, who was not the world's most elegant eater, had to admit to himself that it didn't make him feel great either. It may have been a work meeting but Frank, without realising it, was playing gooseberry. Lesley really wanted was to get Jack on his own.

"She came to London to study fashion design, worked part time as a waitress and shared a flat with two others just north of Elephant and Castle. From what I can tell she seems like a hard-working, normal kind of girl. Her flat mates are gutted. One of them has offered to do the formal

ID on the body if we need her to."

"Was there a boyfriend?" Salazar asked during a break in the chewing.

"Her flatmates didn't seem to know about one, but then again it's not uncommon for people these days to keep their relationships a secret, isn't that right, guv?"

Jack chose not to respond, thankful that either Salazar hadn't picked up on Lesley's comment or had been decent enough not to say anything about it.

"I'm sure they wouldn't admit it even if they knew, but did they give any indication that they thought she might have been working as a prostitute?"

"I asked them about that. They were very careful what they said, probably, I suspect, because they're doing the same thing. They did tell me that occasionally Irina met men that she had connected with online and that sometimes they gave her money, but they absolutely rejected the suggestion that she was a hooker."

"What would they call it… being an entrepreneur?"

Salazar laughed and ordered another doughnut. Lesley wished he would just disappear.

"I think they meant no in the sense that it wasn't organised; she didn't have a pimp or anything like that."

"So if she met this Christopher Sinclair online we should be able to pick up something from her browser history or from her emails. Make sure if she had a laptop or a tablet that we get them and any other variation on a computer she might have owned. Let's have them all and get the geeks working on seeing what they can find. Frank, did you find her mobile phone in the bedroom?"

Frank shook his head as he worked a mix of cream and jam from the side of his mouth.

"Nobody goes anywhere these days without their mobile phone, especially, I would suggest, if you're going to meet a man you've never met before for sex."

"Who said they'd never met before?" asked Lesley.

"Maybe that Sinclair or whoever killed Irina took her phone with them. Lesley, find out from her friends what her mobile number was and call it, you could pretend to be a friend trying to arrange a coffee."

"Or *you* could call it and pretend to be another client?"

Frank laughed. Jack ran a finger round the collar of his shirt to try and release his sense of discomfort.

"DO YOU MIND telling me exactly what you're playing at?" Jack asked after Salazar had left to return to the hotel.

"What do you mean?"

"You know damn well what I mean. Don't pretend you don't."

Munday stood his ground, waiting for an answer.

"Jack, when we started whatever our 'thing' is, I was really clear that it was just between you and me. I didn't want anyone else knowing about it because it's nobody else's business. I certainly didn't want to become the subject of this week's station rumour mill."

"Whoa, slow down. First, I haven't told a single soul. Has anybody actually said anything to your face?"

"Of course not. I can ignore Danny's occasional remark as office banter, especially as he's too stupid to realise how close he is to the truth, but when Jacobs tells me I can discuss the case with you when we're at home, that kind of makes me think she knows something."

"Well, if she does it's because she's put two and two together and got four and not because anyone has told her."

Lesley stirred what remained of her tea as they sat in awkward silence.

"So what do you want to do? Do you want to cool it; do you want to end it?"

"Why does the decision have to be mine?"

"Because you're the one who has a problem with their comments. I say fuck them. It's none of their business."

Lesley laughed.

"This suits you perfectly, doesn't it? You have me to cuddle up to whilst you still harbour dreams of getting back with Elaine. What happens to me if she agrees to take you back?"

"You were the one who said this was just about sex, that you didn't want a relationship."

"Maybe I've changed my mind."

Jack choked on the mouthful of coffee he had just taken in.

"What are you saying?"

"I'm saying maybe I'll really give them something to gossip about. Maybe I'll go back to the station and send them all an email to let them know their suspicions are true and that we are in a relationship."

CHAPTER TWENTY-TWO

THE EMOTIONAL IMPACT of visiting his brother's grave for the first time had weighed heavily on Simon's shoulders. He had been more quiet and withdrawn than usual. Esther had told him to book some time away from work and had reserved a cottage in Norfolk for few days' break with the boys. Simon couldn't deny that he loved the idea that of being able to spend some time together as a family. The boys certainly approved of the idea.

It was a glorious week. The sun shone through a cold but resolutely blue sky. The cottage was picture-box pretty and sat on the edge of a farm close to Hethersett. Charlie and Joe loved the freedom of running through the fields and quickly made friends with the farmer, enabling them to wander across and visit the cows whenever they wanted. With Esther's permission Simon had taken his laptop with him and could check in with the office as often as he felt he needed, allowing him to maintain a balance of control and leisure.

On the second day of four they took the boys to Banham Zoo near Diss. Even though the journey wasn't long, the children fell back to sleep almost as soon as they had left the cottage and it enabled Esther to put some grown up music on in the car. Out went the story tapes and in came the Rolling Stones.

Visiting the zoo made Esther feel like they were a family, carefree, devoid of troubles and emotional baggage. Joe particularly loved the monkeys whilst Charlie made roaring noises eyeball to eyeball with a tiger from behind the safety of the viewing gallery. Simon caught Esther watching his interactions with the boys and they shared a smile as they walked hand in hand, the boys skipping in front of them towards the elephant enclosure. As Simon flayed his right arm out in front of him to make a trunk, causing Charlie to double up in laughter and Joe to copy him, Simon's mobile bleeped twice. He pulled the phone from his pocket. The message had come from his mother's mobile. It was signed by his uncle Bob, Adele's brother, and read simply: "Simon, call me urgently, Mum very sick. It's serious."

They drove straight from the zoo to the cottage, piled their belongings back into their suitcases and headed home. Esther dropped Simon outside the hospital and made him promise to call. He ran through an endless maze of magnolia-painted corridors to reach the place where Adele had been taken. The pungent scent of disinfectant assaulted his nostrils. When he arrived, he was not prepared for what he saw. He knew what he was seeing was true, it was just that his mind couldn't process what his eyes were showing him. His mother, such a stubborn, stoic and redoubtable figure for so many years, lay diminished in front of him. Her eyes were closed, her head to one side. Simon just stood and stared at his mother, not so much enveloped by the cold, white hospital bed linen as consumed by it.

"A massive stroke, they said. But they've told us she can hear us, though I've no idea how they know that," said his uncle, who had greeted him on his arrival. "So talk to her."

"And say what?"

"Whatever you like, I guess; whatever you don't want to be left unsaid."

"I grew up resenting her, you know, after Danny. I didn't hate her. I've never hated her, but just as it looks like we were sorting things out, this goes and happens."

"But you grew up loving her, too."

Simon nodded. "She taught me how to be a parent, you know. I simply did the opposite of everything she did to me."

"You can't blame her for everything. I'm not saying you're wrong, but nobody should have to deal with what she did. Talk to her. I'm going to get some coffee. I'll bring you something back."

Simon sat alone. He lifted his mother's inanimate left hand from the bed covers, the white hospital identity tag slipping down her bony forearm until it made contact with his fingers. He twisted his mother's wedding ring and leant forward until his forehead pressed against her hand and he quietly began to sob. After a minute or so, he sat back in his chair, wiped his eyes on his shirt sleeve and sniffed hard to clear his head. Adele remained lifeless, save for the movement of her chest as she breathed.

"Well, I've got to say, you pick your moments," he whispered. "But then you always did need to be the centre of attention. You know, I only ever wanted your love and approval but you could never quite bring yourself to give it to me, could you? Or Mark? I get that it's somehow more important for you to think about Danny, maybe easier than it was for you to think about us. But once in a while some kind of recognition would have been nice and now you'll never be able to give it. And yet I still love you, and now I'm sad because you're here like this and we can never properly move on from this conversation. We can't move on from where we got to and God knows it took us long enough to get there. I wanted to tell you about all the shit that's going on with me at the moment. Sometimes I wanted to tell you I was scared, and I wanted you to be able to put your arm around me and tell me it was going to be okay and make me believe it. But you can't because you're lying there, pathetic, waiting to die, waiting to be with Danny."

Simon sensed his frustration rising. He got up from his seat and walked around the bed in the small, dimly lit room. He turned and looked at his stricken mother.

"Why can't you fight this, damn you?" he half-shouted. "Why can't you summon up all the anger you've had inside you all these years and turn it against this thing and fight it off? You won't, because you think this is going to reunite you with Danny, so you're going to lie there and give into it. You don't have what it takes to stay here for me and for Mark."

A nurse entered the room and smiled sympathetically in Simon's direction. He apologised for raising his voice.

"You don't need to apologise. People deal with this situation in many different ways," she smiled. She attended to Adele, making her comfortable, taking and monitoring readings from a selection of different machines. *If she's going to die anyway*, Simon wondered, *what's the point?* And then he remembered Mark. They had to find Mark. He had to have the opportunity to say goodbye, whatever it took.

"Her breathing has become shallower over the last couple of hours," the nurse said, quietly, as if not to waken the almost dead. "It's none of my business how angry you are with her. But the best piece of advice I was given when my mum passed was to make sure I'd said goodbye. Don't regret tomorrow not saying something today."

"Tomorrow?"

"It'll be soon."

"Shit, I thought she might have longer than that."

"I'm so sorry. Can I get you a cup of tea?"

"No, thanks," smiled Simon. "My uncle has gone to get some."

FOUR HOURS LATER, Simon and Mark found themselves on opposite sides of their mother's bed. Esther's continual calling finally paid off and she had driven to find her brother-in-law and bring him to the hospital. It was unclear who looked worse, Mark or Adele. He was gaunt, unshaven. His hair was greasy and lank, and he looked shell-shocked. They sat alternately sipping coffee, staring at Adele as she clung to life and watching as the light of the day turned to evening dusk and then the dark of night. By nine in the evening, her breathing had become noticeably more laboured and was accompanied by a loud rattle at the end of each inward breath, which both Simon and Mark found frightening. Nurses came in more frequently now and busied themselves around the bed.

"I was always envious of you, growing up," said Mark, breaking a silence heavy with sorrow.

"What on earth for?"

"Because you were the direct link to Danny, and I don't think she ever held a grudge against you."

"I just don't think she ever knew how to get past what happened. She loved us both in her own way."

"Did she? She had a funny way of showing it."

"Perhaps, but I don't know how I would have reacted in her situation. I know how I *hope* I would react, but I can't be sure. And they were different times."

Simon sipped more coffee and squeezed his mother's cold hand. "Why have we never been close?"

"Probably because we're just different people."

"But we're brothers. Soon we'll be the only flesh and blood each other has got. Surely we could be closer than we are?"

"Why? I had two brothers, but I lost one, and all these years later I'm still trying to put that situation right."

"There's nothing to put right. We need to come to terms with what happened – then and since. I want us to help each other to do it."

Mark laughed. "Simon, I'm grateful that Esther got me here. I am, really. But once this is over and we've buried our mother, we'll go our separate ways; you know we will. You go back to your family and let me go back to doing what I need to do."

CHAPTER TWENTY-THREE

CHRISTOPHER SINCLAIR JUGGLED the young girl's mobile phone between his hands, a little like the hot potato it threatened to become. He could remove the SIM card and wipe the phone but that would make an accident look much more planned. He could have thrown it away as he left the hotel but even though he wasn't thinking clearly, he'd still realised it could be found and handed in. There was enough on the phone's call and message log to tie it back to him; the *real* him, not this Christopher Sinclair creation. He slipped the phone into the already cluttered drawer in his bedside table. It was all meant to be so innocent, just a night of fun between two consenting adults with no strings attached. Why did she have to spoil it like that? They had been getting on fine. He had felt a connection between them despite the age difference, but she had to make it seem somehow sordid with her threats. She'd given him hardly any choice. Once she started screaming and refused to quiet down, he had to do something that would make her stop, but then he hadn't been able to bring her round again. He'd tried; God knows he'd tried. He'd sat beside her willing her back to life, shaking her and desperately trying and failing to come to terms with what had happened. He'd cried, cradling her head in his lap. He'd even prayed. But then his survival instincts kicked in and he'd realised he had to pull himself together and act.

Now he faced a dilemma. He needed to get rid of his clothes and anything else that might have her DNA on it. He had to wash away all traces of her. On the news, they were referring to it as a murder, but that put a much more sinister spin on what actually happened… not that he had any intention of walking into a police station to try and put them right. There would be a feeding frenzy. Nobody would be interested in listening to what he actually had to say.

The water in the shower was searingly hot, just the way he wanted it. He thought that if he stood under the water long enough that it would burn any semblance of guilt from his body. And yet the tightness in his chest was still there as he dried himself off. He had to keep himself together. If he didn't turn up where he was meant to be today, it would ask more questions than it answered. He could call in sick, but everyone would know that it was a lie. He never took time off for illness. Of course, one thing didn't automatically mean another, but he simply couldn't take a risk that people might start turning amateur detective. He thought he had covered his tracks. He had chosen the hotel carefully because he was assured of the manager's discretion once he had been rewarded for his silence, and because too much of his trade relied on this kind of activity. He had always paid cash, had never used his real identity and had always disguised himself as carefully as he could when going to and from the hotel; nothing that arose suspicion but enough to conceal his face.

HE LOOKED AT himself in the mirror, brushed his teeth, swilled mouthwash as if it would disinfect more than just his gums and then shaved, as he always did, using a block and a brush and then a clean, new blade. A styptic pencil lay on the shelf for any unfortunate little cuts. Then he pulled a navy-blue pinstripe suit from his wardrobe, a deep blue shirt and a tie from Liberty's, dressing before slipping on a pair of highly polished black brogues. He grabbed his brown leather briefcase from beneath the hat stand by the door and consciously stopped to take a long inward breadth, holding it for a few seconds before releasing again in an effort to slow down his racing heart. He locked the door behind him and took the lift to the ground floor. He exchanged morning pleasantries with Henry, the regular morning doorman, before climbing into the back of the black London taxi that was waiting for him, engine running, outside. He glanced out of the window at the seemingly endless waves of antlike commuters and reassured himself. Who would care, anyway?

CHAPTER TWENTY-FOUR

THE YOUNG MAN and woman both wore black, which offset their pale complexions. The young woman, Celina, had fading red rings beneath her eyes, evidence that she'd been crying since receiving the news of her friend's death. The young man, Mariusz, clutched her hand tightly. Salazar had offered them tea, but both had declined and asked only for water, which sat on the scratched tabletop in front of them in two white plastic cups.

"Thank you for coming in to see us. I know that this can't be easy for you," Jack began.

"Inspector, we want to do whatever we can to help you find the man who killed Irina," Mariusz replied.

"You told my colleague DC Hilton that the last time you saw Irina was around six on the night she went to the hotel," Salazar interrupted, displaying what Jack thought was a remarkable lack of sensitivity.

Mariusz nodded.

"Where was that?"

"In the flat that we share... shared."

"And when you last saw her, what was Irina doing?"

"She was going out. We were just considering going out to get some dinner and Celina asked her if she wanted to come with us. But she said she was meeting somebody for the evening, was staying out and that she probably wouldn't be back until the morning."

"And what did you take that to mean?"

Mariusz laughed as if to suggest that Salazar was being intentionally naive.

"What do you think? Irina had clearly arranged to meet someone, possibly for dinner, definitely for sex and expected it to last all night."

"Did you ask who or where?"

"We were her flat mates, sir, not her parents. It wasn't our place to tell her different, even if we wanted to."

"And *would* you have wanted to?"

"Not particularly. Irina was hardly the only person in London to use an app to hook up."

"That may be true but not all of them end up dead."

Jack leaned forward.

"Mariusz, how often do you think Irina would meet men like this?"

The young man shrugged his shoulders. "Every few weeks, maybe once a month. As I said we didn't really keep a check on her like that."

"Do you know if she ever received payment from these

men that she met?"

"Yes." Celina spoke quietly for the first time. Mariusz said something to his girlfriend in a language that Jack recognised as Polish.

"What did you say to her?"

"I told her that she didn't have to say anything that she didn't want to."

Jack smiled. "That's true, but what you know could be very helpful to our investigation. Now, how do you know she received money?"

"She showed me a bracelet that she bought. It looked really expensive so I asked her how she could afford it. She told me she used the money that the men gave her. She only ever met rich men."

"And she definitely said men. There was more than one? She didn't meet the same man on more than one occasion?"

"I'm sorry, I don't know."

"Do you know how she met these men?"

"Online, always online. She would chat with them, sometimes they would exchange photographs and then if they wanted to go ahead, they would make arrangements to meet. She told me that she never used her real name."

"But you don't know where online, which websites she visited?"

Celina shook her head.

"Tell me about how you met Irina."

"About eight months ago, Celina and I decided we

wanted to set up home together, so we found this small flat but the rent is very high. We knew from the very beginning that we would need somebody to share with us. We're Polish so we thought it would be best if we found a Polish flatmate, so we advertised in one of the ex-pat groups on Facebook. Irina, even though she was from Ukraine, answered the ad. She came around and looked at the place and we just hit it off. She moved in a few days later. We got on really well."

"Did she ever bring anyone back to the flat?"

"Men?"

Jack nodded. The couple opposite him both shook their heads in response.

"No, sir, not that I know. I mean, she might have when we weren't there, we wouldn't have objected."

"And her family, did she talk about her family?"

"Not much. I think her parents live near Kiev. Have you been able to contact them?"

"Yes," Salazar confirmed. "They'll be arriving in the next few days. Once we have the post-mortem report and the coroner has released the body, I think they plan to take her home for a funeral in Ukraine."

"On the last night that you saw her, you said she left the flat at around six in the evening."

"That's correct."

"She didn't arrive at the hotel where she met the man until around eight. If she was going direct from the flat, I doubt that would take her more than half an hour, forty minutes. So do you have any idea where she might have gone for the intervening hour and a half before she arrived at the hotel?"

Celina whispered something to Mariusz, who turned to look at Jack.

"Irina needed to pluck up the courage to meet these men so she would often go and drink for a while to settle her nerves."

"Why was she nervous? Was it just the fact that she was meeting a stranger?"

"Perhaps. I guess until you actually meet the person face to face you can't be sure that you're going to be comfortable with them, or even that they used a picture of themselves.

"Had she ever told you if she had been hurt by one of these men before?"

Celina nodded and began to cry. "One of them asked her to try and choke him, and then he would do the same to her. He thought it made the orgasm more intense."

"Erotic asphyxiation."

"I don't know what it is called," Mariusz replied.

"Why would she carry on meeting men having been with somebody who had made her do things she didn't really want to do?"

"I guess that the money was too good for her to turn it down."

Jack sighed and took a sip from a mug of cold tea.

Salazar scribbled on a small piece of paper, folded it

and pushed it across the table towards Jack.

"Thank you so much for coming in to speak to us. I'm sure it hasn't been easy, but you have both been really helpful. We'll keep in contact with you. Just wait here for a second and I'll find a constable to drive you home."

"It's okay, thank you. We could do with the fresh air and arriving home in police car will only make everyone talk."

Jack left them with Salazar to escort them out of the station, opening the folded piece of notepaper as he walked back to his office. Scrawled in untidy handwriting it said simply: *tenner says the perv is Christopher Sinclair.*

CHAPTER TWENTY-FIVE

IT WAS MID-AFTERNOON before Simon arrived home. Esther had taken the children to visit her parents, leaving the house quiet and still.

He lay on the sofa and pushed his head back into the cushion, exhaling deeply. Monty curled up to half his size and fell asleep. Simon followed soon after. His dreams, as they often did, took him back to the swimming pool on that sunny afternoon. Danny was there, looking at him in a way that Simon interpreted as a plea for help.

"There really was nothing I could do." He said, his voice deep and adult. "You have to believe me. By the time I realised anything was wrong, it was all too late."

Danny's expression didn't change, save for a slight smile; he remained silent.

"God knows if I could have done something, I would have done. But I was only a kid like you. What did I know?"

In his dream-state, Simon could feel himself begin to

cry.

"I've had this image of you in my mind. Cold, blue, lifeless. Fucking hell, it's been with me for over thirty years. *You've* been with me for over thirty years. It's not right. Every time I close my eyes, I see you; not the happy smiling you, but the lifeless you. And that's not what I want to remember. It's not how I want to remember you."

Danny smiled benignly.

"I was angry at them, *really* angry. I mean, why couldn't they save you? Why couldn't they bring you back? How difficult is it? All they had to do was make you breathe again. I was shouting at them, but they just told me to keep quiet and let them do their job. Except they didn't, did they?"

In his dream the sound of Danny's voice jolted Simon. He remembered the face, of course. Even recalled the smell, but he'd forgotten how his twin sounded. The essence of the person he had lost. It brought the whole reality of it home to him once more.

"Did you want them to save me or did you want them to spare you all of this?"

"What kind of question is that? Of *course* I wanted them to save you. What eleven-year-old kid wants to stand and watch as his brother drowns?"

"It didn't hurt."

"Really?"

"I remember standing on the side with Matthew and I dived in. I guess I must have hit my head, but the rest that

I can remember was okay. Everything went slowly. Very, *very* slowly. The water felt like a warm blanket, but by the time they brought me out of the water, I was already gone. I actually sat on the edge of one of the sunbeds and watched them trying to revive me. I knew immediately it was a waste of time. I could see the horror on your faces and hated the fact that you were all so upset. I could see everyone crying because of me. I didn't like that. I think I even tried to shout across the pool at you not to worry because I was okay, but of course you couldn't hear me. And then I thought about Mum."

"She took it hardest of all. We've never really spoken about it properly; never really dealt with it. I think everyone just wanted to pretend it had never happened."

"Why are you so worked up about it now?" Danny asked after a moment's silence. He appeared as Simon remembered him, but he spoke with the voice of an adult.

"Because you died, mate, and now mum has gone too. It's a big deal for an eleven year old to watch what happened to you. I didn't have any of the counselling I'd get if it happened today. I got a pat on the head, an extra biscuit at bedtime. I was kept home until after the funeral and then I got sent off to school as if nothing out of the ordinary had happened."

"You have to let it go, Simon. It's eating you from the inside out. It's a whole lifetime ago. You have a wife, kids, a dog even. Only one of us died; you can't let it feel like both of us did. You need to let it go and live your life because it won't be long before you turn around and wonder where it all went. All of you."

He's talking about Mark too, Simon realised.

"I guess what happened to you was the first really bad thing I ever remember happening in my life. I've always wondered why it was you who died and not me or Mark or just some other random person. Why you, and why then?"

"You're falling into that trap of trying to make sense of something that just doesn't make sense. It never will."

"That's rubbish. There has to be a reason."

"Why? Who says these things can't just happen?"

"That day set the pattern for everything that's come since."

"Only because you let it."

"Everything I've done since then has been to prove that I was worthy of surviving that day. *Everything* has been about getting approval, being a good guy, succeeding, and every little failure – well, frankly, every big failure too – just makes me think the wrong person died."

"It doesn't work like that. You're holding yourself back and setting expectations that are so impossibly high that you'll never meet them and then you can say you've failed. You're the one being too hard on yourself, nobody else."

Simon processed the idea for a moment.

"Do you think we would still have been friends?"

"Does it matter? I don't know. I'd like to think so."

"Me too. I miss you, you know."

"You don't miss me. We were only kids. You miss what you thought I could have become, what *we* could have become as brothers and friends. It's harder for you. I remember when it first happened being so confused. I couldn't get my head round the terror you were all going through. It ended my life, but it ruined yours. I know I'm alright. You lot left behind only have your memories and your imaginations."

"So I'm just meant to forget, am I?"

"Forget? Well, that's up to you, but move on? Definitely. Don't get me wrong, I'm touched you came to see me. It means everything to know you're always thinking of me, but you can't use me as an excuse for not living your life."

By the time Simon woke up, it was dark outside. The house was still, save for the distant sound of conversation and child-like laughter coming from the direction of the kitchen. He lay still for a few moments and tried to recall and preserve each element of his conversation with Danny. Monty sensed him stirring and began to lick the back of his hand, which had slipped off the side of the sofa. Simon pulled it away. He could hear the boys chattering. He sighed deeply, rubbed his eyes and shook his head vigorously as if trying to pump life back into himself. Slowly, he got up off the sofa and went to join his family.

CHAPTER TWENTY-SIX

JACK NEEDED TO escape, if only for an hour. Spending so much of his time surrounded by acts of the greatest depravity or perversion made them seem somehow normal and he always felt the need to remind himself that they weren't.

He walked the ten minutes from the station to the nearest cafe that he knew was unlikely to be frequented by colleagues, turned his mobile phone off and sat himself at a table in the corner as far away from the door as he could get. He didn't even want to risk somebody walking past and noticing him through the dirty glass windows. He had a lot to think about and not just about the case. Lesley's change of heart had thrown him completely. He thought they had an understanding, one where both of them knew what they wanted and what they expected of the other and now she had gone and thrown this curveball. He loved Lesley, he didn't doubt that, but he had always felt that he and Elaine were soul mates. He just needed a few minutes of peace, some time alone.

Some days, deciding between whole milk and semi-skimmed in his caramel macchiato was the most difficult choice in Jack's first world existence. Then there were days like this. He ordered a coffee and a bacon sandwich and sat back to read the sports pages of one of the red top tabloids that had been left folded on the edge of his table. Bloody Chelsea, top of the Premiership; it seemed as if nothing was going his way. He'd always wanted to be a policeman but sometimes he envied all those people who had what he thought of as ordinary jobs, where they could leave everything behind them at the end of the day and simply go home to an evening of domestic bliss. Harry had told him that not only would he be bored and frustrated at having to do any other job, but also that he *could* have had the family life he craved so much if only he had kept his temper in check. He smothered the bacon in ketchup and pushed the sandwich into his mouth before taking a mouthful of sweet, warm coffee to wash it down. He continued to read about some minor politician caught with his trousers down and now forced to apologise, but mostly the paper was filled with economic doom and gloom. *Surely*, he thought, *there must be something good happening somewhere; why not make everyone's day and report that for a change?* He held his mobile and thought about sending Elaine a text, but what did he have to say? She knew where he was. If she really wanted to see or speak to him, she could also pick up the phone. He was even less sure about Lesley. He had concluded not long after Elaine threw him out that he wasn't the type that was built to be alone. He needed the company, but until he sorted his head out and decided how he felt about both of the women in his life, he resolved to stay at his tiny rented bedsit.

He paid for the sandwich and the coffee and took a chocolate bar as well to keep in his jacket pocket for later and left, still not ready to return to work. He crossed the road to look in the window of an electrical store before, on impulse, walking into the florist next door.

Sending bouquets to both his estranged wife and his girlfriend would be something a psychologist could have a field day with, but he did it anyway, knowing that it would make his already complicated private life only harder to negotiate. So, fifty pounds lighter, he strolled back to the station where Salazar had been frantically looking for him with a copy of Irina Kostyshyn's post-mortem report. He professed to not knowing that his mobile phone had been switched off and speed-read the report. Then, recalling her request to be kept in every loop, he called Jenny Jacobs before walking down the bleak and bare corridor to appraise her of its contents.

"The fact that the girl died from strangulation is no surprise. The issue now is whether it was murder, as in did he go into the meeting intending to kill or was it a sex act gone badly wrong. It may not alter the final outcome; God knows, it didn't for her, but we should be sure we know the whole story."

Jack stood holding the post-mortem report, rolled in half like a tube in his right hand, as Jenny Jacobs sat back in her desk chair gripping a pen between her teeth like a cigarette.

"Whether he intentionally killed her or not, the fact remains that he left her dead in a hotel bedroom without calling for help. He's still looking at manslaughter at the absolute minimum and regardless of whether he says she consented, use of excessive force could still equate to murder."

"The guys are doing their best to find him."

"Tell them to do better. Jack, *you never really understand a person until you consider things from his point of view, until you climb inside of his skin and walk around in it.*"

"Boss?"

"It's from *To Kill A Mockingbird*, Jack. Surely you've read or seen *To Kill A Mockingbird*? I thought everyone had."

"I have but I was what, fourteen when I read it."

"Then you should read it again. Think about the words though. If Christopher Sinclair, or whatever his real name is, is paying East European girls for sex, the last he thing he wants is to be found. He's probably quietly shitting himself somewhere. Get inside his head, get under his skin and you're more likely to find a way to bring him out in the open. Find him, talk to him and show him you understand that it was all a terrible accident."

"And then?"

"Well then, you nail the perverted, murdering bastard. Make the team try harder because he isn't going to walk through the front door and hand himself in."

Rob Shaw and Lesley were both waiting for Jack when he returned to his office.

"And to what do I owe this unexpected pleasure?"

"Do you want the good news or the less good news?" Lesley asked.

"I'll start with the less good news and build myself up to a climax." Lesley gave him her most unimpressed look. He seemed to be getting them more often these days.

"I tried Irina's mobile phone about five times but on each occasion it went straight to voicemail. I think we're going to draw a blank there."

"Okay but speak to the networks. Find out which one she was with and let's at least find out the last time the phone was used and where."

Lesley nodded.

"I take it that's the less good news."

"I think so," Rob started. "We did some searches for a Christopher Sinclair online and found some old posts on websites where people go looking for sex. We set up a fake profile ourselves, emailed each of them and about an hour ago he replied to one of them."

"Did he now. What did he want to know?"

"He wanted the usual stuff about what we looked like,

whether we had a photo but he also wanted to know what we were into. What should we tell him?"

"How about we like five minute sex and then we like to grunt, roll off and fall asleep?"

Jack was going to have to have a word with Lesley. Comments like that were just not helpful. He smiled at her and tried to force a laugh to convince Rob it was just a poor taste joke.

"Don't send him a picture. Let's play it coy for a while, a bit hard to get. Maybe ask him if he'll send us a picture of him? You know the kind of thing; you show me yours and I'll show you mine."

"What about what we're into? I think we need to give him something."

Jack inhaled deeply.

"Tell him we're into edgy stuff. Tell him we've never done anything too kinky but have always wanted to try and now we feel we're ready to. Don't be any more specific than that; certainly, don't mention anything about erotic asphyxiation – and certainly not those words – but let's just see what he comes back with."

Rob nodded and rose to leave the room. Lesley did likewise.

"If he replies, I want to know immediately," Jack called after him, raising a finger to Lesley indicating he wanted her to stay. He waited until he was certain Rob and, frankly, everyone else was out of earshot before closing the office door. He turned back into the room. Lesley was smiling.

"Want to tell me what the fuck you're playing at? You're the one complaining that you think people know about us and here you are making it easy for them by making inappropriate comments. Don't you think they're going to guess what you're playing at? They're fucking detectives, for Christ's sake."

"I'm sorry," she whispered, her quiet voice cracking a little. "I just want to know where I stand."

In that moment she seemed fragile. Her vulnerability made him want to wrap his arms around her and pull her close. But he knew if he did, somebody would walk into the office and that would open a whole new can of worms.

"We can't talk about it here. We have to keep it separate from the job otherwise we really will have problems. I'll come round tonight and we'll talk, I promise."

She nodded, and walked towards the door.

"Lesley," Jack called after her, "I do love you."

"I know you do."

Suddenly, for Jack, with those words everything had simultaneously become both clearer and much more complicated.

CHAPTER TWENTY-SEVEN

HARRY HAD COFFEE waiting by the time Jack arrived in the small office they were sharing.

"How are you getting on with Salazar?"

"The guy's a Muppet."

"You don't have to like him; you only have to be able to work with him."

"That's what Jenny said."

"You should listen to her; she speaks a lot of sense."

"What makes you think I'm *not* listening to her?"

"Because you're so frigging defensive about it. If you're going to make the step up to DCI, you can't pick and choose which members of the team you're prepared to work with and which ones you aren't."

"That's true but it doesn't mean I can't think the guy's a Muppet."

"No, Jack, but you have to be a bit more careful not to show it."

The phone rang.

"Saved by the bell," Jack muttered.

Duggan took the call, which lasted a matter of seconds.

"It's your lucky day; Danny Thorne's coming into see you."

At almost the same moment that Duggan finished his sentence, Danny Thorne wrapped rhythmically on the office door, bursting in before waiting to be invited.

"Aye aye gentlemen, how's life in the love shack today?"

As much as Jack wanted to bawl him out for insubordination, he just couldn't. You could say many things about Danny Thorne, but you could never accuse him of being disloyal.

"It's not a love shack, it's an office but you're welcome anyway. Pull up a chair. What's on your mind?"

He sat, brushing his shirt down with his hands and looked directly at Jack as if he were sitting in front of the headmaster or attending his first job interview. Jack pulled a small bottle of water out of the bag by his desk, opened and gulped half of it down. Lesley had shown him an article in a magazine about the importance of staying hydrated, especially if you need to concentrate on your work. It made perfect sense but really, he was doing it just to earn some brownie points with Lesley.

"Christopher Sinclair."

"What about him?"

"I went to the hotel and started poking around. It

turns out the other night wasn't the first time Mr Sinclair had stayed there. In fact, it was the fourth time in the last three months, and always just for one night at a time."

"In London on business?"

"Maybe, but the manager's reluctance to answer questions makes me think he uses the hotel specifically to meet women. He always pays cash. If you're staying for work, they either pay for you or you settle it with a card when you leave."

"Don't tell me he always insists on the same room?"

"No, but the room service order is always the same, always a bottle of Cristal champagne and a tray of strawberries."

"Classy," commented Jack.

"Bet you're more of a Nutella and spray whipped cream kind of guy, Danny?" ventured Harry.

"What else does he do when he's at the hotel, apart from the obvious? Does he have dinner in the restaurant or a drink in the bar?"

"It seems not. He seems to arrive, collect his key and then heads straight up to his room."

"So presumably he arrived before Irina the other night?"

"Yes, he arrived a little before seven thirty, she arrived just after eight."

"And when he books, does he give any other contact details, an address, a mobile phone number, an email?"

"Nope, not a jot."

The door opened and Mike Sheridan's face appeared.

"Can I have a word, guv?"

Danny smiled at him.

"The grown-ups are just about done, Mikey, I'm sure the DI doesn't mind reopening the crèche for a while."

Sheridan raised his middle finger, which only prompted another round of laughter.

"What do you need, Mike?"

Danny rose, blew Sheridan a kiss and made his exit.

"These threats, guv, the ones that Karen Westcott has been receiving?"

What with the murder enquiry underway, Jack had almost forgotten about the other enquiry and had certainly lost a degree of interest in it. But if they were part of Jacobs' test, then he knew he had to give the impression, at least, of being on top of events.

"What about them?"

"So, she received emails from someone purporting to be this kid Danny Carter, who died in seventy-five. Yes?"

Both Duggan and Munday confirmed the point.

"So, I rang her to introduce myself and to find out if she had received any more messages. Not only has she had a new one saying that soon..." Sheridan looked down at his notebook, "...one of the old gang would be getting a surprise, but that she'd heard from another old friend, who was also present on the day Danny died, with whom she's still in contact. He's also been getting messages from Danny Carter, pretty much the same thing, but this time with a picture of himself attached."

"This is getting a bit weird now. Who is this guy?"

"His name's Kevin Simpson and he lives in Manchester."

"She mentioned him when we saw her. Okay, track him down and give him a call."

"Do you want me to ask the Manchester boys to send round a couple of constables?"

Harry stared at Jack and knew instinctively what he was thinking.

"No but ask them as a courtesy if they mind us popping up to have a chat with him."

"To Manchester?" Duggan queried.

"It isn't that far on the train and if this has been set as a challenge from above, it's time we started rising to it."

"Challenge from above? Not sure I understand guv."

"Silly private joke, Mike. Pay no attention. Do a search and see if anybody else has reported anything similar."

Sheridan nodded.

"When do you want to go to Manchester?"

"Well my mum used to say there's no time like the present, so why don't you see if Mr Simpson can see us tomorrow."

CHAPTER TWENTY-EIGHT

ADELE'S FUNERAL HAD brought Simon and Esther even closer together. She saw the sadness behind his eyes, and it drew a tenderness out of him that she felt had been missing for far too long. He may have been approaching middle age with children of his own, but Esther recognised that there's nobody as vulnerable as a child who has just lost a parent. At a time where Simon seemed distant, despondent and forlorn, Esther took it upon herself to try and build him back up.

The morning after the funeral, Charlie climbed into bed with Simon. He laid his head against his father's shoulder and tapped rhythmically on his T-shirt covered chest.

"Are you sad about Grandma?"

"Of course."

"You're not crying, though. Are you?"

"No, I'm not crying on the outside. But when you're grown up sometimes you do your crying on the inside."

Charlie found the concept amusing.

"Why did Grandma die?"

"Well," Simon swallowed hard. "She got very sick very suddenly and the doctors, even though they tried their best, just weren't able to make her better."

"They're not very good doctors, then, are they?"

Simon smiled at the simplicity of his rationale.

"Probably Grandma was just too sick."

Charlie took time to absorb this information before coming back with his next question.

"Are you and mummy going to die?"

"One day. But not for a very long time."

"How do you know that? There might be better doctors then so they could save you."

"Maybe, but everyone has to die sometime. It's nature. It's just the same as flowers dying, or even Martin."

Martin had been Charlie's hamster who had passed away and been buried with much ceremony the previous spring.

"Martin got very old and very sick and it was just his time."

Charlie considered and processed this piece of information.

"Sometimes, when somebody who is old dies and they've had a long and happy life, we need to do our best to remember them and do our best to smile when we think of them. That's the best way to try and keep them with us."

"Why didn't we bury Grandma in the garden with

Martin?"

Simon was completely nonplussed by this latest quest for information. He pulled Charlie closer to him and ruffled his unbrushed hair.

"You, young man, ask too many questions."

Simon knew that being a father was the most important job he would ever have. When the boys were babies, he had slept with them laying on his chest and across his shoulder, feeling their little hearts beat faster and yet somehow still in time with his own. He would study them as they slept; the long, thin, elegant fingers with their soft, tiny little nails; their pink downy skin and their button noses and rosebud mouths. This was evidence enough for Simon that miracles existed, and he felt sad that Mark had never experienced it. As the boys had gotten older he wished he had made the conscious decision to stop from time to time and step back to watch their progress, to note and enjoy each little change or development in their personalities, each growth in confidence, each step onto the next rung of the ladder towards independence.

More than anything, he wanted to be more of a parent to them than ever his mother had been to him. Thinking about it made him happy, and yet it made him melancholy too.

CHAPTER TWENTY-NINE

ANDERSON JAMES LOOKED hassled when he walked into the café, pushing past the queue and sitting down at Matthew's table. There was no handshake, no small talk, just a nod in the direction of the waitress and a point at Matthew's coffee to indicate that he would have the same. He looked a little less immaculate than usual. Beads of sweat bubbled across his brow. This time there was no tie, just an open necked shirt and he spent much of his time looking around the café at who was in the queue and who was watching them. Nobody was.

"Fucking busy," he started, gasping a little for breath.

"That's a good thing, right?"

"Well, kind of; just too much to do and not enough hours in the day, brother."

"Millionaire Boyfriend going well?"

"Going mental, mate, and in no small part to you. It's seriously doing the business."

"So you're happy?"

"Happy, brother? Fucking ecstatic. Registrations have almost doubled and we're now getting around fifty dates a month organised. Revenue is topping twenty grand a month and climbing, which isn't half bad given how long it's been going. I reckon we could double that by the end of the year. We've just got to keep pushing it and then you and I need to have a talk about taking it global."

"Global?"

"Worldwide, brother, we're not stopping at the UK. We've got to take this baby to the world. I need you to keep it going here as I'm off on my travels for a while, promoting the music and the fashion."

"I thought you wanted to build it up and then sell it; you know cash in and split the profits?"

"We will. That's still the plan. But why stick with what the UK has to offer when we can maximise our potential by taking it international? There's a lot of very horny millionaires out there and we're providing a service they're happy to pay for. I reckon it would be selfish not to give them the opportunity to benefit, don't you?"

Matthew felt a little deflated. He was hoping to begin to see some more money out of the project; perhaps even enough to make a dent to his debt and enable him to show Susie that they were on the road to recovery. Whilst Anderson's rationale made perfect sense, it also meant that the timescales he was banking on to recoup some serious money were now going to be extended.

"Where are you travelling to?"

"To Africa, my man. I've got meetings in Ivory Coast and Nigeria in the next few weeks about all my normal stuff, but I'm also going to talk to them about Millionaire Boyfriend. I think it could work well out there with the high up government types. So are you cool with minding the shop here?"

Matt nodded. What other choice did he have?

"Cool. I can carry on with the registrations remotely while I'm out there. I can continue to organise the dates and deal with the payments, I just need you to keep an eye on the site. Keep it refreshed and make sure it doesn't go down. The only thing going down should be the girls," said Anderson, with a wink.

"Business is still tight, you know," said Matt. "If there's any other work I can do that will give me some money, just throw it in my direction?"

"Of course, brother, of course. There's nothing this minute but there will be."

Then Anderson looked around the café once again and lent into his black Mulberry messenger bag, retrieving a white envelope, unsealed and bulging at the sides. He passed it across the table and handed it to Matthew. Matt opened it and looked at the inch-thick wide stack of used twenty-pound notes. He looked up and made direct eye contact with Anderson.

"What's this?"

"It's three thousand pounds, that's what this is."

"And it's for?"

"Let's just call it a down payment on future earnings. I know you're finding it tough, so I want to help. We're brothers, man. Take it. It has to help, right?"

Matt smiled and offered his hand for Anderson to shake.

"Don't give me no sentimental shit, just take the money."

"Thanks. It will make a difference and it goes without saying that you can rely on me."

"Yeah yeah, whatever. Let's just make it happen. Now while I'm away, email is going to be the best way to try and get me. Not sure I'll have much time for talking. If I get time, I'll call but whatever decisions you need to make, make them and I'll back you."

"No worries. Leave it with me."

Before Matthew had even finished his sentence, Anderson was out of his seat and brushing imaginary crumbs off of his lap. He smiled, offered a clenched fist for Matthew to self-consciously bump and then he was gone; almost as quickly as he'd arrived.

MATTHEW SPENT THE rest of the day moving from one cafe to the next, particularly searching out those that offered free WiFi to keep his costs as low as possible. Occasionally, more in hope than expectation, he would fire off a speculative email or two looking for work, but nobody replied. He began to think about what would be needed to take Millionaire Boyfriend global and started to sketch out some ideas that he could have in his locker to show Anderson the next time they met.

A year from now, Matt thought to himself, it would all be very different. Millionaire Boyfriend would not only be bringing in regular income, but they'd be close to selling and he he'd have a raft of other projects on the go. Debts would be being paid off, life would be more stable, he'd feel more content in himself and perhaps even Susie would like him again. Perhaps.

He returned to his laptop and wandered onto Facebook to check up on the mundane comings and goings of people he once called friends, but who now had been reduced by technology to little more than virtual contacts. As ever, nothing dramatic had happened so he resolved to click on the one message waiting for him and then head home. It was from a name that he hadn't seen written in years. Danny Carter.

"Hi Matthew. 30 years is a long time, isn't it? Not *that* long, though. Did you get my text? I'm going to start setting a few wrongs right; can't wait to see your face."

Matt slammed the laptop shut, to the evident alarm of the others around him. If this was somebody's idea of a sick joke, then it wasn't very funny.

CHAPTER THIRTY

THE ANALYSIS OF the contents of Irina Kostyshyn's laptop gave a much clearer picture of her activities in the weeks leading up to her death. From her email account it became apparent that she had been communicating with Christopher Sinclair for around ten days. Mostly the communication had been flirtatious, what Jack's mother might have called 'saucy', but in the last few days, after she had agreed to meet him, the correspondence became much more formal, almost business-like. They not only discussed what Sinclair wanted to do and where, though there was no mention of asphyxiation, but also emails relating to the financial transaction, which were particularly interesting.

"I've printed them all out for you but there's one particular email that I want to draw your attention to," Paul Price began. "In it Sinclair asks how much she expects as payment for meeting him, to which Irina replies five hundred pounds. He then asks how she wants payment to be made, cash on the night or how? Irina replies that she wants payment to be made to MMB."

"MMB?"

"We started looking back through her emails even further and also through her web browsing history and the only MMB we could come up with was a dating site called My Millionaire Boyfriend. This offers the chance for predominantly young women to get in contact with very wealthy men."

"Get in contact?"

"As far as I can see and in as much as I know from my very limited experience of dating websites, you put up a profile of yourself, pay a membership fee to join and then you get to view the profiles of other members. Then, if you see someone that takes your fancy, you can message them through the site and potentially arrange a meet."

"But she said that she wanted payment for services rendered to be made through this website?"

"And if that's the case that means this website, particularly if it's taking a commission, could in fact be a high-class prostitution organisation."

Jack nodded.

"The first thing we need to do is gain access to Mr Sinclair's profile. That should help get us closer to him. Contact MMB but don't give them any indication that we suspect them of prostitution. Even if they are, they didn't kill Irina and our first priority is to catch the person who did. We can come back to them for the pimping later."

Paul nodded just as Lesley stuck her head around the door. Momentarily Jack's heart sank, but she was determined to be a paragon of professionalism.

"Irina's mobile."

"What about it?"

"The network tells me that the signal from her phone was last detected around ten in the morning *after* she died in the Mayfair area of London. I'm just waiting for them to come back to me with a more accurate area reading."

"Keep on it. I think the net's closing around Mr Sinclair. Let's not let anything slip."

CHAPTER THIRTY-ONE

KEVIN SIMPSON SAT in his large, plush office on the fifth floor of a modern glazed block just off of Deansgate in the heart of Manchester. He sipped a skinny vanilla latte from a white mug that was a little too elegant for his stubby fingers as he scanned Facebook on the MacBook that sat on top of the smoked glass table that passed for his desk.

Even though his working day had barely begun, he had undone the top button on his shirt, and loosened his tie such that it gave the appearance of being drunk, hanging lopsidedly over his chest and on top of the ridge that the top of his stomach created. As a younger man his body had been something of a Temple; these days it more closely resembled a bouncy castle. He had resolved again to get fitter and had even joined a gym but on almost every occasion that he had visited, hadn't made it much further than the coffee shop in reception.

Kevin wasn't an active Facebook user, in the sense of

placing on public record the minutiae of his everyday life, but his ex-wife Denise had harassed him to sign up as a way of keeping tabs on what their two teenage daughters were doing online; he thought she was being unduly paranoid but had learnt a long time previously to carefully choose the battles he wanted to fight, particularly with Denise. However the more time he began to spend on the site, the more he had begun to enjoy the experience and, recently (in fact ever since Karen Westcott had been in contact with these strange stories of messages supposedly from Danny Carter), he had found himself logging on every day or two rather than every week or two; occasionally he would comment on another person's status, mostly though he would just silently prowl, restricting himself to inhabiting the online shadows. And then, of course, he began to receive similar messages. He didn't particularly feel threatened by them but they intrigued him, perhaps even disturbed him a little.

On this particular morning, something new had caught his attention. On the right hand side of the screen was a list of other Facebook users helpfully gathered under the heading "people you may know." Indeed, Kevin knew most of them, some well, others quite distantly, but it must have been more than thirty years since he had seen the name Matthew Baines.

He clicked through to Matthew's profile and searched through the photo library. The guy had failed to set almost any of his privacy settings so there was plenty to see. The images bore little resemblance to the boy he remembered. Matthew was the kid at school who never quite fitted in; the one who wore the grey shirt when everybody else was wearing white, his trousers were shapeless, his shoes scuffed and he always seemed to be wearing a grey v-neck sweater regardless of how hot it was outside. Matthew had been the piece in the jigsaw box that had come from a different puzzle.

They had been friends, once, both inside school and outside where their parents' acquaintance kind of forced them together, but he hadn't seen or heard of him since Matthew's whole family had upped and moved away apparently without warning. His parents had never mentioned the Baineses again, or not in front of him at any rate. Now it seemed Matthew was married and had a family of his own, a girl and a boy as far as Kevin could make out. They were good looking kids.

Momentarily it made him smile and long for the lost simplicity and sense of freedom from before *that* day. He had been thinking a lot about it recently and, though they had never realised it at the time, he had reflected on how that one incident had ripped that small group of friends apart when, perhaps, it might reasonably have been expected to have brought them closer together. Back when they were kids, kicking a ball together against the playground wall and pretending it was Wembley, how could they have known that things would have turned out the way they had?

He looked back at his screen and wondered if Matthew ever thought about that day; whether he spoke about it and whether he was still in contact with Simon, Mark and the rest of Danny's family. He wondered whether the Matthew he remembered had changed and become more comfortable in his own skin or whether he was just a grown-up version of the child riven with anxiety. Most of all, he wondered if Matthew Baines had also received a message from whoever it was pretending to be Danny Carter.

Kevin had bumped into Simon once himself, probably ten years previously, coming out of an exhibition that both of them had attended at the cavernous Earl's Court centre in West London. It had been an awkward encounter; an effected handshake and a brief attempt at small talk. Such things, Kevin had found, were almost impossible after a lengthy time apart and with such an unspoken tragedy between them. Thankfully Simon had mentioned something about having an imminent meeting and had scuttled off, head bowed, mobile phone locked between his shoulder and his cheek as he wrestled with the briefcase in his other hand. Neither of them had offered contact details, exchanged business cards or suggested getting together later for a coffee or a beer. He sensed that both had walked away a little sadder, but probably also breathing a sigh of relief.

Part of Kevin had wanted to take Simon aside and get answers to his many unanswered questions and, almost as soon as they had gone their separate ways, part of him regretted not having done so: what had really happened that day? It had felt like he had been whisked away faster than his feet could touch the ground. Would Simon have liked to know that Kevin thought often about that day or would the sight of him have been little more than a painful and unwelcome reminder? But he didn't take Simon to one side, and to ask those questions would have been to invite himself into Simon's private grief simply to satisfy his own curiosity, so they had exchanged stilted pleasantries but said goodbye.

The events of that day had always been like a troublesome itch in a place he couldn't reach which, every now and then would resurrect itself and demand to be scratched. Sometimes his recollections were vivid other times so diluted with the passing of time that he had cause to question whether they had happened at all. Seeing the horror that still lived behind Simon's eyes that day reminded him they had. Kevin held the on-screen cursor hovering over the 'friend request' icon on Matthew Baines's Facebook profile before moving it sharply away and closing the browser tab. Nothing good would ever come from going back, he thought.

Kevin's secretary, Jane, had already told him that the police officers he had been expecting had arrived. He closed his laptop, straightened his tie and rose from his seat to introduce himself as she showed Jack Munday and Harry Duggan into his office.

"It's an impressive view." Jack looked out of the floor-to-ceiling windows behind Kevin's desk.

"It is Inspector, provided you don't suffer from vertigo. I've had a number of people who've come in here, made similar comments until they've got close up to the glass, then you see them slowly but surely edging their way back into the safety of the centre of the room."

Almost through the power of suggestion, Jack began to step back.

"What line of work are you in?"

"Commercial property."

"It looks like it's good business?"

"I started out at an estate agent's as a kid, doing residential sales and lettings. I enjoyed it, but I always thought there was potential to earn better money in the commercial sector so I made that my ambition when I first moved up here."

"A man with a plan?"

"Not a plan as such. I just looked at who had the biggest houses and drove the flashiest cars and decided to try and do whatever it was that they did."

"So when did you move up here?"

"When I was about twenty-six. I married a Manchester girl who had absolutely no intention of coming down to London, so here I am. We're not married anymore but I've been here long enough for it to feel more like home than London, though no matter how long you live up here, Inspector, don't let anybody try and tell you it's easy being an Arsenal supporter living in the shadow of Old Trafford."

Duggan took out a notebook and began tapping the page with a ballpoint pen; Jack knew from experience that this was one of Harry's telltale ways of nudging him to get on with the matter in hand. This only made Jack determined to extend the pleasantries for a few minutes more. Jane entered the room and laid down a tray with three mugs of coffee and a plate of shortbread biscuits; the kind often bought as a Christmas present in a tartan-covered tin. Jack leant forward and took one from the plate without waiting to be offered. He could hear Harry's sigh of disapproval.

"Do you go back home much, Mr Simpson?"

"From time to time. My parents still live in the house where I grew up and we try and get together four or five times a year. I usually go down there two or three times and they come up here for the others. There's more chance of them seeing their grandchildren if they come up here than if I have to try and persuade the girls to put their busy social lives on hold to go and see them with me. But my parents are getting older and aren't in the best of health, I'm afraid, so it's becoming less easy for them to drag up here than it used to be, especially as my Dad still insists on driving."

"And do you see or speak to any of the people you were friendly with back then?"

"Back around the time that Danny died?"

Jack nodded as he wiped a crumb of shortbread away from the corner of his mouth with the thumb on his right hand. He didn't need to imagine too hard what Duggan was thinking.

"Not really. I mean I am still in contact with a few through Facebook and the like but it's a fairly superficial friendship. I haven't seen any of them. I just comment on the odd funny post or old photograph. We haven't had any big reunions, if that's what you mean."

"And that's how Karen Westcott got in touch? Through Facebook?"

"Yes, she sent me a message, out of the blue really, and asked me if I'd had any messages about Danny Carter's death. I thought it was a really strange thing to ask. I mean, it's been thirty years. I hadn't had any at that stage and to be honest I didn't really know what she was talking about until she told me about them in a bit more detail."

"And then you got some?"

"Yes, mine were pretty similar to Karen's, to be honest, except whoever it was hasn't attached any photographs to mine. They just seem to be almost reminiscing about the day."

"Do you mind if we see them?"

Kevin pushed a white envelope across the desktop, which Jack took and handed immediately to Harry.

"I printed them all out. They're in there."

"You know, Mr Simpson, Danny's death must have been a pretty huge thing to have witnessed when you were as young as you all were."

Kevin sipped from his coffee cup and allowed the question to sit in his mind for a moment.

"I've thought about this a lot over the past few weeks, since all this stuff with the messages started, but the problem is that when I think about it, I seem to do so from the perspective of being the age I am now. We knew that it was bad; we knew that Danny was gone. It affected everybody but, you know, we were back at school the next day."

"That couldn't have been easy?"

"To be honest, I don't know. I remember it feeling weird that we had all experienced this horrible thing and then, so soon after, nobody was talking about it. There were whispers and stuff, but I don't remember any big assembly or anything."

"And what about those of you who were actually there when it happened?"

Kevin shook his head slowly, as if his recollections had momentarily transported him back to 1975.

"We never spoke about it."

"Don't you think that's odd?"

"Well, you have to ask yourself what we could possibly have discussed at eleven and twelve years old? We didn't want to relive it; we couldn't have put it right and I don't think any of us wanted to talk about it behind Simon's back."

"But didn't your parents talk to you about it?"

He shook his head again.

"It hit my mother hard. The Carter boys had come with us that day so, in a sense, they were her responsibility."

Jack leant forward and sipped a little of the now tepid coffee.

"Tell me about Danny."

Kevin inhaled deeply and exhaled with equal force.

"Danny was an ordinary kid. It's a long time ago but I remember him being funny, outgoing. Simon was the more reserved of the two, but they were both just normal kids."

"And they had an older brother?"

"Yes, Mark. He was a bit more intense; he was a few years older than us and, at that age, a few years is a big gap. I think he thought we were a bit of a pain in the arse to have to hang around with. He never seemed to have many friends of his own. Not when we were all together, at least."

"When was the last time you saw Simon or Mark?"

Kevin outlined the chance encounter with Simon at the NEC, adding that he couldn't really recall the last time he saw Mark.

"I'm not sure that us growing up and apart had anything to do with Danny. I think it's just what happens. Occasionally, I'd see Simon or Mark out and about. Simon would nod or say hello, but we didn't hang around with the same people and I think anything more than being polite could have brought all of those feelings to the fore again. I had heard that their mother had never really adjusted to what happened to Danny, and who could blame her, so seeing any of us who were there that day couldn't have been easy. We would just have been a reminder."

"And Mark?"

"On the rare occasions that I used to see him, Mark wouldn't even make eye contact. He seemed quite intense, angry even. I think he started drinking and dabbling in things he shouldn't have in his late teens to try and cope with whatever demons he was dealing with because of Danny."

"You say he was angry?"

"Yes. I don't think he ever came to terms with the fact that what happened to Danny was just a nasty, freakish accident. But then when the rumours started swirling around, he seemed to take that as proof that it wasn't quite the accident people had made it out to be."

Kevin picked up the desk telephone to ask Jane to replenish the coffee when it would probably have been just as easy to open the door and call.

"Tell me about these rumours," Jack began, hoping Jane would bring fresh mugs so he didn't have to pour fresh coffee onto the inch of cold liquid that lurked at the bottom of his existing cup.

"I've never been one to spread rumours, Inspector, or tell tales out of school."

"I think we're way past the telling tales out of school phase, sir, so why don't you just fill us in on the rumours like the Inspector asked." Harry looked like he was trying to combine menace with a polite smile.

"I was beginning to wonder whether or not you spoke, Sergeant."

"He only speaks when he thinks we're being bullshitted," Jack interjected.

Kevin Simpson coughed to clear a throat that nobody in the room, least of all himself, seriously thought was blocked.

"Now, I'm not for a moment suggesting there was any truth behind these rumours." His voice wavered enough to betray his nerves. "I've always thought they were just hearsay."

"We get it," snapped Jack. "We've heard the health warnings loud and clear, but we can't make a judgement on them until you actually tell us the rumours."

Simpson nodded. "Soon after Danny's death, Matthew Baines and his family suddenly moved away from the area, without warning. One day they were there and the next day they were just gone."

"I have to tell you it's not the most exhilarating rumour I've ever heard."

"Well, no, quite. The rumour mill had it that the family moved because Matthew had been responsible for Danny's death and they were worried that it wouldn't be long before the shit hit the fan. I suppose they thought it best to get him out of the way and deal with whatever might be coming from somewhere else."

"And when you say he was responsible, how exactly would that have been?"

Kevin rose from behind his desk and stood with his back to the panoramic window.

"I mean, I don't know exactly but I think the suggestion was that they'd been horsing around outside, on the edge of the pool and that as Danny was running to dive or jump in, or whatever, Matthew tripped him, which caused him to enter the pool at an angle, causing him to hit his head on the side."

"Even if that was true, it hardly makes him a murderer. It's still just a horrible accident."

"True, Inspector, but not if you're looking for somebody to blame."

"Mark?"

"Far be it from me to cast aspersions but…"

"… but you think, all these years later, that Mark Carter could still be looking for somebody to pin it on."

Kevin Simpson nodded.

"Even if that is true," interrupted Duggan, "wouldn't he be sending his messages to Matthew rather than to Karen Westcott and yourself?"

"Who's to say he hasn't, Sergeant? I'm no longer in contact with Matthew Baines."

AN HOUR LATER, as Jack and Duggan drank Starbucks

coffee on the concourse at Piccadilly Station, watching commuters running for trains they weren't going to catch, Munday acknowledged that maybe, just maybe, there might be more to this case than he had originally admitted.

"We should probably talk to the Carter brothers and Matthew Baines as well, just to tie up the loose ends so we can write a neat and tidy report for the Super."

"You mean so *I* can write a neat and tidy report? You wouldn't know how to."

Jack's chuckle recognised the truth of Duggan statement.

"What did you make of Mr Simpson, then?"

Duggan reflected on the question.

"I thought he was dodgy as fuck."

"Me too," Jack laughed. "Fancy a muffin?"

CHAPTER THIRTY-TWO

DEEP DOWN, CHRISTOPHER Sinclair knew he shouldn't reply to the message, but he couldn't help himself; what had happened with that other girl had just been a freak accident. It wasn't the sort of thing that would happen twice and, well, if here was another girl willing to indulge him, willing to experiment with him, where was the harm in that? He was only human, after all.

This new girl had responded to an old profile, one that he had almost forgotten; she intrigued him. She wasn't prepared to give much away and at the moment she wouldn't even send him a picture of herself. He liked it when they played a little hard to get. He enjoyed the thrill of the chase. She might be a timewaster, but he was prepared to go along with her a little longer. After all, he had precious few other options at the moment.

He had to try and keep himself calm, to put that Irina girl to the back of his mind, even though every time he closed his eyes, hers was the face he saw. It seemed as if her perfume always carried on the air around him and her little murmurs always in his ear during quieter moments.

In the first few days after it had happened and he had read about her true identity, he was aware that the case had become the subject of water cooler conversation. He had convinced himself that friends and colleagues were looking at him differently, as if they somehow suspected he had been involved. At one point, when one of his colleagues asked him if he was okay, he had snapped back a response so quickly that he would later worry that this alone might have aroused suspicion. He had apologised as profusely as he had been able, blaming his agitated state on too little sleep and far too much coffee. In truth, most of the time since it happened, he'd been able to keep a lid on his anxiety, particularly if he immersed himself in work. But every now and again, usually when he least expected it, he would see the image of that beautiful young girl lying naked and lifeless on the bed where he had left her.

He returned his attention to his laptop. He needed to give the new girl just enough information to tempt her to respond a second time and, once she did, he was confident she would be hooked. He had an impressive track record when it came to this, yet it was still important for him to prove to himself that he could have what he wanted again without any of these unfortunate consequences. He had told her as much as he was prepared to about himself at this stage.

He had undercooked his age a little but that shouldn't be a deal breaker; he had even indicated, as subtly as he could, that he was prepared to reward her for her time. He had been careful not to be too obvious as some women didn't like the suggestion, however carefully it was couched, that they might be interested in accepting money for sex. Others, of course, like the Ukrainian girl, were only ever looking for a transactional relationship. He could be patient. He had time on his side; there was no particular rush. For now, he closed his Christopher Sinclair email account, reopened his real one and returned to his work.

CHAPTER THIRTY-THREE

"YOU DON'T HAVE to stay with him, you know. You deserve better. It must be such a drag for you and the kids, him being so, you know, unreliable. You're entitled to be looked after the way Ricky looks after me."

Donna Christie and Susie Baines had been close friends for longer than either would want to admit. Donna was tall, not far short of six feet in heels, even when she wore her thinning hair down rather than up. Some would have called her statuesque, whilst too much exposure to tanning beds had given her skin a texture not dissimilar to the hide of an elephant with a colour that matched 'ochre' on the Dulux chart. Susie could already smell at least one glass of white on her friend's breath, even before eleven in the morning. She had often thought of broaching the drinking issue but had never uncovered the courage to do so. The Ricky to whom Donna referred was her husband, a man who wore his self-confidence the same way as his designer clothes: at least a size too small and more suited to somebody fifteen years his junior. It was, Matt had said on more than one occasion, a reflection of an ego the same size as his bank balance and yet in direct contrast to the size of his penis; classic small man syndrome. Susie and Matt had talked about how Donna and Ricky had changed in the time they had known them, how they had seemed to have forgotten what life had been like before they found their fortune.

Matt disliked them both. He didn't trust them, and he didn't like the way their success had prompted them, perhaps subconsciously, to treat others with a casual disregard that sometimes bordered on disdain. They seemed so preoccupied with their new material lifestyle, with its many trappings of success, that he knew others had also noticed how their children seemed to yearn for the affection and attention of their parents and not just an allowance. But most of all Matthew hated the hold that Donna seemed to exercise over his wife. The teeth-whitened smile, the holiday home on the Catalonian coast, the sporty Audi and the need to be with the in-crowd meant Susie had, in some way, become seduced by Donna. Susie had never felt able to say no whenever Donna came calling.

Now here she was, in Costa Coffee, Norah Jones singing *Come Away With Me* in the background, their marriage the subject of Donna's cappuccino counselling.

"It's really not that easy," said Susie, as she dipped half a biscotti into a skinny latte before licking the foam off the biscuit. "This is the first time since the business collapsed that I've plucked up the courage to come out. And even now I'm worrying about how quickly I can get back to the kids. Matt's had it even tougher. He blames himself for everything that's happened and I can't find a way to convince him that the only person pointing the finger is himself. It's like he *wants* me to shout and scream and blame him because in some way that will vindicate how much he hates himself. You and Ricky are lucky. You've not been under the same kind of pressure, and you don't have the kind of strain on your relationship that we're under."

"So tell me that you love him – that you *really* love him – and I'll shut up. Tell me that deep down there isn't even a *tiny* part of you that blames him for what happened."

Susie stirred her coffee.

"Exactly… are you sleeping with him? I don't mean are you in the same bed."

Susie carried on stirring.

"Point proven. Susie, we've been friends for eons. I only ever want what's best for you. I really do think it's time for you to consider moving on."

"It's not proven, though, is it? Because he's my husband and I still have feelings for him."

"So why don't you run home now and shag him senseless?"

Susie felt embarrassment burning into her skin at how

her friend's voice had carried. She sipped hard from her coffee glass but kept her gaze fixed downwards.

"Because not everything is about sex. When he touches me, he makes my skin crawl and when I touch him, I sometimes feel like I'm going to be sick. But we have two great kids and a history together, and I still love him. I'm just not *in* love with him."

"But, honey, he's damaged goods. That's not necessarily his fault, but it's the truth. Things *aren't* going to get better. You only live once and I don't see why you should make do and mend, when you could be out there getting yourself some genuine happiness. Why is he such a fucking misery anyway?"

"You really have to ask that? You know he suffers with depression, how much of a struggle things can be for him. And before you say something you might regret, just remember it's an illness. He gets treatment for it but just because you can't see it, doesn't mean it isn't hurting. And then on top of that the recession rolled the business downhill and we're in debt up to our eyes. I can hardly hold him responsible for the recession, can I? It's getting to me, but it's really getting to him. I mean, *really* getting to him."

"Well, tell him to work harder."

Susie responded with an involuntary, exasperated sigh.

"It's not quite as simple as that. Just because you and Ricky have been lucky doesn't mean we're all in the same boat. It also doesn't mean he isn't working hard. Everything is just a struggle."

"Luck doesn't come into it. Ricky's a talented guy and he works so hard. Matt could learn a few things from him; on how to work, on how to value his wife and how to provide for his family. Maybe they should spend some time together."

"That's harsh. You have enough money to keep yourselves insulated from what's happening in the real world. Not everyone is quite so fortunate. I've hidden my jewellery in case anyone comes calling, I'm planning for what would happen if we lose the house and I'm sick of cutting the kids' pocket money just so I can buy them the basics. We need our friends to stand by us now not stab us in the back. If you don't feel able to do that, then maybe we shouldn't spend time together until things have worked themselves out."

Donna looked hard at Susie, nothing soft or sympathetic about her features at all.

"Susie, darling, you make your own luck in this world. Stop defending him, start getting real and accept that Matt's letting you all down. There are plenty of people still working their socks off and doing okay. It's only Matt who's lying down and giving in. You know I'm right."

As much as Susie wanted to disagree, part of her couldn't. She never expected to be living the Donna and Ricky lifestyle but neither did she expect such a hand to mouth existence. Perhaps she didn't blame Matt but subconsciously she couldn't deny that in her frustration she had started to resent him.

"But what would you do now if everything went wrong with you and Ricky? What would you do if you found out, for example, that Ricky had blown all of your money gambling or had been cheating on you for the last few years?"

The notion was preposterous. Donna looked at Susie with pity in her eyes. Susie could think of nothing worse than being pitied.

"The one thing that separates a marriage from a friendship, my darling, is the intimacy. If you haven't got that, you haven't really got anything," Donna said knowingly. "Ricky and I are emotionally and sexually in sync and always have been and I think we've achieved what we have because of that connection. It's not an accident. We really are a team."

"So you're telling me if Matt and I had sex more often, we'd be better off?"

"Of course, darling, because the connection between you would be that much stronger and then you'd also have something to use as a bargaining chip to make him deliver more for you."

"That's way too simplistic. But if Ricky cheated?"

"I'd forgive him."

"Just like that, you'd forgive him? How much of it is about loving Ricky and how much about loving Ricky's money?"

"Both, and there's nothing wrong with that. I don't mind admitting it. I'm here to have the best life I can. What is it they say? We're here for a good time not a long time? I don't want to be lying on my deathbed looking back on a struggle. Where's the fun in that? When you got married, Matt said he'd provide for you, look after you. And he's not. It's as simple as that."

"But we also said something about for better, for worse, for richer, for poorer, in sickness and in health."

"Susie, you're so intelligent and yet in many ways still so naïve. If you want to put up with second best, then that's your choice, but you don't have to. How are Millie and Leo by the way?"

The question burnt hard into Susie's consciousness and she unclenched her jaw to reply.

"They're coping. We all are. Well, all of us except Matt."

Donna's iPhone rang, her loud Kylie Minogue ringtone causing others to stop what they were doing and stare. She halted their conversation by raising one finger to take the call.

"That was Ricky; he's taking me to Ramsay's for lunch so I'm going to need to cut this short. But Suse, do the decent thing, put Matt out of his misery and fly down with the kids and spend some time with us over Christmas in Cadaqués. Give yourself a brand-new start."

And with a flourish of a fawn pashmina and a Mulberry handbag Susie was alone with Norah Jones, a cooling cup of coffee, three surrounding tables of gossiping middle-aged women and a whole lot to think about.

AS SUSIE WAS meeting Donna, Matthew was out walking. He had turned up the collar on his black coat and tightened the striped multi-coloured scarf in a fashionable loop around his neck. The brisk, late November wind was stinging his face and the leaves under foot on the forest path resembled a colour-chart carpet of browns, reds and oranges. They crunched like milk bottle tops beneath his scuffed Timberland boots.

The Autumn sun pierced through the trees' branches the way an interrogator shines a light into a prisoner's eyes, sometimes forcing him to move his head from one side to the next to avoid its most penetrating power. Ahead, Crisp, the family's six-year-old Weimaraner, slate grey like a December sky, darted in and out of the trees, always looking back to assure himself of his master's presence. Matt reached into his inside pocket and retrieved a silent mobile phone, checking for messages that simply weren't there. Frequently, he imagined he had felt the phone vibrate only to find it still and undisturbed; one of the minor frustrations of his modern, connected life.

He walked on. By now Crisp had a small branch perched in his mouth like a cigar and patrolled the path ahead studiously. Matt both liked and disliked the solitude of the forest walk. He liked it because it gave him time to think; he disliked it for exactly the same reason.

Most times he would come with Susie but today she had made the short journey into town for coffee and muffins with people like Donna, people she called friends and he called acquaintances.

Nineteen years married, almost half his life. He knew they loved each other but these days he wondered how much. How much did she blame him for what had happened? And wasn't he kidding himself about the impact of it on their relationship? Hadn't they long stopped feeling passion towards each other before what had happened? The past few months had made him question if Susie would miss him if he was suddenly no longer there.

To Matt, it seemed like he and Crisp were alone in the forest. They could often walk for an hour or more and not see another soul. He bent down and picked up a stone from the side of the track, drying it on the corner of his coat. He called to Crisp, who stood statuesque on the path ten or fifteen metres ahead of him, branch still protruding from his mouth and awaiting instruction. Pulling his arm back like a baseball pitcher he hurled the stone into the trees and watched as the dog dropped the branch where he stood and set off in hot pursuit of a quarry he was never going to find. As he waited for the dog to return, Matt wondered to himself how it was possible that he couldn't find peace in even this most tranquil of settings.

He unfolded his scarf, placed it carefully on the fallen log beside him, and twisted the plastic screw cap on the bottle of water in his hand. At first he took more water down his throat than he was able to cope with. He gasped a little for breath, but it refreshed him nonetheless. He poured some into his cupped hands and let Crisp drink away. This time he knew his mobile vibrated in his side pocket, but he ignored it. It wouldn't be good news so why allow himself to be distracted? He thought instead of the plans for a new exciting life that he and Susie had once dreamt of building for themselves. So many years on and that's all they remained, plans they had never realised.

Matt sat on the log, his legs straight out in front of him, his back upright against an invisible wall. He closed his eyes and tried to take himself back to the days when they not only dreamt but when it also felt okay to dream. He wished that he could smell the optimism he remembered from that time. Were they really the days when anything was possible, or had it just seemed that way at the time?

Susie's spontaneity had enraptured him; when they'd first met he had almost been intimidated by the freedom with which she seemed to live her life. She showed him how to enjoy life, to take risks, to feel liberated and to give and receive love; to him it was reckless, to Susie it was merely living. It was Susie who had persuaded him to strip off and make love in their local park. It was the first time Matt had ever felt genuinely carefree and he'd relished the thought that people may have seen them. It was Susie who had taken him against his more conservative judgement on a protest against the poll tax; who had forced him to go to the Free Nelson Mandela concert and who had set up a table for two and served a candlelit dinner on Millennium Eve at the top of Parliament Hill so they could enjoy the fireworks and the magical transition of one century into another alone and yet together.

She rooted him, and acted as the constant upon which he could always rely.

Susie was two years older than Matt, but he was four inches taller. It was a trade-off they had often played on down the years. They had met in their mid-twenties when he was working for a boutique advertising agency, assigned as the gopher on his first account; she was the brand manager for the client, a range of hair care products infused with some long winded, supposedly revolutionary scientific formula that promised far more than it ever delivered. Promoting that promise was their joint responsibility and that had meant spending considerable time in each other's company. They had bonded over music. He had been the first person to play her Tracy Chapman's *Fast Car* and had bought her one of those Sony Walkman things to listen to it on; she had bought him tickets and been next to him at Wembley Stadium when he fulfilled a lifelong ambition to see Bruce Springsteen and his E Street Band complete a marathon three and a half hour set. Initially he had been reluctant to move beyond friendship, concerned primarily about what sleeping with the client might do for his fledgling agency career.

He needn't have worried. For the agency, it was seen as just another way of "improving client relationships", the importance of which could then be dismissed as irrelevant to work when the affair inevitably ended. Only this affair didn't end. In meetings they began to finish each other's sentences and, occasionally to try and catch her off guard, he would throw a hacky-sack across the room to check that she was still paying attention. Only once did she fail to catch it, but then it was thrown back with interest. It helped, of course, that the campaign on which they were working was successful, but within two months, Matt found that he was spending almost all of his free time with Susie; within six months, they were living together.

Matt particularly loved the weekends; waking up alongside Susie on a Saturday morning, lying with her beneath the cool white Egyptian cotton duvet in a double bed secured within a wrought iron frame felt perfect. He would lie and watch her sleep and ask himself what someone as vibrant and self-confident as Susie could possibly find attractive in him. Maybe, looking back, the signs were already there. Then she would wake, smile a warm and all-embracing smile through her still-sleepy eyes, before rolling towards him and lying within the security of his arms. He enjoyed the closeness of their physical connection and would sigh the sigh of a contented man. He liked their weekend routine. They would make love, then shower and then dress quickly to walk to one of the several cafes that ran down the hill on Hampstead High Street away from the Heath in the general direction of Belsize Park. In the warmer weather they would sit outside, their table balanced on the uneven pavement, and drink freshly squeezed juice and eat almond croissants; in the winter, they'd huddle indoors, close to the open fire, read the weekend newspapers, coddle a hot chocolate and eat buttered fruit toast.

Matt was still imagining hot chocolate and fruit toast when an elderly woman stopped to make friends with Crisp. Matt looked vacantly at the woman as she held out the back of her clenched fist for the dog to smell, attempting to engage him in small talk as she did so. Matt had never understood the bizarre, unwritten rule of it being okay to approach and make conversation with another dog owner, even if they were a stranger, and so he answered a question he didn't hear. The woman moved on and Crisp curled back obediently beside his feet.

It had been years since he and Susie had coddled hot chocolate and eaten fruit toast together. There were always other things to do; tasks, chores, calls or paperwork that simply couldn't wait another hour or two. He had long since accepted that he was just another item at the bottom of her in-box. And now, if he even suggested it – or anything similar – she just became exasperated. Matt knew, of course, that this had nothing to do with drinks or pastries. She was exasperated with him. And their children saw it too.

Millie's birth nine years previously had been the last time Matt could remember feeling genuinely happy; that lightness of being that comes with real contentment when you don't need to think consciously about how you feel and can go about the business of living day to day. Now, everything seemed like a conscious decision, an internal debate, a deliberate discussion in his mind between himself and the comments of the voice that constantly told him he was wrong and unworthy. The psychotherapist had called it his 'inner critic'. He had another, less polite name for it.

He had been proud and excited when Millie was born. He had held her in one arm and wondered at the beauty of this little life he had helped to create. He wrapped her securely in a pale lemon blanket as they brought her home from hospital. Susie's bag was gripped tightly in one hand, Millie in the other, as their son, Leo, at that time a boisterous two year old, marked out his territory from this new 'invader' by claiming all of his mother's attention as they walked back to the car. As any new parent will testify, those first few months are anything but easy. The regimented routine of feeding, sleeping and sterilising bottles removed all spontaneity from their relationship; when Susie was sleeping, he was attending to the children and vice versa. Yet, although they were caught up in the maelstrom of raising a young family with all the deprivations that attend it, Matt remembered being happy and from the distance of hindsight he recalled them as serene days.

That serenity began to dissipate as the children grew and became increasingly independent of him but less, it seemed, independent of Susie. He would read to them, play with them, sleep, and hold and try to bond with them. He had done but not the way Susie had. Perhaps children always replace the husband in the mother's affections and, like it or not, there's nothing you're ever going to be able to do about it. One thing he knew is that it wasn't the way he had expected it to be.

By the time Leo was seven and Millie was five, during the day he was out of sight and out of mind; at night, they were often asleep before he'd return home and when they were together, he couldn't share the experiences, the private jokes and silly stories they had enjoyed in their time without him. It felt as if they had stopped being a family of four and were now a family of three plus one. Only later would he question whether it was he that moved away from them rather than the other way around.

And so it continued. Matt wasn't sure how aware Susie was of how he felt; she stopped asking him about his day and at night she would climb into bed next to him, roll over in a single movement so she lay with her back to him and sometimes blew him a kiss goodnight; but more often not. At weekends he would try to gain ground, but there were grandparents to see, parties to attend or friends to hang out with. Matt never quite felt like a fully-fledged member of the team. There were times when he wanted to scream out for attention, for a hug or a kiss; just to get a reminder that Susie knew he was still there. But he equally knew this would be dismissed as self-indulgent and nonsensical. There were times, like now, when he wanted to ensure that he wouldn't be a problem for her much longer.

CHAPTER THIRTY-FOUR

DESPITE THE COLD, Jack wiped sweat from his brow, as he rang the bell at Lesley's place that evening. He felt as if he was going on a first date, and he had never been much good at those. Lesley answered the door. She wore a long sloppy joe type T-shirt that hung loose off of one shoulder, and grey tracksuit trousers. Her hair was still done the way she had it for work and the combination of the casual and the formal made her look all the more attractive. She beamed, and he sensed that she was genuinely pleased to see him.

"Ringing the bell, Mr Munday? Why didn't you use your keys?"

"Well, Miss Hilton, I thought it would be impolite given that it's been a few days since I was last here."

Lesley stepped back to open the door wider and allow him room to enter.

"You'd better come in then. If you stay standing on the doorstep, people will talk and we wouldn't want that, would we?"

"I guess not."

Jack entered the familiar surroundings, placing a box of chocolates and a bottle of red on the table that had already been laid. Two candles burnt in the centre, permeating a vanilla essence around the room and flickering as if the draught from the nearby window was making them dance on command. Lesley had gone straight into the apartment's small but well-equipped kitchen, from which aromas heavy with basil and oregano seeped out.

"Thanks for the flowers," she called out. "I forgot to mention it at work. It was very sweet of you."

"I'm glad you liked them," he replied. *But you wouldn't think so if you knew I'd sent some to Elaine as well.* "It was just my way of saying sorry. I hadn't told anybody about us, but I didn't like the fact that the rumours had you upset."

"I was probably overreacting," she lied. "Sit yourself down; I'm almost ready to serve."

Jack turned to the music collection on Lesley's iPhone, which was sitting prone in its speaker dock beside the wooden fireplace. Getting the music right was critical; they couldn't have a serious and romantic conversation about their future with ACDC playing in the background. He skipped over Duffy and Laura Marling, The Killers and Coldplay and settled instead for Elbow's *Seldom Seen Kid.* The angst in their music sometimes made it feel as if the songs had been written with him in mind. *One Day Like This* had become one of his favourite songs. If it were possible to wear out a download, he would have been the first to do it.

"I just want us to have a nice chilled evening, no stress," Lesley called from the kitchen.

"Sounds good to me."

"Hope you're hungry?"

"Always. You know me."

Jack took a seat at the table. He leant back in the chair and looked around the apartment. After all the time spent living on his own after the break-up with Elaine, he was definitely ready to settle into something more permanent. This was a proper home unlike the place he had been renting, which felt little more than a depository for his belongings. He wanted to be in a relationship, and perhaps moving on would be best for everybody, best for him, best for Connor and, yes, best for Elaine too. Maybe they would find it easier to rebuild their friendship and be better parents without any expectation or desire from either of them to get back together.

Lesley emerged from the kitchen with a basket of bread balanced on top of a red casserole dish that she was carrying with both hands encased in floral oven gloves. She laid the pot down on a mat in the centre of the table and lifted the lid, allowing steam to escape and dissipate before it reached the ceiling. God, it smelt good. She ran back into the kitchen and returned with a ladle and two bowls.

"Tomato and basil soup," she announced grandly, lifting one of the bowls and spooning in the thick, rich red liquid.

"It smells amazing."

"It's one of Jamie Oliver's recipes."

"Well, next time I see Jamie, I can tell him you've done him justice."

And she had. The flavours were such a contrast to the sterile station food or the microwave boxes that Jack had become accustomed to when he was home alone. He took some bread, tore it into small pieces and dropped it in the soup as some kind of informal crouton.

"So do you think we can make a go of it?" Lesley asked, holding her spoon centimetres from her mouth until she completed the question.

"The soup? I think so."

"I meant us. Be serious for once."

Jack put his spoon down.

"Of course we can if that's what we both want."

"Is it what we both want?"

He poured some wine into Lesley's glass before filling his own. He raised his glass as if in a toast and clinked it against hers.

"I love you, Lesley Hilton. I have done since the first day we got together. I respected the fact then that you didn't want a relationship, so I had kind of put that out of my mind. I'm not going to lie; you raising the prospect of a proper grown-up relationship gave me plenty to think about. You know that I come with baggage."

"Yes, but I'll take you warts and all."

"If we do this there are going to be some hurdles we'll need to jump. I'll need to talk to Elaine because, whatever else, I need to try and keep some kind of friendship going with her for Connor's sake."

"Of course."

"And then there's Connor. I'll have to think how to tell him and how we introduce you to him as more than just one of my work colleagues. Then we'll have to deal with what Elaine thinks about you and Connor."

"There is no 'me and Connor'. I don't want to be his mum. He has a mum. I just want to be his dad's partner."

Jack nodded, waiting whilst his brain caught up and processed this new information.

"We'll have to be careful about how we play it at work. We'll need to think who we tell and when we tell them. They may not like us still working together if we're a couple."

Lesley got up and took Jack's bowl without waiting to ask if he had actually finished. He looked longingly after it and reached out to try and bring it back.

"Will you just stop for a minute and listen to yourself? So far all you've talked about is everybody else. I'm not denying that's important but, for now, can we just focus on us? We're not doing anything wrong here. We're two grown-up, single, consenting adults who want to take what was a bit of a fling to the next stage and have a proper relationship. Will it be forever? I don't know. Is it the real deal? I hope so, but there's only one way to find out. And is it really anybody else's business but ours? No. Now change that music to something a bit more upbeat whilst I go and get the rest of the food."

She was right; he knew she was right.

THROUGHOUT THE REST of the meal – beautiful pink lamb with roasted rosemary potatoes and vegetables and a sticky toffee pudding for dessert – they laughed like teenagers. They joked about each other, about the things they would do, the places they would go, the dog they would one day own and even growing old together; all the things that Jack had once joked about with Elaine. After they'd finished eating, he cleared the table whilst she stacked the dishwasher. He made fresh coffee, which they drank, sitting on the sofa. He handed her a small glass of brandy and she draped her legs over his. Later, they fell into bed and made love. As Jack lay in the still of the night and listened to Lesley breathing, he felt elated and, in some way, protected. *Perhaps this is the way other people feel*, he thought to himself, and he allowed himself to drift slowly off to sleep.

CHAPTER THIRTY-FIVE

SIMON CARTER RETURNED home in an uncustomary buoyant mood. The fog that had enveloped him since his mother's death seemed, at last, as if it was lifting a little. He had found himself thinking – and then found himself feeling guilty for thinking it – that perhaps Adele's passing would enable him to draw some imaginary line. That he could, if not begin again, then at least move forward without feeling weighed down by the shackles of his youth. He always wanted to remember Danny; but it was okay for Danny not to dictate the life he wanted to lead. He had spent too many years wondering what the purpose of his life should be and now he had come to the conclusion that it was also okay not to know. He wanted to be a dad to his boys; not just their father. He wasn't sure he could explain that to Esther, let alone anyone else, without it sounding as if he'd been away on a long retreat in an ashram and not told her, but then he didn't think she would really need to be told. She would recognise it soon enough by the change that he was sure she would see in him.

He was returning home earlier than usual. He wanted to spend time with Joe and Charlie before they went to bed. In fact, what he really wanted was to get home early enough to persuade Elaine to allow him to take them all out for an early supper, even though it was a school night. So instead of parking on the driveway, which would risk alerting them to his arrival, he squeezed past a Ford Mondeo that had been unhelpfully parked outside the house and stopped the car a few yards further down the road. As he lifted flowers, a bottle of wine and enough sweets to guarantee the boys the kind of sugar rush that he would regret come three in the morning, he felt a childlike excitement that seemed both new and yet, at the same time, strangely, like the return of a long lost friend. The closest comparison he could come up with was like late on Christmas Eve, when he, Danny and Mark would pretend to be sleeping as his parents brought pillowcases stuffed with presents into their rooms and left them perched at the end of their beds. They would lie still in the darkness, stifling laughter until they were sure their parents had turned in for the night. Danny would get out of bed, close the door as quietly as he could, turn on the bedroom light and then the unwrapping would begin. Momentarily, he slipped back into reflecting on how different his life might have been, but only for long enough to snap himself out of his memory and back into the present.

Simon turned the key carefully in the lock, the way a

safebreaker might if he knew the combination, and crept into the hallway, closing the door softly behind him. Ordinarily, the boys would have bounded down the stairs with the vigour and excitement of a queue outside a cinema for the first showing of a new Marvel film, but today there was nothing. All was going to plan until Monty came charging out of the kitchen, barely able to control his canine excitement, leaping to the point where all four paws were fully off the ground and he was in mid-air coming towards Simon.

"Simon, is that you?" called Esther.

"The very same," he called back, setting the sweets and the wine at the foot of the stairs and carrying Monty in one arm and the flowers in the other as he entered the lounge. "Why, were you expecting your lover?"

That was the moment Simon noticed the two police officers sitting with Esther, awaiting his return. Simon instinctively felt as if he had done something wrong; like when he used to get his name called out in school assembly because Danny had got them both into trouble. He handed the flowers to Esther without ceremony. The two men returned coffee cups to the side tables and got up as he entered the room, offering him their warrant cards and introducing themselves simultaneously. The taller of the two, Detective Inspector Jack Munday, immediately reclaimed his seat whilst the other, Sergeant Duggan, waited until Simon had taken a seat on the empty sofa.

Simon glanced at Esther as if to ask *what the fuck is*

going on here? She responded with a calming smile that gave no kind of answer to his unspoken question. Both policemen picked up their mugs of coffee again. Esther asked if her husband wanted one as well, but he waved the offer away.

"The officers want to have a chat about Danny." Esther felt the need to provide some kind of explanation for the presence of the police in their house.

"Danny? Is this some kind of joke?"

Of all the things he could think the police may want to discuss, Danny would have been very low down his list of likely possibilities.

"What happened to Danny must have been very difficult for you," the Inspector asked in a manner so casual that Simon started to feel as if he was being lulled into a false sense of security.

"It was and it doesn't get any easier."

"I understand."

"With all due respect, Inspector, I don't see how you can."

Esther had moved and now sat on the sofa's arm next to Simon. He reached behind him to place his left hand on hers as she gently squeezed his right shoulder.

"So how can I help you?"

"Mr Carter, does the name Karen Westcott mean anything to you?"

Simon rolled the name around his mind the way someone might swill a good red around a glass.

"No," he replied after a few seconds, "I don't think so."

"Perhaps you remember her by her maiden name. Blakemore. Karen Blakemore."

Simon scratched the top of his forehead.

"Karen Blakemore. Wait a moment, yes; we went to school with a girl called Karen Blakemore. But that's more than thirty years ago."

"Do you remember if she was present on the day that Danny died?"

Simon adjusted his seating position, betraying nervous discomfort for the first time.

"What's all this about?"

"Please, for the moment, could you just tell us if she was there when Danny died?"

On some subconscious level Simon objected to Munday referring to Danny by name, as if pretending he had known him; perhaps he was being overly sensitive but it felt like an unwanted incursion into Danny's memory. Esther had clearly picked up on his anxiety because she gently squeezed his shoulder again. Simon threw his head back and for a few seconds that seemed like longer, he took his mind back, consciously trying to bring forward every face and then recalled the conversation he'd had with his mother.

He brought his head forward again, opened his eyes and stared directly at Munday.

"Yes, Inspector, I believe that she was."

"And what about Kevin Simpson?"

The pauses in the conversation were becoming longer than the conversation itself.

"Kevin was definitely there; it was his mother that took us swimming that day. Why do I suspect you already knew that?"

Munday leant forward, coffee cup down, and put his hands together so that his fingers were interlocked and sighed.

"This is going to sound strange, Mr Carter, so hear me out. Kevin Simpson and Karen Westcott have both been receiving messages from somebody purporting to be Danny."

"Messages? You mean, like, psychic messages from the afterlife?"

Munday laughed a little. Simon felt a little sick at someone he had only just met laughing – even just a little – while talking about Danny.

"No, Mr Carter, I mean emails. Facebook messages."

"Well, that's not possible."

"Clearly not, which means they're obviously not from Danny."

"What kind of messages?"

"Well, they started off talking about a reunion and gradually became a bit creepier, asking how often they thought about the day that Danny died. The later ones to Karen included some pictures of her kids, as if whoever had been sending them had been watching from a distance."

Simon straightened, before leaning forward and bringing his hands together as if in prayer. He brought his fingertips up to touch his lips. He looked at Esther and then looked back at Jack Munday.

"And you think I've been sending them?"

Munday replaced his coffee cup carefully onto the glass table top next to where he was sitting.

"No, I don't think you've been sending them, but you might be able to shed some light on who has. The kind of information included in these messages could only have come from somebody who was either present on the day that your brother died, or who has a very detailed knowledge of that day."

"I'm sure you already know the details of what happened that day and I don't know what new perspective I could offer, given that it all happened a long time ago and none of us have really seen each other since."

"Tell me about Matthew Baines."

"What about him?"

"I'm told that there were some rumours doing the rounds after Danny died that Matthew might have been responsible in some way; that this caused enough of a stir to prompt his parents to move the family away."

Simon nodded. He swallowed hard.

"I only heard those rumours recently myself for the first time. My mother told me shortly before she passed away. Esther had always said I'm the last to find out anything. I guess this proved her right."

"And did you – or your mother – think these rumours had any truth in them?"

Simon shook his head. "I really don't think so. Even if what they said about Matthew tripping Danny is true, it still doesn't make it any less of an accident. People were looking for an explanation for something that seemed inexplicable. You know what people are like, Inspector, everybody wants to be able to blame somebody when something goes horribly wrong."

"What about your other brother, Mr Carter, what does he think?"

"Mark? I don't know, I guess you'd have to ask him if you could find him. We're really not that close, I'm afraid."

"That's a shame. How come?"

"I don't know that there's a single answer. We're different characters; we always have been, even before Danny died. I guess we've just grown further apart."

"We've been told that Mark took Danny's death particularly badly. Is that true?"

"We all took it badly, Inspector, not just Mark."

"Of course, but there have been suggestions that Mark had difficulty managing his anger over Danny's death; perhaps that he wanted somebody to blame, some kind of retribution."

"Maybe at the time, Inspector, but Mark's in his forties now. That's not the same as being a teenager."

"That's true, but it's not uncommon that untreated

anger issues have a tendency to flare up again as you grow older. It can manifest itself in different ways; sometimes it affects relationships, or your ability to hold down a job. It can show itself in things like anxiety or depression; you know, panic attacks and things like that."

"What happened to Danny isn't the kind of thing you can ever get over, but you come to terms with it and you move on with your life."

"And that's what you and Mark have done?"

Simon was about to speak until Esther, squeezing his shoulder, interrupted.

"I'm sorry, Simon, but this could be important."

"Mrs Carter?"

"I'm not saying that he hasn't tried, but Mark has never been able to come to terms with what happened and…" she looked down at her husband, "…we need to be honest with you about that. Mark is one very angry man and he's never had a constructive outlet for that anger."

"That might be true," Simon rebutted, "but he's not going to be stalking and threatening people thirty years after the event."

Simon watched as the two detectives tried to process what Esther had just told them, silently trying to assess whether their case had just become clearer or a whole lot more complicated.

"Well, at the moment, whoever's sending these messages is only guilty of being a bit of a pest. We need to work out who it is and get to them before it becomes anything more serious than that, whether it's your brother or somebody completely different."

Simon reached into his trouser pocket and pulled out his mobile phone, pressing a few buttons before turning the screen to face Munday.

"That's his mobile number, or at least it's the last mobile number that I had for him. He's not an easy guy to reach and I don't have an address for him or any real idea where he might be living. As I said, we're not close."

ESTHER CLOSED THE door behind the two detectives as they left, placing her forehead against the glass and exhaling deeply, before turning to face her husband in the hall. All of the positivity with which Simon had come home armed with had deserted him. He looked exhausted.

"Thanks for the flowers, by the way." She kissed him on the cheek.

"He wouldn't have, would he? I mean, it couldn't be him."

"Let's hope not," she replied, "but when he's really struggling, there's nothing I wouldn't put past Mark."

CHAPTER THIRTY-SIX

IRINA KOSTYSHYN'S MURDER and subsequent funeral had become front-page news at home as well as back in her native Ukraine. Jack folded a copy of the previous day's newspaper, which carried a picture of her coffin being borne aloft into the church in her home town of Lutsk, her parents following behind, bent double by the mass of their grief and clinging to each other like driftwood in a stormy sea. He handed it across the desk to Duggan to read.

"There's one bit of reporting in there I'd really like to take issue with," Jack mentioned as he stood, glancing out of the dirty office window over the station car park. He couldn't even begin to guess when the last time somebody had wiped a wet cloth over the outside of the glass.

"There's some posh twat in there talking about Irina's death as being the wakeup call we all need to put a stop to the sex trafficking of young women from Eastern Europe. I'm not saying sex trafficking isn't a problem and I'm not saying that we shouldn't put a stop to it..."

"So, stop telling me what you're not saying and tell me what you are, before one of us dies of old age."

Jack threw Duggan an unimpressed look.

"I'm saying that, whatever did or didn't happen to her, Irina Kostyshyn wasn't trafficked into the UK for sex. She came here legitimately and of her own free will. She made the decision to offer herself up as a high-class hooker. Nobody forced her to do it and to use what happened to her to suggest otherwise is a bit disingenuous."

"Or she may not have felt she had another option? And disingenuous, that's a big word for you. Where did you read that?"

"In *The Times*. I had to Google it to see what it meant."

"So, you think Irina was just being entrepreneurial? I think that's a bit insulting, to be honest."

"Perhaps, but maybe she was driven to the more extreme stuff because she was finding it harder to get normal clients – and I use the word 'normal' advisedly – now so many of the bankers are up shit creek without a paddle."

A cough caught their attention. Danny Thorne had slipped into the office unnoticed through the open door and had been listening to their conversation.

"Make a habit of eavesdropping into other people's conversations, Danny?"

Thorne held up his hands in apology.

"What can I tell you, I'm a detective, it's kind of what I do."

"So, are you here for a reason or is the eavesdropping purely social?"

Duggan laughed a deeper, dirtier laugh than any of them had been expected. It prompted both Jack and Danny to look at him like a parent disappointed with their small child's table manners.

"The point you made about the bankers having no money, I can tell you that's true in this case, at least."

"And what makes you so sure of that, Danny?"

"Because our friend Christopher Sinclair isn't a banker. I think he might be a lawyer."

"How do you know?"

"Let's just say I managed to have a full and frank discussion with the manager of the hotel. We understand each other now."

"Please tell me that doesn't mean he's in hospital. I can't face the paperwork if it does."

Thorne smiled. "No, he's still in one piece and his pretty little features are all intact. But it's amazing what you can get out of people if you show them a fake piece of paper giving you authority to shut their hotel down on grounds of kitchen hygiene."

"I never heard that."

"Never heard what?"

"Exactly."

Duggan moved quickly to pull Thorne further into the

office and close the door securely behind him.

"What have you told Salazar?"

"Nothing. He was far too busy changing the battery on his fucking Bluetooth headset."

Munday sniggered. Now he knew what he had always suspected, that he wasn't the only person irritated by both *it* and *him*.

"So what did the guy tell you?"

"Sinclair wasn't a regular as such, though he *had* used the hotel before, but this is the first time he can remember Sinclair leaving the hotel before the girl he'd brought to his room. They never arrived together, and they never left together."

"And the girls he had been there with previously, was there any pattern?"

Danny smiled. "Always East European, always very slight, always very pale in complexion. Comrade Sinclair has a type."

"Always very dead by the end of it?"

"I ran a check on the system to see if anything similar cropped up, but nothing rang any alarm bells."

"What makes you think that Sinclair is a lawyer?"

"I asked the manager what else he knew about Sinclair. The answer, unsurprisingly, was not much but he *did* mention that a few months ago, the hotel was getting some hassle from the local authority about a late night drinks licence, people complaining about the noise at night. Sinclair told the manager that it was in his line of work and that he would look into it for him. The manager couldn't be sure if he was saying it because he genuinely wanted to help or because he was just trying to curry a bit of favour."

"It's got to be worth speaking to the local authority and finding out if they have the names of anyone who has intervened or made an enquiry with them on behalf of the hotel."

Danny, chewing the end of a ballpoint pen, nodded.

"Just an off the wall idea," Duggan began. "If this guy is a lawyer and isn't averse to using his status, if not his real identity, to win people over, what are the chances that he might also have helped one of these East European girls he's been consorting with – maybe one he's really fallen for – with immigration papers, a job application, anything that might make him think that she really loves him and wants him for his personality rather than his cash?"

"It would be a hell of a foolish thing to do, wouldn't it? A bit of risk to take."

"Love makes fools out of all of us. You should know that by now, Jack."

The ghost of a tumbleweed floated across the office. Jack looked towards Danny who tried to give some indication that the comment had gone way over his head. Grateful though he was, Jack didn't believe it for a moment.

"It's a long shot but we should look into it, nonetheless. Danny, ask DS Salazar, once he's fitted the new battery into his Bluetooth headset and checked it's working, if he could get onto it."

"But DS Salazar is a senior officer, boss. I'm not sure I should be telling a senior officer what to do."

"It's never stopped you in the past," Duggan butted in. Munday sniggered.

"Just mention it to DS Salazar and, if he has a problem with it, he can stick his head round the door and tell me."

Jack reached into the top drawer of his desk and took out an open packet of chocolate digestive biscuits. He helped himself to two before throwing the packet at Thorne, who caught it one handed.

"What does your gut tell you about all of this? Irina, Sinclair, the hotel. What do you think we've got going on? Isolated incident or something more serious?"

Danny brushed crumbs from the front of his shirt and held a half biscuit pointed towards Munday like some kind of prop.

"I think what happened to Irina is the tip of the iceberg. I'm not saying many of them end up dead, but I don't think Irina – or Christopher Sinclair, for that matter – are the only ones doing it."

"I think you're right. I'm all for the enterprising spirit and all that, especially in tough times like this, but not when young girls start turning up dead. While you're dishing out the instructions to DS Salazar, ask him to take a closer look at the website Sinclair used to meet Irina. It might be time to increase the scope of this investigation and start putting the heat on a few other people."

"Salazar won't be happy taking instructions from Danny Thorne," Duggan noted after Thorne had left the room, "I know I wouldn't be."

"And what would you do in that situation?"

"I'd come and have a go at you about it."

"Exactly. Let's see if Frank has the balls to do it. In the meantime, we need to try and locate Mark Carter and find out if he's the guy behind the creepy messages and, if so, why he's getting off on sending them from his dead brother."

CHAPTER THIRTY-SEVEN

MATTHEW BAINES HAD woken up in a fighting mood. He stood in the shower and encouraged the powerful jets of hot water to run first over his hair and then directly onto his face even though, for a moment, he sensed the heat might scorch him. He grabbed Susie's Lemon and Tea Tree shower gel from the chrome cage beside the shower and squeezed it purposefully onto his scalp. The scent of the gel as he worked it in with his fingers made him feel as fresh as the water made him feel warm. He rubbed the foaming liquid into his chest and then leant down to rub the soap into his thighs – one of the features that Susie had always found most attractive in him – as he became aware of a stream of hot water running down the centre line of his back towards his bare buttocks. It caused him to arch his back and even hold his breath for a moment or two.

Having completed the washing regime, he stepped out of the shower, shuddering slightly as the cold air hit his wet skin. In some ways he felt cleansed as well as clean. He wrapped a towel around his waist and draped another round his shoulders and rubbed slightly to dry the wettest parts. He ruffled his hair with the towel and, with it wrapped around his index finger, ensured the inside of each ear was soap-free.

Matthew looked at himself closely in the mirror, sure he could detect new lines and silver hairs on his temples brought on by the stresses of the previous months. He sometimes thought about using one of those hair dyes for men that seemed to be constantly being advertised on the television, but considered that Susie would find it ridiculous.

What Matt wanted more than anything was a degree of perspective; this, he had concluded, was what had been missing most from his life. Removing any sense of objectivity was one of the ways in which depression had come to distort his mind. He saw enemies around every corner; anyone who paid him a compliment wasn't to be believed or trusted and, at its worst, he was sure everyone was meeting up behind his back to discuss what a wreck he had become. He could take their disgust, but he couldn't tolerate their pity.

After all, he'd seen it before all those years ago; the disgust in the eyes of those kids in the playground in the days after Danny had drowned and the pity in his mother's eyes around the same time. Perhaps he'd done her a disservice; maybe he'd mistaken pity for concern and it had been this that had prompted his parents to take him away and not expose him to whatever those friends were speaking about in huddles in playground corners.

He towel-dried his hair properly and then, glancing around to make sure he wasn't being overlooked within his empty house, he reached for a tube of moisturising cream. He pushed a penny-sized swirl onto the palm of his hand before rubbing the cold lotion onto his newly-shaved face. It felt soft, cool and strangely comforting. He dressed to reflect his new-found confidence; a crisp white shirt, clean blue jeans and his favourite Timberland boots. Perhaps this was the key: making time for himself in the morning instead of rushing around in a frenzy to get things done; more haste less speed, as his mother would have said.

There was work to do. Anderson's faith in him, coupled with the undeniable growing success of Millionaire Boyfriend had lifted his mood and had begun to discernibly boost his confidence. If every day was an internal battle, for the time being at least he felt he had the upper hand. He may have been playing second fiddle to Anderson on this particular project but surely not even Susie at her most frustrated would deny him just a little bit of self-satisfaction. Moreover, if Anderson was as good as his word, and Matt increasingly thought he might be, then perhaps there would be a golden pot of money at the end of this particular rainbow after all. He held onto that prospect as the key to fulfilling what he saw as his responsibility to Susie and to the children. He could even conceive of a moment when, one day, he might be in a position to reflect on where his life stood now and not regard himself as an abject failure. That may still be some way, off but the fact that he was allowing himself to consider the possibility was progress that, just months previously, would have been unthinkable.

Matt took an espresso pod from the box in the kitchen cupboard and slotted it unconvincingly into the black and chrome coffee machine that Susie had bought for herself in the previous January sales. Its sleek finish made it look like the interior of a German car as it fizzed and gurgled into life; a lot of noise and action, thought Matt, to produce a single trickle of dark coffee into the white mug he had placed on the shiny metal grille. He didn't understand what was wrong with a kettle; why suddenly it was no longer good enough to make coffee the old fashioned way, other than the fact that Donna had one and so Susie needed one too. But, as he lifted the mug to his mouth, it undeniably smelt good and this fed into his new-found sense of control.

Those strange messages from someone pretending to be Danny Carter had still been coming, in more of a trickle than a flood, and he thought the fact that he hadn't responded was probably irritating whoever was sending them and prompting them to send more. As they had climbed into bed the previous night and she had turned her back towards him in the darkness, Susie had urged him one more time to call the police.

"And tell them what? They're not exactly threatening messages. They don't actually say they're going to do anything to me, do they?"

"It's still not right. Whoever's sending them is playing games with your mind."

"Best thing to do is to ignore them completely. If I don't respond, whoever it is will just get fed up and move onto some other poor bugger."

Matt was unsure who he was trying to convince, Susie or himself. He knew the messages related to Danny's death but why now and, more to the point, why him? His memory of the event was so sketchy that he struggled to remember everybody who was there that day let alone anything else. Over and again he ran through who could possibly be making these threats; forget what he'd said to Susie, Matt recognised them for the threats that they were.

He held the coffee up to his face, taking in the aroma before he chose to take in the taste. Susie had taken the kids to school and was then driving on into town for some retail therapy, though Matt couldn't imagine what she proposed to use to fund her excursion.

Maybe that wasn't what she was doing at all; perhaps it was just a ruse. Maybe she was meeting another man, someone who treated her the way she deserved to be treated; a man who could afford to take her out for retail therapy. His imagination was in overdrive. Matt pictured them sitting together in a town centre cafe sipping cappuccino with chocolate sprinkles on top, the way he once had with her; they were laughing together, carefree, Susie with her head on the shoulder of this mystery man. He felt as if he was watching from a distance. She looked younger and happier than he had been able to make her feel. The man dabbed her lips with a white napkin and then leant forward and kissed her tenderly. She reciprocated. Neither of them cared who saw.

In the scene he was directing, would she be giving any thought to him? Would this mystery man even know that she was married, or would she have conveniently airbrushed him out of her life? Who could have blamed her if she had? He sipped the black coffee and told himself that he needed to stop creating these images in his mind; it wasn't helpful, and he knew he was wrong. Or, at least, he hoped so. But the voice in his head urged him on.

His phone sat on the kitchen worktop, near to the coffee machine. As it rang, its jaunty tone splitting the silence, the vibrations caused it to move dangerously close to the unit's precipice. He grabbed it just before it fell. The moment he heard the urgency in Susie's voice he instinctively knew she wasn't sipping a macchiato and eating a croissant with some unknown beau in a cafe in town and yet, strangely, the realisation didn't comfort him at all. His breathing had sped up, his arms felt suddenly heavy, his chest tightened, and he began to feel sweat bubbling up around his neck. He already felt nauseous even though not a single word had passed between them.

"Suse?"

"Is Leo with you?"

"What's wrong?"

"Just answer the bloody question, Matt, is Leo with you?"

"No. I thought you took him to school."

"I did. The school rang to find out where he was. I dropped him off outside like usual, but he never made it inside. Matt, I think somebody's taken him."

"Whoa... you don't know that. Calm down. He's probably wandered off to get some sweets."

"This is Leo. He doesn't wander off. He doesn't go to the toilet without telling somebody. Leo is *missing*. He's vanished. I told you to call the police, but you didn't listen to me. So, don't you *dare* tell me to calm down."

The implication was clear. This was *his* fault. Matthew began to shake; almost imperceptibly at first but enough to heighten his unease as adrenalin began to pump around his body. In a split second he saw the whole of Leo's life to date played out before him; football in the park, the time he fell off his skateboard and cut open his leg, even the time he was a "star" in the school nativity, having to leave the Bethlehem skyline hastily with a teacher for an urgent toilet break, only returning after the Baby Jesus had already been born. Precious Leo, who with Millie had been all that had sustained him, could now be somewhere that his love and his protection simply couldn't reach. He was impotent. And Susie, still waiting for a response, thought it was his fault. "I'm going to call the police now," he told her. "Come home. And drive slowly. There's got to be a simple explanation. We'll find him, I promise."

"I'm going to get Millie and then I'll be back. I'm scared Matt. I'm really fucking scared."

Her use of bad language shocked him. It demonstrated how helpless she felt; how complete her despair.

"Me too. But we're going to find him. I promise you, Suse, we're going to find him."

"Words don't mean shit, Matt. Don't promise me things. Just *do* something. Just get my boy back."

My *boy*, thought Matt, *not* ours.

He punched 999 into his phone.

CHAPTER THIRTY-EIGHT

JACK MUNDAY'S HEAD felt as if a Salvation Army band was marching through it and his mouth tasted the way he imagined an ashtray might, but with a lingering aftertaste of Jack Daniels thrown in for good measure. He sat at his desk; his eyes closed to protect them from the daylight. In front of him stood a chipped white mug with black coffee stains around the rim. He ran his tongue across the roof of his mouth to get some saliva moving and, in its further reaches; he could still taste the last knockings of the previous night's Rogan Josh. It had been a good night, or at least as much that he could remember had been, but he wasn't sure how long he could keep burning the midnight oil at both ends. These 'team building' nights were a dangerous invention.

"Quite a nice routine you had going there last night." Harry Duggan smiled a little at his boss' indisposition. "I don't think they've seen anything quite like that in the Star of India before."

Munday lifted his eyes; as heavy as lifting the shutters on a shop front without a prop. Christ, they hurt.

"Like what?"

"Like a Detective Inspector standing on a table singing 'I Want To Break Free' to anyone who wanted to listen? Or, at least, *you* might call it singing."

"Serious?"

"Serious."

"It wasn't…"

"Recorded? Of course it was," Duggan laughed. "But strictly for internal consumption. No danger of it going on YouTube and no danger of you winning a record deal any time soon either. You even mimicked Freddie's vacuuming technique. Don't worry, your grubby little secret is safe with us."

"And if I believe that…"

"Yeah, you'll believe anything."

For half an hour, whilst he waited for the paracetamol to kick in, Jack had been attempting to bring himself back to life by trying to do a crossword. He hated crosswords but he'd being trying to convince himself they represented the first step on the path to self-improvement. He had initially tried Sudoku but had come to the conclusion that that was merely the product of a particularly warped mind. He had the *Daily Telegraph* folded into quarters, a blue police-issue ballpoint pen lodged between his teeth, using his tongue to swing the exposed end back and forth like a horizontal, plastic metronome. There was probably a form somewhere that he should fill in requesting permission to use the pen for non-police activities. Duggan had just brought coffee into the office and had laid two ridged, cardboard cups down on the table, moved the white mug to one side for later transmission to the sink, and thrown a small pack of fruit shortbread biscuits in Jack's general direction. Catching sight of them as they travelled, Munday stretched out his right arm and snatched them out of the air.

"I should play for England with reflexes like that," he said.

The coffee was in an unnecessarily cheery, brightly coloured cup, with a cardboard cup holder and a plastic lid, which, if you tried to actually drink from its narrow aperture, would sear your lips for the rest of the day. Munday looked at the cup as if it were an alien being.

"What the hell is that? Where are the proper cups?"

"Canteen's been outsourced to a new provider," explained Duggan. "I think they think they're Starbucks."

"Is nothing sacred!"

"Well, you can forget about getting your toast from there in the mornings. It's all granola, muesli and pain au this or that down there now."

"This is a hard enough job as it is without having to put up with poncy food as well. I might have to lead a revolution."

"And do you think you'll persuade many people to man the barricades with you Jean Valjean?"

Munday looked blank.

"Who?"

"Jean Valjean. He was the main man in *Les Miserables.* You know, the musical? Don't let the Super hear you don't know about *Les Miserables* otherwise your career is properly coming to an end."

Munday took the chewed ballpoint out of the corner of his mouth, slid it over his left ear and shook his head.

"Mate, I gave up on musicals after *Saturday Night Fever.*"

Duggan sighed. "You're an uncultured heathen, Jack."

"Thank you." A line of cappuccino froth had given Munday a temporary comic moustache.

"It wasn't a compliment." Duggan muttered inaudible abuse under his breath. Jack took one of the biscuits and snapped it high above the cup, watching the crumbs fall like snowflakes into the tepid brown liquid.

"How are you getting on with the crossword? I mean it's nice to see you buy a newspaper for more than just the pictures for once."

"It's not easy, I have to say," Jack replied, his delicate disposition rendering him ignorant to the sarcasm. "I mean, what the hell could this be – eight down, eight letters, the clue is 'American toll' and, unless I've screwed up on six across, it's got a k in it?"

"Turnpike."

"Eh?"

"Turnpike. It's what the Americans call a toll road, as

in the New Jersey turnpike. Have you never listened to *America* by Simon and Garfunkel? Great song."

"You worry me sometimes," Jack filled in the letters, laying the paper flat on the desk and taking another sip of coffee. A mountain of paperwork sat in front of him, tilting unevenly to one side. He needed to review the contents and sign the folders but over the past few days he seemed to find almost any reason for not doing so. It could wait until the next angry email arrived.

"It's too quiet at the moment," Munday started, sipping again from the coffee cup.

"What do you mean too quiet? We haven't nailed this Christopher Sinclair guy and we still need to find the sender of the creepy messages. Anyhow, wouldn't some people say quiet is a good thing in our line of work?"

"I suppose. I was expecting to have nailed both by now. I get uneasy when there are so many loose ends. It all still feels a little bit up in the air. I prefer it when we're all run off our feet."

"Do you want me to get the guys to go out and rustle up some civil unrest, maybe start a riot or beat up a granny or two?"

"Now you're speaking my language." Jack picked up a half-eaten hobnob that he'd found sitting on the corner of his desk. Who knew how long it had been there? In the corner of the room, behind Jack's desk and slightly to the right, a window opened as a far as the catch on it would allow, permitting a cooling breeze to refresh the stale environment. Next to it a small radio crackled, just about conveying a song called *Mercy* from a new female artist that the DJ said in his stereotypical DJ voice had a "big bright future". Munday turned the volume up.

"Don't get me wrong, I love the song but who gives a girl a name like Duffy? I mean it's a really shit name for a pop star."

"So because you don't like the name, nobody can use it?"

Munday shrugged his shoulders. Duffy sang on regardless of Jack's criticism.

"They're kind of appropriate lyrics for coppers, if you think about them," said Duggan, leaning right back in his seat, his head touching the back wall.

"You think way too hard about things, you know. It's just a song."

"Did you and Elaine have a special song?" Duggan knew he was on difficult ground but stepped on it anyway.

"A special song? Do people really have those?"

"Of course they do. Ours is *It Had To Be You* by Harry Connick Junior."

"Why does that not shock me?"

Duggan was mildly offended but unsurprised that his long term friend and colleague did not share what some people would regard as his romantic sensitivities; he was unsure if his shock related to his choice of song or simply the fact that he and Caroline had a special song at all.

A loud rap on the glass pane of the office door caused

it to shudder in its insecure wooden surrounds and stopped the conversation in its tracks.

"I hear you knocking, but you can't come in; I hear you knocking, go back where you been."

Munday sang loudly, channelling his inner Dave Edmunds. Mike Sheridan, the youngest, most inexperienced member of his team, peered nervously around the door.

"Can I come in? Only you shouted that I couldn't."

"The DI was singing, Mike," called Duggan. "Honestly. I know it may not have sounded like it, but he was singing."

Munday looked towards the door. "Ignore Sergeant Duggan, Mike, he's just a bitter and twisted man, probably with no friends and blighted by his envy of my talent. Now how can we help you?"

"Guv, we've had a call. A kid was taken from outside a school this morning."

There remained a high possibility, even a likelihood that the child had just wandered off on an adventure and certainly nothing that Mike could tell them provided anything approaching conclusive evidence that the child had been taken. And yet they all knew how crucial it was to work on the basis that it was an abduction and make the most of the window of opportunity that the first few hours afforded. As soon as they heard the child's name – his surname in particular – both Munday and Duggan sensed they knew where this might be heading. Leo Baines had been missing for approaching two hours.

JACK MUNDAY HATED the media; aside from a few journalists he liked and respected – the ones he drank with and 'curried' with from time to time – mostly he found them to be an irritant that got in the way of him doing his job the way he wanted to. They probably thought of him in much the same way. But in cases like this even he wouldn't be able to deny that they had a role to play; when it came to a missing kid, everybody wanted to do what they could to secure a happy ending. They could then claim their own particular piece of the glory afterwards.

The force would need to get their information out as far and wide as quickly as possible and the media was still the quickest way of doing it. If the child had been taken and put in a car or a van, within a few hours that vehicle could be literally hundreds of miles away. It could also be just around the corner.

"Let's go meet the family. Mike, find out what CCTV footage there is available around the school and the surrounding area and let's take a look at it. But do it quickly. Send a couple of the guys down to the school and get uniform on standby to do some door knocking. Let's see who saw what. Get Rob or Paul to check on any known sex offenders in the area and see what they've been up to but tell them to do it discreetly. I don't want some vendetta on top of everything else. We'll bring back pictures of the missing kid and we'll try and get one of him in school uniform so we can show what he looked like when he went AWOL. And I want everybody – and I mean everybody – back for a team meet at two."

Sheridan turned on his heels and scurried out of the door, trying to temper his excitement with the sobriety of the circumstances. Duggan closed the door behind him.

"The Super, Jack?"

"What about her?"

"Don't you think you should inform her that she has a potential child abduction on her watch?"

Munday considered the point. It wasn't without merit.

"I'll call her from the car."

CHAPTER THIRTY-NINE

THE SOUND OF the doorbell jarred against the sense of fear enveloping the house. Matthew Baines, ashen-faced with reddened eyes, opened the door to the police. Two older women walked past the house and waved. He ignored them both. Matthew ushered the two officers down the narrow hallway of the Edwardian home into a converted through-lounge. His wife Susie, who appeared to be consumed by the deep blue sofa on which she sat, was pale, shaking and distracted. She cupped a glass of water in her hands but didn't look as if she had even sipped from it. She glanced up, glanced back down again and held her daughter Millie, who only wanted to escape her mother's clutches, close to her side. Matthew made tea and brought it into the living room on a small tray. Crisp sniffed disinterestedly around a plate of biscuits before curling in a foetal heap on the floor by Susie's feet.

"When I got the call from the school and realised what had happened, I felt my legs give way."

Susie spoke almost in a whisper and without making any effort to achieve eye contact. She clutched a teddy bear tightly, as if channelling the hug to her son. She seemed to stare beyond them as if the distance would reveal the whereabouts of her son. Inside she wanted to scream whether all this conversation, all of this polite questioning was really necessary or whether time couldn't better be spent just looking for Leo, but she knew it was unavoidable. Munday asked her to recall the morning's events in as much detail as she could. She spoke as if retrieving each memory one at a time from her subconscious.

"I called Matthew and screamed at him to find Leo. I drove around the school a few times trying to see him; one of the other mums came with. But when I hadn't seen him on the second or third time round, it began to sink in. I became a bit hysterical; people must have thought I was mad, sobbing and screaming like that. I felt sick deep down in my stomach. Maybe if I pass out, when I come round it will all have been a mistake."

Jack Munday sat on a second, sagging sofa, facing Susie; momentarily wondering how he'd be able to haul his hungover body back up again. He was gasping for a cigarette even though he had assured everyone he had given up. Matthew stayed standing behind Susie, his right hand resting on his wife's head, stroking her low-lighted hair as tenderly as he dared. She pushed his hand away. Munday let Susie say her piece and listened sympathetically and intently. He explained slowly that roadblocks were already being put in place along the routes in and out of the area, and that officers would be conducting house-to-house enquiries and talking to people outside the school to see if anyone saw anything that morning. He was keen to know if anyone saw Leo being put in a vehicle and, if so, any information they might be able to get about the vehicle in question. He told her, in the hope it might reassure her, that a police hotline had been set up and later that day the number would be circulated nationally. It only seemed to scare her more. The key, he told them both, was to get the message out as quickly and as widely as possible.

As time went on, he explained, they might consider a direct appeal to whoever might have taken Leo.

"What do you mean 'as time goes on'," interrupted Susie. "How long do you think this is going to last?"

"We have no way of knowing that at this stage," replied Jack, now seeing his own son, Connor, in his mind's eye. *Never let anybody tell you the crimes we investigate don't affect us police*, he thought.

"Let's just see how things play out. All I'm saying is there may come a point where we would want to reach out to whoever's taken Leo, if he has been taken, to urge them to let him go or to make contact before the situation deteriorates further."

He wanted to tell them that direct appeals had worked in the past. He also wanted to tell them his colleagues would be consulting the Missing, Abducted and Kidnapped Children unit at the Child Exploitation and Online Protection Centre, but he worried this would serve only to strike new fear into Susie's heart. Instead these two distant and vulnerable parents listened without taking in most of what was being said to them. They nodded nonetheless.

"What do you mean *if* he has been taken?" Matthew asked.

"You'd be surprised how many cases of missing children turn out to be the child disappearing of their own volition, for a few hours or for longer. I'm not saying that's what Leo has done but could you think of any reason why he might have run away?"

Susie shook her head in a manner that suggested she had already forgotten the question's content but Jack could already see that her husband was hesitating.

All morning Matthew had found himself trying to make sense of something that simply didn't. He also found himself being selfish. Leo was gone; Susie had let him go and yet she obviously held *him* responsible. It had taken all of his willpower so far not to shout or scream at her, not to ask her the many questions that were going round and round in his head.

He wanted to know in the tiniest of details what had happened, what had she done at each point on that journey to school and immediately afterwards and why? He wanted to know how it could possibly have happened in broad daylight outside school; how she could have *allowed* it to happen, but there was no way he would ever be able to give voice to that kind of thought. Leo had been taken. In his mind he went over every shocking detail of every terrible kidnap he had ever read about. Were these things happening to Leo? His Leo. Where was he; was he hurt, was he being tortured or mistreated, was he even still alive? Or worse was he alone, terrified, and unable to help himself?

"Leo knew that we had financial problems. He overheard conversations, arguments between us. I think it'd begun to affect him. I'm not saying it would have made him run away but you asked me if anything was bothering him." Susie threw her husband a withering glance.

"Tell me about the financial problems. How extensive are they?"

"Oh, they're extensive alright, aren't they Matthew?"

Matt stared at his wife.

"They're bad," he begun. "My business collapsed, we've had little or no money coming in, the credit cards are maxed out and I'm waiting for a call any day about the mortgage payments. Things have not been great."

"And aside from the credit card companies and the bank, is there anybody else you owe money to?"

"Are you suggesting somebody might have taken Leo because of a debt?"

"It wouldn't be unheard of."

"Fortunately, if that's the right word, those kinds of people owe me the money not the other way round, not that I ever expect to see any of it."

Susie's voice jolted Matthew.

"You should tell them about the messages," she whispered croakily, red rings encasing her hazel eyes.

Jack Munday glanced across at Duggan, whose newly found interest had prompted him to sit up straight. Munday looked up at Matthew Baines.

"I was coming round to asking you about the messages," Jack mentioned.

Matthew looked as if the conversation had moved into a language he knew he was supposed to understand but simply didn't. Jack explained about the messages to Karen Westcott and Kevin Simpson and the conversation with Simon Carter. He recounted how they were planning to speak to him anyway before the call about Leo's disappearance had come in. Talking through these messages and the background to them could be time well spent.

Matt inhaled deeply and told them the story, as far as he knew it. He recounted that day in 1975 in as much detail as he could remember and then brought them up to date on the most recent communication, talking them through each message in chronological order. With the benefit of hindsight, each threat in each message now seemed more obvious and loaded in its intent. Matthew felt exposed; naïve, complacent, and maybe even inadvertently complicit, a view he had little doubt that Susie shared. The pain of his recollections, however, paled compared to the pain of Leo's absence. Duggan took down each and every detail as Jack pushed him for more.

Susie's mother, a slight, white-haired woman, trying to put on a brave face for her daughter's benefit and failing, brought in a fresh tray of coffee from where she and some other family members had been quietly talking in the adjoining kitchen. Jack noticed how she tenderly squeezed her son in law's arm as he opened the door to allow her to retreat to the sanctuary of the kitchen. Maybe not everybody shared Susie's view of her husband. Millie, becoming frustrated that the attention was not on her, was tempted into the kitchen by her grandmother by the promise of chocolate.

"I understand from our other enquiries that your family moved away soon after Danny Carter's death?" Jack restarted once they were alone again.

"Is this relevant?"

"At the moment, everything's relevant."

"Yes, we did. My father was starting a new job."

"Do you know how long after Danny died?"

"I can't be certain; two or three weeks maybe."

"Everybody we've spoken to seems to think it was all a bit of surprise, like they didn't know you were moving away."

"I didn't really have any friends, Inspector. They were just kids I went to school with. I only spent time with them outside school because our parents knew each other."

"Are you aware of the rumours that were doing the rounds in connection with your family's move away?"

Matthew nodded. Susie looked up.

"What rumours?" she asked, glancing swiftly between the policeman and her husband in confused disbelief.

"They were saying that I tripped Danny as he ran towards the pool and because of that he hit his head as he entered the water."

Munday coughed. "And was that true?"

"No. I'm pretty sure I was already in the pool when Danny dived in because I remember my mother screaming at me to get out of the water when somebody first noticed Danny at the bottom."

Jack considered his next question, but Matthew continued.

"But what does it matter where I was? If the kids in the playground say I tripped him then that becomes the truth. Kids can be cruel."

"And the others who were there that day? Have you seen them since?"

Matthew shook his head. "What was the point of keeping in touch? Clearly some of them held me responsible and, given that they never really liked me anyway, I don't think we would have ever got past that. Nobody ever sat us down and talked things through with us, individually or together. Maybe that would have made a difference. Anyhow, it's all a long time ago now."

In the first moment of tenderness he had seen between them, Jack noticed Susie reach out and take her husband's hand. She didn't hold it for long, but long enough to show that a connection remained.

"So, you think what's happened to Leo is linked to Danny's death? It seems a bit far-fetched to me."

"Maybe not Danny's death directly but these messages might; we can't be sure, of course, but it's a bit of a coincidence if they're not and I don't generally do coincidences."

Jack coughed some phlegm into a creased white handkerchief that he had removed from his pocket. Duggan glanced down in disgust and asked for copies of all the messages that Matthew had received.

"An officer is going to come and stay with you. She'll be here in a few minutes and will help you, liaise with you, and keep you informed. Talk to her. Please don't go off doing your own thing, no matter how tempting. There will be times when it will seem to you that not a lot is happening, that maybe things are going more slowly than you would like..."

"Like now," Susie interrupted.

"Like now," Jack conceded. "But you have to trust us. You have to let us do our jobs and let us bring Leo back for you. I'll be back to see you tomorrow unless, of course, we have any news before then. And, please don't take this the wrong way, but the only person to blame for what has happened is whoever has taken Leo. Blaming each other doesn't help anybody."

OVER THE ENSUING hours family and close friends came and went almost unnoticed from the Baines house, smiling as they stepped past the uniformed police officer outside and uncomfortably exchanging pleasantries with the support officer inside.

Susie's parents made up the spare room and took it upon themselves to keep Millie occupied, giving Susie and Matt the time and space they needed to sit reflectively and worry. Much of that time was spent looking at photographs of Leo, from a baby to the young man he had become. But nothing could breach the tension that engulfed the house and everyone within it.

SUSIE AND MATT finally climbed into bed shortly after midnight, but neither could sleep. She wanted to stay awake just in case of a call or a knock at the door; she didn't want to take the risk that she might sleep through it. He wanted to cuddle up against her; he needed the human contact and, after all, she was the only other person who could possibly know how he was feeling. But he didn't try. Instead, he lay on his back, staring up into the darkness and listened to Susie as she tried to stifle her crying. The longer he lay awake, the more sinister were the thoughts that entered his mind. He'd heard all of those news reports over the years say that if a kidnapped child hadn't been found within the first twenty-four hours, the odds suggest that they wouldn't be found alive. The more Matt stared at the ceiling the harder he found it to escape the thought that time may be running out for Leo, and that perhaps it was all down to him.

CHAPTER FORTY

"YOU AND THE Super seem to be hitting it off," Duggan smiled as he handed Jack a coffee that he'd just bought from a mobile refreshment truck parked in a lay-by along the side of the road. It had been an unscheduled stop on their way back to the station. Jack had declared himself desperate for a "comfort break". Harry organised refreshments whilst Jack relieved himself discreetly behind some bushes, something for which his colleague could probably have issued him with a caution.

"And when you say *hitting it off*, what exactly do you mean?"

"I mean getting on well. Not everybody's mind is a sewer. It's just that a couple of weeks ago you were talking about her as if she was Satan's daughter."

"I never did. I reject that suggestion categorically."

"Okay, but you can't deny you weren't exactly excited about her arrival."

Jack sipped the coffee, enjoying the sweetness in his

mouth and the warmth as he felt it travel through his body and counter the residual alcohol in his blood stream.

"That might be true but she's alright. I think we're going to get along just fine. After all, we both want the same thing, to catch the baddies."

Harry chuckled as they climbed back into the car. "Is that so? You just want to catch the baddies. And how are things with Elaine?"

Jack was so expecting Harry to say Lesley's name that the question took him a little by surprise. Harry took Jack's momentary pause as a sign of reluctance to talk.

"I'm sorry, I was only asking. I'll change the subject."

Jack turned his face away from Harry. He thought about his night with Lesley and smiled. A jolt of excitement pulsed through his body.

"There's no change with Elaine but I have a feeling things are about to get a whole lot more complicated there."

"How come?"

"Because Lesley and I are an item and don't for a minute pretend that you hadn't guessed. It's just that now we've decided we're going to do it properly."

"You're going to be a couple rather than just fuck buddies?"

Jack choked a little on his mouthful of coffee, spraying foam across the car's leather look fascia. He wiped it off with his jacket sleeve.

"Don't let Lesley hear you say that if you value keeping

hold of your testicles."

"I think there's probably just one elderly lady living on a remote island off the coast of Northern Scotland who hasn't guessed but, her apart, I think it has to have been the worst kept secret in modern history."

"Everyone knows?"

"Everyone."

"But we were always so careful." Jack appeared genuinely mystified, serving to make Harry enjoy the moment even more.

"You work every day in a building full of people who are paid to solve horrible and difficult crimes and you say you're surprised that they manage to work out that their boss is shagging one of their colleagues. Honestly."

"Well, when you put it like that."

"When are you going public?"

"Don't know. We haven't decided yet so keep it to yourself for the time being. I need to tell Connor and Elaine first, which isn't going to be easy, but they need to hear it from me rather than find out from somebody else."

"How do you think they'll take it?"

"I think Elaine will go properly mad and make life really difficult. I just hope she doesn't try and twist Connor's mind the way she did when we first split. It's taken ages to get that relationship with him working and I don't need to have to start from scratch again. I mean, I know she'll have a problem with the thought of Connor and Lesley getting to know each other but she'll just have to get over it. I had to when she moved her boyfriend in that time so she can't really throw her toys out of the pram now the boot's on the other foot."

"And what about Connor? What if *he* has a problem with it?"

Jack shrugged. "I hope he won't but I guess we'll have to cross that bridge when we come to it. I can't put my life on hold just because other people may not like my choices. I'm entitled to a life as well, aren't I?"

Harry took the question to be rhetorical and just allowed the conversation to lapse into silence.

THE JOURNEY BACK to the station took them through the leafier northern suburbs of London, with their manicured lawns, prep schools and SUVs on the driveways. Jack watched the world go by from the passenger window. He found himself wondering how far this world was from the one that had left a young girl from Ukraine dead in a hotel room and a young boy taken from his parents. Was the distance really as great as he thought? There are secrets behind every window, he had once been told. He could only imagine what secrets lay behind these. How many of the people they had passed so far had a son the same age as Leo Baines or driven past Christopher Sinclair going about his business without giving him a second glance.

"How are things working out with Salazar?" Harry asked.

"The guy's a twat."

Harry laughed. He could imagine Frank saying exactly the same thing about Jack.

"You don't have to like him, you just have to be able to work with him."

"Have you been talking to the Super?"

"Were those her orders?"

"Kind of. The 'if you're going to be a DCI you have to get the best out of all your staff and not just work with the ones you like' conversation."

"She's got a point."

"I know, but I'd still rather transfer him somewhere else."

"He's a decent copper, though; experienced."

"Since when were you in charge of his fan club?"

"I'm just saying, that's all."

"Maybe say a little less and drive a little more."

CHAPTER FORTY-ONE

THE FOLLOWING DAY dawned brightly, the sun causing a kaleidoscope of colours to bounce off of the car windows parked along the street outside Elaine Munday's house. The sense of optimism that invariably followed the sun was, on this occasion, completely out of keeping with the way both Matthew Baines and Jack Munday were feeling.

MUNDAY HAD SPENT the night asleep in the armchair in Connor's bedroom, his leather jacket half draped over his torso like some kind of makeshift blanket. It had been an uncomfortable night with tranches of sleep interrupted by back pain caused by his unnatural sleeping position. He woke feeling anything but refreshed and, in the half light, watched the rise and fall of his son's breathing, bringing back to mind the many nights he had spent in the same position as Connor had grown from baby to toddler to child to teenager; that closeness had seemed behind him until last night. When he'd arrived, unannounced, late the previous night, Elaine had initially been reluctant to let him in. At first, she suspected he might have been drinking, but the need to see and be close to his son seemed so intense that she could neither bring herself to ask him why or deny him the opportunity.

Jack was in that place of semi-consciousness, awake yet not ready to take on the responsibilities of the day, when he felt Elaine's hand, more tender than he had expected, rest on his shoulder and hand him a white china mug giving off the comforting aroma of freshly ground coffee.

"It's seven o'clock. I'm not going to ask, but I need to get him up soon. Why don't you take a shower?"

Jack nodded and sipped from the cup. How different from the last time he had been here, he thought. He needed to send Lesley a text to let her know where he'd been all night, though God alone knew how he would explain it or whether she would even believe that explanation. Who, he thought to himself, decreed that life had to be so fucking complicated?

ACROSS TOWN MATT woke to find the space in the bed alongside him empty. He lifted his upper body off the pillows before the sheer weight of what yet faced him forced him back down onto the mattress as if a concrete block had been placed across his chest. Sunlight speared its way through the points where the curtains failed to meet or overlap. It all felt worse this morning. The adrenalin that had kicked in the previous day had given way to the whole, naked, horrific reality and the lactic acid that now inhabited the muscles where stress had previously been, made it harder than he had imagined it would be to move. He laid flat, head on the pillow and staring directly upwards. Yesterday, the police had asked basic questions, like Leo's height, weight and eye colour and he felt ashamed that he'd struggled to provide the answers they were looking for. Susie had known them instantly, of course, and she had also provided the recent picture of Leo that they needed. It felt like they were scoring points on who was the most caring parent. How, he wondered, had things turned so sour?

As Matthew lay in silence trying to summon up positivity from somewhere and channel it into his veins, the sound of conversation drifted up from downstairs. It wasn't animated or excessively loud, but multiple voices vying for attention was enough to make it audible. As he strained to make out actual words, he heard somebody firmly close the kitchen door.

His legs felt heavier than he expected as he swung them round until his feet were on the floor, pulled on some blue checked pyjama bottoms and crept towards the top of the stairs as if desperately trying to avoid waking a baby.

Despite the closed door, the conversation downstairs was still audible, and he stopped as each step creaked to make sure he hadn't disturbed them. He knew it made no sense but something inside him still wanted to retain some kind of element of surprise.

Six faces looked around in unison as Matthew turned the wooden knob and forced the door open in a single motion. Susie and her parents were sitting around the kitchen table, papers spread out across the varnished wooden surface, and a three-quarters drained cafetiere nestled among five mugs. Two of the other mothers from Leo's school were also around the table and the police officer assigned to stay with the family stood at the back of the kitchen filling the kettle from the tap.

"What's going on?"

Susie smiled, but the disquiet behind the expression couldn't be disguised.

"The girls came round to see if we were okay. We've been talking. We've decided we can't just sit back and wait for something to happen. I… *we*… have to do something. The girls have suggested that we make some flyers and organise some search teams. We've drawn up some maps of the area to hand out to anyone who wants to volunteer."

She pushed the maps forward for him to look at, as if waiting for his approval.

"And what, this is Mission Control?"

"I can't just sit here and wait for the police to bring us news. We need to get out and find him. He has to know when we get him back that we were out there looking for him all the time he was away; that we didn't spare a single moment."

She seemed genuinely strengthened at having stumbled upon something tangible she felt she could do. Matt understood exactly the point she was making and, though he didn't want to stifle her energy, neither did he want to do anything that might compromise the actions taken by the police. He glanced at his watch and felt sick as he realised that time was closing in on their chances of getting Leo back alive. The 24-hour marker had hooked him in, and he knew that it had done the same to Susie. They had been told how crucial it was to establish a clear timeline of where Leo had been in the hours and days before and at the point he went missing, to determine if someone had been watching him. As they had laid in the dark the previous night, they had tried to piece together the minutes before he was taken.

The police had warned them it might be a process made more difficult by the young age of any witnesses, but that they were sending trained officers into the school that morning to try and draw out any friends who may have seen Leo getting into a vehicle. They wanted to know whether there had been a struggle, or whether he went willingly, which would suggest that he might have known the driver. The police still believed that abduction by a stranger was both the worst-case scenario and still the most unlikely. Matthew knew they were almost certainly right.

Munday and Duggan arrived unannounced; the loud

rap on the front door caused glances to be exchanged between everyone around the kitchen table, at once raising hopes and then almost immediately dashing them again. It had only been a matter of hours since the detectives' first visit but already Matthew had sensed that there would be no reprieve from riding the emotional rollercoaster. He had always hated funfairs.

Matthew ushered the officers into the living room, whilst those in the kitchen busied themselves washing up cups and making fresh coffee, even though nobody had requested any.

"I want to talk about nineteen seventy-five a bit more," Duggan started, addressing his comments directly to Matt. "Talk me through it again. I want to know everyone who was there the day Danny Carter died."

Jack Munday sat squarely in an armchair, his left leg crossed over his right, hands clasped around his knee. He didn't move his gaze away from Matthew's face. The insistence in Duggan's voice and the urgency with which he asked his question unsettled Matthew. He took one long, deep breath, feeling it stretch his diaphragm, sunk back into the sofa, put his hands together in supplication and breathed hard across the top of his fingertips.

"It's a very long time ago but there was me and Danny, obviously."

"What was Danny like?"

"He was quite a cool kid, funny. He was about a year older than me and the fact that we were friends meant that

I got to hang around with a group of kids who were all older than me. That kind of stuff is important when you're nine or ten."

"So if he was older than you, presumably you weren't in the same class at school?"

Matt nodded his head to confirm.

"So how did you become friends?"

Matt exhaled to what seemed like the full capacity of his lungs.

"I was friends with Kevin, because our parents were close, and Kevin also used to play with Danny and Simon, so that's how I had got to know them."

"And are you still in touch with him?"

"Who? Kevin? Simon? Jesus, no. I mean, I suppose I must have seen them again after that day, but I can't recall it. I remember the whole thing being talked about in the school playground on what I think was the day after, but we moved soon after anyway and we lost touch. There were no mobile phones or Facebook in 1975."

"So, do you think about that day much?"

"I do now. I didn't then really. Perhaps when I became a parent myself, I found myself thinking more about Danny and what happened that day. At first, I thought it wasn't discussed because we moved away soon after it happened but somehow I still think there might have been more to it than that. I just don't have anyone I can ask so it's all guesswork."

"And what does guesswork tell you?"

"It doesn't really. Maybe that I could have understood it, come to terms with it better, if it had been explained to me at the time."

"And the other kids there that day? Any of the parents still alive?"

"Honestly I don't know who is or isn't alive. Kevin's mum would be the person to speak to because she was looking after Danny but I don't know what happened to her. As for the kids, other than Simon, Mark and Kevin, there was Karen's older brother Christopher. He was a bit of a weird kid, but that might be the pot calling the kettle black. There was, I think, a kid called Paul Cherry and another one, too, whose name, don't quote me on it, was Swain. Timothy Swain. Yes, definitely Timothy Swain."

"Would it surprise you to know that we've already spoken to Simon, to Kevin and to Karen?"

Matthew laughed a little and breathed into his closed fist.

"In connection with Leo?"

"Not directly, but Karen contacted us because she'd been receiving messages very similar to the ones you've been describing. She had confided in Kevin and so, naturally, we also wanted to speak to Simon."

"And did they know anything?"

Munday shook his head.

"Nothing earth shattering, no. But you see now why we're keen to know who has been sending the messages."

Matthew nodded.

"You mentioned that you felt as if you were kept away from the others that were there when Danny died, or that they were kept away from you. Don't you think that's strange? I mean you were friends, you share in this very intense and very tragic situation and none of you meet up, keep in touch, or ever even speak about it, talk it through."

"The older I have got, Inspector, the more I *have* thought about it, and the stranger it seems. But we were nine, ten, eleven years old, so those decisions were made for us. It wasn't like a movie. I don't know how you start re-engaging after all this time especially around something so awful; it's not something you meet in the pub over a pint to reminisce about."

The tautness of the atmosphere was broken by the ringtone of Harry Duggan's mobile phone. He hauled himself up off the sofa to answer the call, acknowledging Mike Sheridan at the other end, whilst simultaneously exiting the lounge to take the conversation into the hall. Munday returned to the questioning.

"Tell me some more about Leo."

"What do you want to know?"

"I want to know what kind of kid is he? How do you think he'll be coping at the moment?"

"What kind of question is that? He's eleven years old. He'll be shit scared. Wouldn't you be?"

"I'm not asking you these questions because I want to upset you, but I need to get inside Leo's head, if you get my drift. Will he be calm? Will he try and argue with whoever has him? Will he be compliant? How do you think he will be handling things?"

Matt sipped from a glass of water that Susie's mum had brought in for him. She smiled benignly as she moved backwards out of the room.

"I think he'll do whatever he thinks he needs to do to not make matters worse. He's a bright lad. He won't want to get whoever it is angry, but I think he *will* try and ask why. He'll want to know why he's been taken."

"Do you agree, Mrs Baines?"

Susie nodded, her paper tissue clutched so tightly around her left hand that it started to resemble a new wedding ring.

"I just want to go back to your financial problems. What do you do for a living?"

"Why is that relevant?"

"At the moment, we have no idea what may be relevant and what may not. I'm just trying to build up a picture. If somebody has taken Leo as a way of getting at you or your wife, then we need to start thinking who that might be and why."

"I'm a graphic designer."

"And business hasn't been good?"

"No, it's shit, but then it's the same for everybody."

"A sign of the times. When you say 'shit' just how 'shit' do you mean?"

"What are you driving at?"

"Do you have business enemies?"

"Enemies, I don't think so. Yes, I owe money but only because I'm owed so much, but not in the way you're suggesting; I don't have big gambling debts that people are looking to have repaid or they'll break my legs…"

"…or kidnap your son?"

"But if that was the case why hasn't anyone asked for a ransom?"

"Yet…"

"Yet."

"So, I'll need a list from you of everyone you owe money to and how much."

"You can have whatever you need as long as you get my son back."

Harry Duggan opened the door and looked first at Matt and then at Munday, his mobile phone clenched so tightly in his fist that when he realised, he felt his fingers ache a little as he released his grip. He tipped the phone in his colleague's general direction.

"What?"

"Mike's found a kid who thinks she saw Leo being bundled into a car outside the school yesterday morning."

Munday pursed his lips in concentration and nodded as he rose, irritated that Duggan had disclosed the news in front of the parents.

"Don't pin too much on this," he cautioned. "We're out there looking as we speak. As soon as we find anything, you will be the first to know. We'll let ourselves out."

CHAPTER FORTY-TWO

DANNY THORNE PUNCHED the air the way a golfer might when he sinks the putt that wins a major championship. His follow-up reaction was similarly colourful.

"Get in," he shouted, causing at least half a dozen fellow officers, some of whom were on calls, to stop what they were doing to see what the commotion was all about. A few put their hands over the handsets; others placed them back on their cradles completely. One of those was Frank Salazar.

"Danny, something to share with the class?" he bellowed from across the room.

"He's only gone and taken the bait, boss. He's fucking taken the bait."

"Who?"

"Christopher Sinclair. He's taken the bait. Lesley's got herself a date with a killer."

The full, potential horror of Thorne's pronouncement

rendered Lesley Hilton momentarily speechless. She felt suddenly nauseous as all adrenalin seemed to depart her body at once. She sat at her desk, opposite Thorne, and rested her head in her hands, staring down at the tabletop as Salazar walked around the central bank of desks that he had once remarked made the department more closely resemble a call centre than a police station. He huddled up alongside Thorne, leaning forward to get a closer look at the computer screen, the smell of his sweat-ridden body forcing the younger officer to stifle a retch. Thorne doubted that Salazar had ever been introduced to a can of deodorant.

Thorne's initial inclination was to make a flippant remark or two in his usual way as the fount of the station's light entertainment. But Lesley's silence, followed by a lift of her head and a nervous, fixed stare stopped him in his tracks.

"BEFORE YOU SAY anything Danny, I know it's not a term you're particularly familiar with, but can we try and keep this at least vaguely professional?"

"You tell me, Lesley. You're the one that's going to be the pro."

"You see," replied Lesley, more for anyone who could hear than Danny in particular, "that's what I was talking about."

"Enough," interjected Salazar, bringing the palm of his hand down firm and flat on the pile of papers stacked precariously on the corner of Thorne's desk. It was hard enough to send a few from the top scattering onto the floor and loud enough to cause an uncomfortable silence to fall across the room. He looked up at Thorne.

"Stop playing the joker for five minutes, will you? You'd better hope that you're as professional as she will be because we're all depending on you to make sure she gets out of there without even a hair out of place. Understood? Now, what're the arrangements?"

"It's on Thursday, boss. He's booked a room at a hotel called The Middlebank over in Kensington and we have to get Lesley there, looking voluptuous for him, by nine pm. If he follows his previous pattern, he'll already be there and, of course, we'll have people there to watch him arrive. We'll wire up his room and the moment Lesley gives the signal, we can charge in so mob-handed, he won't even have time to take the condom off."

"Thanks for the unwanted image."

"I thought I'd go down to the hotel a bit later and make sure we've got both rooms either side of the one he's booked. I'm not going to go in too heavy this early, in case the manager and Sinclair have an understanding, if you know what I mean. I'll just be some corporate punter."

Salazar nodded and then stood, arched his back and stretched his arms out wide before locking his hands together behind his head. This only served to reinforce the impact of the lack of antiperspirant. Thorne coughed.

"What it does do, of course, is put us under even greater pressure to find out who Christopher Sinclair actually is."

Thorne nodded. "We're already on it."

"And put together a detailed plan of action for the night of the Sinclair meeting that we can show the DI and the Superintendent. Nothing, and I repeat, nothing can be left to chance."

"Aye aye Captain."

Lesley studied a fresh email. She stood, turned and looked towards Mike Sheridan a few desks away.

"Mike, the name of the father of the kidnapped boy, what is it?"

Sheridan looked up, flustered, before looking down again and consulting his notebook.

"Baines. Matthew Baines," he called across the room. "Why?"

"Where does he live?"

Sheridan looked down again. How difficult could it be to remember such basic facts on a live case, Lesley thought to herself.

"Pilgrim Avenue."

"Shit," Lesley exhaled loudly. "Jack's not going to like this."

Salazar looked round.

"What's up?"

Lesley sighed.

"Just had some information in from Companies House. One of the directors of My Millionaire Boyfriend is one Matthew Baines of Pilgrim Avenue."

"Call Jack now," Salazar replied.

CHAPTER FORTY-THREE

FIVE MILES ACROSS town Christopher Sinclair felt buoyant. After the stress of the past few weeks, the fact that this latest girl had accepted his offer to meet had reassured him that perhaps everything would work out okay. After all, one unfortunate accident shouldn't be allowed to define a life. He was doing nothing wrong; two adults consenting to sexual intercourse should not incur the approbation of society. So what if he paid the girls. They were willingly providing a service that he was happy to pay for. Anyone who disapproved but were in favour of the basic principles of a supply and demand economy were merely hypocrites. He had always gone to such lengths to conceal his real identity because of them; *they* were the ones who had a problem, the ones who didn't understand. And yet, he could only imagine the consequences if everything came out.

He had often wondered why sex had become such a taboo; it wasn't as if most of the people he knew or saw on the underground in the morning weren't doing it in some form. What was it, he wondered, that they would have the problem with? That it was paid for? That some of his predilections were, in their view, a little extreme? Sometimes he'd felt a genuine affinity for some of the girls he had met, and was sure that one or two would have reciprocated that affection. But in the final analysis, he liked the variety and, if truth be told, part of him enjoyed the element of danger. Being so risk averse in almost all other aspects of his life made having this one secret let him feel so much more alive.

It was something that had started unintentionally. He had been a late developer and didn't lose his virginity until he had completed his law degree. There had simply been no opportunity before then but he had found a sympathetic prostitute in Cambridge after he stayed on to complete his Masters and she offered discounts for multiple visits. As he became more confident in her company, he felt freer to explore some of the darker fantasies that had been forming in his imagination. She didn't mind, she simply took more of the money he earned waiting tables for doing so. By the time he had been called to the Bar and money was a little more free flowing he felt free enough to indulge again. It was the ability to hide in the online shadows that persuaded him to adopt an assumed identity and he quickly and unexpectedly found that this added to the frisson that he felt. He could do things, say things and generally behave as Christopher

Sinclair that would have been impossible as his true self. And as for the name? It had been a two-minute thought process. Sinclair had been his mother's maiden name and Christopher his best friend at school.

And as for Thursday's meet-up, well, he wanted that to be special, unhurried and to take him back to the edges of what others might find acceptable. He also planned for it to eradicate the memory of that last, unfortunate appointment from his mind. He slipped the debit card back into the black leather wallet that sat on the corner of his desk, breathed deeply and picked up the new brief that the clerk of chambers had left for his attention.

CHAPTER FORTY-FOUR

JODIE BARRETT SAT on a functional blue-cloth chair outside the Head Teacher's office at Bridleway Foundation School. Her mother, Ellie, a stubby woman whose facial features seemed as if they had all been forcibly squeezed closer together, had just arrived after receiving a call from the school office. She fidgeted in the seat next to her daughter, who looked flushed and nervous, intermittently twisting her wedding ring, checking her watch and running her hands through her poorly dyed red hair, the greying roots more than passingly visible. She smiled to herself as if pleased, proud even, that her daughter had summoned the courage to come forward with such potentially important information, whilst the greater part of her was exasperated at the amount of time it was going to take out of her day.

Her mother's obvious frustration was putting Jodie on edge and the young girl was willing the questions to start as soon as possible. School friends who passed by threw her an occasional, sympathetic smile but mostly she went unnoticed.

The Head Teacher, a middle-aged man with a shaving rash and flaky skin, wore an ill-fitting suit, a cheap, crumpled shirt and a shiny red tie. He ushered them into the office; a cavernous, soulless room, with a mahogany desk and a whiteboard on the wall behind it, bearing unintelligible scribbles in at least four different colours. Munday sat in a hard-backed chair beside the head teacher's desk. Duggan remained standing.

"Hi Jodie."

Jodie smiled. Her mother continued to twist her ring.

"I understand that you may have seen something yesterday morning that might be able to help us find Leo."

She nodded again.

"Can you tell me more?"

In a gesture that Jack was sure was meant to be encouraging, Jodie's mother rubbed her daughter nervously across her back. The child shook her upper body until the mother withdrew her hand.

"I saw Leo being pushed into a car."

"And you're absolutely sure it was Leo?"

Jodie nodded. "He had his red Adidas bag on his shoulder; the one he takes everywhere. I didn't see his face because the man had his hand on the back of his head and was pushing him down into the car, but I know it was Leo."

"So, it didn't look like Leo wanted to go with the

man?"

"I don't think so. I mean, he wasn't screaming or shouting or anything but the man had grabbed him and then it was all over really quickly and they just drove away."

"Did you see if he put Leo into the back of the car or the front?"

"Definitely the back."

"Perhaps he'd been threatened," interjected the Head Teacher. Munday's glance at him should have been enough to tell him to keep his mouth shut.

"Can you tell me what the man looked like?" Duggan asked.

Jodie looked down at her lap and then back up again, directly at him.

"I didn't see much but he had dark hair."

"Okay. Long hair, short hair or about collar length like mine?"

"Like yours."

"Curly or straight?"

"I don't know."

"Go easy officer," interjected Jodie's mother, "you're firing questions at her as if she's a suspect. She's only a kid and she's trying her best."

She gave Jodie another patronising pat just above the knee. For the second time the young girl shook herself away from the older woman's grasp. The Head Teacher, frustrated at feeling redundant, tapped irritatingly on the top of a hole punch from his position behind the desk. Munday reached out to indicate that he should stop. The Head went back to silently running through the different statements he would make to the press dependent on how this whole scenario played out. Harry smiled and turned his attention back to the schoolgirl.

"I'm sorry, Jodie, you're doing really well but I need to ask these questions. It's really important that we find Leo quickly. You understand that, don't you? Now, do you remember the man's clothes?"

The girl considered her answer.

"Jeans. I only remember jeans."

Munday cleared his throat to suggest he wanted to ask a question of his own. Duggan carried on regardless.

"Was he short or tall, thin or fat or was he just average?"

"He was thin. His clothes looked baggy on him."

Munday sighed, frustrated that Duggan might be putting words into the girl's mouth, but more frustrated that the abductor seemed to be average in every respect. Why couldn't he have been huge, with ginger hair, a scar on his face and distinctive tattoos?

"And did the man get into the driver's seat or the passenger seat or did he climb in the back of the car with Leo?" Munday wanted to regain some control over the conversation.

"The driver's seat."

"Now, think very carefully. Where were you when this

happened and when did you first notice that Leo was in trouble?"

The girl thought carefully and sipped from a plastic cup of water; the kind given by a dentist to swill your mouth out after an appointment.

"Mum dropped me off in the usual place, just around the corner near the shops. I was walking across the crossing and I noticed Leo further down the road, nearer to the school gates. Normally he's on his own, like in his own little world, but today I saw a man tap him on the shoulder and start talking to him, like really close to his ear. Leo looked a bit freaked out, but then he got pushed into the back of the car and driven away. It all happened really quickly."

"And the car? Was it big, small, what colour?"

"Small, a bit like mum's car and dark blue or black."

"What does Mum drive?"

The question, directed at Jodie's mother, caught her slightly off guard.

"Oh, dear, yes, well... what do I drive? Erm, a Ford Focus." She twisted her wedding ring again and looked at her watch all in a single motion.

Duggan wondered how the mother would cope under serious and sustained questioning and then thanked the Lord she wasn't actually a suspect.

Munday lifted himself off his seat, putting his hand on the small of his back to try and ease the bit of pain running down the outside of his right leg.

"What's Leo like?" he asked.

Jodie shrugged her shoulders.

"Were you friends?"

"Not really. We were in some classes together but he was quite quiet."

"But he must have had friends. Everybody hangs around with somebody."

"He was friends with some of the boys. They talk about computer games the whole time. It's really boring."

"But he was definitely on his own this morning, when you saw him with the man?"

Jodie nodded. Her mother looked at her watch again.

"Okay, can you give Sergeant Duggan here the names of some of the boys that Leo was friends with? We may need to talk to them too, but I think, for now, we've taken up enough of your time. So, thank you, Jodie, you've been very helpful."

Much to the relief of her mother that the interview was drawing to a close, Munday shook hands with the schoolgirl first and then the Head Teacher before both officers began walking out of the school. Jodie's mum wondered how long she needed to wait before being able to rush away herself.

"PENNY FOR YOUR thoughts," started Duggan as they reached the car.

"Not much value for money, I'm afraid."

"You're convinced it's something to do with the

messages, the boy that drowned, aren't you?"

"I don't know. But if it's not, why kidnap a kid whose parents can't afford a ransom?"

"Sex… paedo ring?"

"It's a possibility, I guess. See how they've got on chasing up details on anyone on the sex offenders register. I'm interested in anybody within a twenty-five-mile radius with a taste for young boys, especially anyone who's been recently released."

"And the messages?"

Munday looked away from Duggan, out of the car's side window as if expecting clues to be written on the clouds. The lack of any communication from the kidnapper worried him. He knew the clock was ticking.

"I know they've looked at the CCTV from around here, but we need them to look at it again, frame by frame, to match it up with what the girl said. They need to try harder to identify the car. That can't be beyond them, surely. They get paid enough. And we need more information on the Dad's old friends. Get the guys digging again into the ones we know and let's have Rob and Paul start on the other names he mentioned this morning – Swain, Cherry – anything that's not quite right, and I mean anything."

"So, find a motive?"

"That's why it's called detective work."

CHAPTER FORTY-FIVE

ALTHOUGH IT HAD been a comparatively short life so far, Leo Baines had never felt so scared. This was way above and beyond the punishment he'd received in the past for the occasional bit of backchat. He concentrated hard to control the rampant fear and the racing heartbeat that had overtaken his breathing since he had been bundled into the car. What could he do to calm his shaking body? Twice he thought he was about to be sick but he was terrified what kind of punishment that might incur.

He knew, of course, that something was very wrong and yet the more he tried to understand, the less he could make sense of anything that was happening.

At least now the thick tape that had bound his hands and his ankles together, rendering him unable to climb out of a sitting position, had been removed from his mouth. It meant he could at least breathe a little more easily even though it had come at the cost of a promise to remain silent. He could still taste the bitter adhesive on his lips. Fabric still covered his eyes so he couldn't be sure of his surroundings. He couldn't even hear traffic in the distance, so he doubted there was anyone nearby to hear him even if he found the courage to call out. He had considered ignoring the man's instruction and screaming with all the energy he could muster, but he had no idea where he was, and he couldn't see an upside to antagonising the man without good reason.

In the extended hours of silence, he asked himself what his Dad would do, and the answer was always the same: *don't do anything that could make the situation worse.* He knew the place where he'd been taken was large, because whenever he'd heard footsteps coming or doors shutting, the sound had echoed, reverberated and had come back towards him, like in his school science lessons. He hated science but he would have given anything to be back in that classroom right now.

The hardest part so far had been having no idea *why* he'd been taken; the man had given no reason. He assumed there was only the one man, but he couldn't be certain of that either. He had only seen and spoken to the person who had taken him from outside of the school, but that didn't mean that there couldn't have been others. His eyes had been covered almost immediately; a black hood placed over his head as he was bundled into the back of the car, his hands tied together behind his back.

In the long noiseless, hours between meals he had

concentrated as hard as he could on trying to remember what the man looked like, to picture everything from the colour of his eyes to the way his hair was cut, and even the smell of his breath. But everything had happened so quickly that Leo had found it hard to be sure that anything he could recall was accurate. Instead he found himself thinking about his parents and how scared they probably were. He'd been ten minutes late coming back from the shop on the corner once and his mum had been ready to send out search parties. This would have taken her panic to a different level.

Time continued to drag and with his eyes covered he had no concept of night and day, light and dark. When he drifted into an uncomfortable sleep, he couldn't be sure if it had been for five minutes or five hours and now he was even less certain how easy he would find it to lie down rather than remain seated in this weird position, let alone stand again.

Sometimes, like now, he sensed that the man was present, as if he could feel his gaze actually touching his face. The man would speak to him, softly, almost too softly to hear properly, and ask if he was okay, as if reassuring himself. After all, if he'd been that concerned about *him*, Leo thought, he wouldn't have taken him in the first place. He always nodded and tried to be friendly and talkative even if he felt awful because he didn't know how the man would react to any other response. Sometimes it appeared, bizarrely, as if the man needed to feel that Leo knew he was being cared for. Leo thought it was weird.

During the periods of silence, Leo wondered what was happening outside. Was there a dramatic search going on to look for him? Was his photograph in all of the newspapers? Had his parents been on television asking for his safe return? Had the man asked for money? What if his parents couldn't afford it? What would the man do if his plan went wrong? Leo felt the tension rising again through his body and turned his attention to thinking of other things.

The man gave him food from time to time, left beside him on the same type of plastic plate his parents would pack when they took him on camping trips. The food was always the same. A sandwich, where the bread was neither fresh nor hard enough to be stale, and a single square of processed cheese; even worse than the one his father had once grabbed him from a run-down petrol station on the way home from a school football match. Unlike his father, though, the man had given him a bag of crisps as well, which offset the taste of the sandwich.

The man would remove the tape from his hands and guide them to the plate so he could feel for the food. If he strained his eyes downwards as low as he could without giving himself a headache, he could only see the freckles on his bare arms. He had always hated those freckles; he made a mental note now to never complain about them again. A bottle of water, cap unscrewed, was placed by his side but the man would always stay with him until the food had been eaten and would then tape his hands together again, apologising as he did so. Once, Leo was sure he could hear the man quietly crying. He wanted to ask why but the moment hadn't seemed right.

There had been a moment, he couldn't be sure how long ago, when he'd sensed the man sitting close to him. He could hear him breathing and, at times he thought he could feel warm, nicotine-stenched breath on his own skin. He found it unsettling.

"Do you love your family?" the man had asked.

Leo had nodded. Part of him didn't want to have a conversation but he knew to just go along with it and to try to be as co-operative as was possible.

"They seem a nice family," the man continued. "Your dad, Matt, your mum, Susie, isn't it? And little Millie, she looks like a cute one."

The significance struck Leo dumb. He knew their names. He felt panic rising again from his stomach and up through his chest towards his throat. Before, Leo had guessed he'd been taken randomly, just the wrong kid in the wrong place at the wrong time. He couldn't think of any other explanation. But now, suddenly, everything was different. The man knew who he was; he knew his family; who else did he know?

"How do you know my family?"

"We go way back," said the man, "me and your dad."

"Are you friends? Do I know you?"

"We were friends once, kind of." And then the man

laughed a little. "And no, don't worry, you don't know me."

There was a moment's silence between them, but Leo could still sense his proximity.

"So how do you know my dad?"

No reply. Leo waited a little longer. Now he actually wanted conversation, wanted to understand why he had been taken. "So did you take me because of something to do with my dad?"

Leo could hear the phosphorus tip of a matchstick scratch against the side of a matchbox, followed by the aroma of smoke beginning to irritate his nostrils and line the back of his own throat.

"You're asking a lot of questions."

"Sorry."

He heard the man inhale again and waited for another cloud of smoke he couldn't see to dance across his face.

"Don't be. I understand. You want to know why I took you."

Leo, his knees pulled up to his chest, his hands clasped tightly around them, nodded to the invisible voice.

"Sometimes, Leo, we do things as children without being fully aware of the consequences, without understanding the effect our actions have on the people around us. Do you understand me?"

"Kind of." He didn't.

"But just because we were children, it doesn't mean there weren't consequences then or aren't consequences now. It doesn't mean we can – or should – escape the impact of our actions one day, one week, one month, one year or even thirty years after the event. Especially if it still affects other people all those years later."

Leo wondered if the man was talking more to himself now. Leo couldn't understand the point he was trying to make, or how it connected to himself or his family.

"So when something happens today, that may be as a result of something someone did years ago, do you think they should just get away with it?"

"I guess not."

"So you agree that there has to be payback?"

Leo sat quietly for a moment. The man had begun pacing around him. He could hear his shoes stamping on the cold, tiled floor. He would shout at himself, swear out loud and kick the tiled wall with his boots. Leo sat, his body rigid, too afraid to move. The smell of nicotine and heavy breathing made Leo realise the man had come closer.

"Answer me," he shouted, "do you agree there has to be payback?"

Leo's innate sense of fight or flight caused him to nod.

"Good," the man hissed, "at least we agree on that."

Leo swallowed hard. His voice, when it came, was quiet and shaky.

"But what has all this got to do with my dad?"

The man laughed.

"Probably best you don't know. Yet."

CHAPTER FORTY-SIX

"THIS IS NO random abduction," Munday told the assembled team during the morning briefing. He stood in front of a notice board, which held a school photograph of a smiling Leo Baines. Alongside it were images from where he'd been taken and an artist's impression of both the car and the abductor drawn from Jodie Barrett's recollections and other sketchy witness statements.

"But let's deal in the facts first and then we can come on to the theories."

He handed over to Harry Duggan who reviewed the abduction's details as they now knew them, including the messages sent to the boy's father and those received by others present on the day that Danny Carter drowned.

"I've been taking a closer look at the father," interjected Lesley Hilton. "The guy has been in serious financial trouble. His business has been struggling and he's been scratching around for work. We now also know that he's a director of a dating site called My Millionaire Boyfriend, the one used in the Irina killing, but we don't know if the two are connected. The other bit of feedback I'm getting is that the relationship between the mother and the father is a bit strained."

"Well, we certainly picked up on his financial and marital trouble when we spoke to them," confirmed Munday, "but are you suggesting the father might have been involved? I'm prepared to keep an open mind about the dating site, and I'll pick my moment to talk to him about it in connection with Irina, but I don't see a connection between the two."

Lesley nodded.

"What's the father's finances got to do with his kid being taken?" asked Paul Price. "There's been no ransom note. What would his motive be?"

"I'm not suggesting he has one, but it wouldn't be the first time parents had been involved in their child's kidnapping," replied Lesley. "You know, you try to raise cash through a fund and then the kid mysteriously turns up safe and sound. Remember Louise Jenkins?"

Louise Jenkins had disappeared one afternoon from outside her school near Sutton Coldfield. The search for her had become a major missing persons operation for the police. Louise had been found two weeks later at a house a short distance away. The abduction had been planned by Louise's father and his friend with the intention of generating cash from the publicity in the form of a reward.

The plan had been for the friend to 'find' Louise, return her to the family via the police and claim the reward money, which he and the father would then share. The case had captured the public imagination, probably far more so than they had ever envisaged, and had resulted in the two being charged, convicted and imprisoned for kidnapping and perverting the course of justice.

"So, all these messages that the father's been receiving? Are you suggesting he's faked them? And what about the similar messages received by the others present when Danny Carter drowned… just a coincidence?" Duggan asked.

"I'm not saying that. We don't know *who* has been sending the messages. He could have been sending them to everyone including himself as some kind of smokescreen. All I'm saying is that we look into it and, if the messages are genuine, then maybe it gives us a steer."

Munday coughed to clear his throat. Duggan looked towards him, expecting him to speak, but he remained silent and allowed Harry to continue.

"So now we need to talk to others who were there when Danny Carter died that we may have missed, not just those who've been getting these messages, and find out how they remember it. Perhaps they've been getting similar messages and have done nothing about them. It may be a wild goose chase, but it might also be a way of joining some dots."

Munday looked towards Danny Thorne.

"Danny, help Rob and Paul scour the files and track down as many as you can. Keep it nice and on the lowdown at the moment. Let's not worry anyone or rattle too many cages. And Lesley, can you do some of the family liaison bit? Go spend some time with the boy's parents, support them, talk to them but also watch them. Give me your honest view on what's going on between them and whether your idea that the father might be involved could have any legs."

Lesley knew Jack well enough by now to know that yes, the mother might be more likely to open up to her because she was a woman, but she also knew Jack rated her the best detective on the team. If anybody was going to sniff out family involvement, she would.

"I shouldn't need to tell you that time is of the essence. We've circulated Leo's picture to the media but we're only going to give the bare facts of the disappearance to them. We're not saying anything else at the moment so be careful what information you give out."

The team murmured its agreement.

"DS Duggan and I will be on our mobiles. You call us the moment you have anything."

CHAPTER FORTY-SEVEN

THE LAST THING Marion Simpson ever wanted to be reminded of was that day. Despite her newly styled hair and immaculate make up, she looked more frail and vulnerable than her seventy two years.

She listened quietly as her husband, Derek, a thick-set man of around five feet ten with thinning hair and a ruddy complexion, asked the two police officers whether this uninvited intrusion into their lives was absolutely necessary. The anticipation of merely having to talk about *that* day had provoked pains in Marion's chest to flutter, prompting her to discreetly pop one of her angina tablets under her tongue. She lay back into the embrace of the armchair and tried to calm her breathing. The heavy net curtains made the compact room appear darker than the sunshine outside should have made it. Notwithstanding the odd lick of paint in the intervening period, Jack could believe that the photograph and knickknack-bedecked room probably hadn't changed much since Kevin had been a boy and since Danny Carter drowned.

"See," Derek implored at the officers, pointing to his wife's obvious discomfort, "do you have to do this now? Can't it wait? If she gets any more worked up than this, I'm going to have to call a doctor or something and then it takes her days to properly recover."

"If Mrs Simpson is in pain, we can call an ambulance and come back another time," Munday spoke slowly and calmly and in as understanding a manner as he could muster. He had no wish to open up old wounds but neither did he want Leo Baines to become the latest postscript to Danny Carter's tragic death. "But whether we do it now or we do it later, we *do* need to talk to you about the day Danny died and I would rather we did it soon. We believe there may be a direct link between what happened that day and the abduction of a child that we are currently investigating."

"What boy? And that's ridiculous. It's years ago."

Marion coughed, as a schoolteacher might when she wants to regain control of a class. In that split second Jack felt ten years old again, sitting up straighter as a consequence. All three men instinctively turned to look at her.

"Let's do it now, Inspector. I'm trying to stay calm but, frankly Derek, I know your intentions are good but you're not really helping very much. If we can do anything to get this boy back to his family, then we should. Now, go and make us all a cup of tea, and there's a packet of chocolate chip cookies in the kitchen cupboard. Bring those back in with you. I'm sure these gentlemen would like one with their tea. I know I would."

There was something about Marion that Jack rather liked, a kind of assurance that he figured she would have needed to draw on to get her through that day and many others since. She may not have been expecting it today but given the conversation she must have had with Kevin, he doubted that she wasn't expecting it at all. Derek, suitably admonished, left the room as instructed.

"Marion… can I call you Marion?"

She smiled at Jack as if to thank him for having the courtesy to ask.

"Marion, I don't want to take you through the events of that day particularly. We're pretty clear on what happened. I want to talk to you about the days that followed Danny's death."

She nodded.

"Kevin told us that at the time this all happened you were working in the school the kids attended?"

"Yes, Inspector, I was the school secretary."

"So, you were used to seeing how the kids interacted with each other?"

"Well, to an extent. I wasn't a teacher, so I wasn't in a classroom with them, but I would wander around the school in the course of my work. Sometimes, I'd stray out into the playground, though not too often. As ridiculous as it sounds, I was always afraid of getting hit by a stray ball. But I used to hear the teachers talk in the staff room and, of course, as a parent of a child there myself, we would talk about Kevin."

"What would the teachers say about Matthew Baines?"

She considered the question carefully.

"That he was a quiet boy, some would say a little withdrawn. He was bright enough, don't get me wrong, good at his work, but I don't think he found it easy to make friends."

"And do you remember how he was in the days after Danny's death?"

"Not really. I think he may have taken a couple of days off. Everybody was in shock, so it was understandable. He probably wasn't the only one. It was a small school and it might sound like a cliché, but you never think that kind of tragedy is going to happen in your own little community. You're certainly not prepared for it when it does, I can tell you that for nothing. It's impossible to underestimate its impact. I didn't want to take time off myself. I wanted to be in school to show that life goes on, to be with the children, but everyone – Derek, the headmistress, my doctor – they all suggested that taking a little time away was the sensible thing to do."

"And yet you sent Kevin to school?"

"I know, it sounds hard, doesn't it? I don't know if I would do that now if it happened again, God forbid. Children, though, have a much better capacity to compartmentalise things. They can go from being in the depths of despair one minute to playing football on the field the next. We thought they would probably all be better with some degree of routine, of structure and the ability to be with each other."

"You thought they'd be able to run it off?"

In that moment that Jack first became aware of Marion's piercing blue eyes. They seemed to communicate both the anger and the hurt she obviously continued to carry without her having to actually say anything. Jack immediately felt bad but not bad enough to stop.

"So, Matthew Baines? You must be aware of the rumours?"

"That he tripped Danny?"

Jack nodded.

"The rumours weren't true. I'm not even sure where Matthew was when Danny was spotted, but it was just an accident."

"So why do you think the rumours started?"

"I have no idea. I suspect it was just cruel playground chat. Perhaps it was because he wasn't in school the day after and people began to talk."

Derek pushed open the door to the sitting room with his left hip and entered carrying a tray of tea that he set down on a small table in the corner of the room, almost knocking the telephone onto the floor in the process. Marion struggled to conceal her frustration. He handed around the tea, offered biscuits that both Harry and Jack accepted, and then sat in the armchair adjacent to his wife, sipping from his own china cup.

"What were the Baines family like?"

"Unremarkable, Inspector. The whole Danny Carter incident was a remarkable event that happened to unremarkable people. None of us stood out from the crowd. We just went for a nice day out and something terrible happened. All we wanted afterwards was to get on with our lives and raise our kids. I don't think that has changed much."

The tea was stronger than Jack would normally have taken it, and it left a slightly bitter, malty aftertaste. Jack sweetened it with the chocolate chips in the cookies, letting them melt against the side of his tongue.

"I wonder if you remember Danny's funeral?"

Marion inhaled deeply. Derek reached across from his armchair and placed his hand over hers. How wonderful it must be to have enjoyed a relationship that had sustained over so many years, Jack thought to himself, momentarily seeing both Elaine and Lesley appear in his mind's eye.

"I'm sure you wouldn't believe me if I said that I didn't."

Jack smiled sympathetically. "What can you tell us about it?"

"That it was a devastating occasion for all of us, of course. Immensely sad. I think we all felt weighed down by the sadness, or at least I know that I did."

"Did the children attend?"

"No. I mean Simon and Mark, Danny's brothers did,

but they were still in such shock that I would be surprised if they remember much about being there, but not the others."

"But the other families attended?"

"The ones who were present at the swimming pool?"

Jack nodded.

"Yes, I believe so."

"And Matthew Baines's parents? They were there?"

"I think so."

Derek coughed, almost as a reminder to all that he was still present in the room. Jack turned to look at him.

"Inspector, how does any of this help you find this missing boy?"

"That's a good question. Well, the boy is Matthew's son. The nature of the messages that have been sent to Matthew, Kevin and others suggest that they're coming from somebody who was present that day. So it follows that whoever's taken Leo Baines was also present that day and that something has triggered them now, at this point, to take action against Matthew. They likely hold him responsible for what happened to Danny, and possibly for something else that has happened to them more recently as a consequence. Time is against us. We need to find that person fast."

Marion reached out to put her empty teacup on a small, wooden coffee table to her right.

"So, is there anything else I can tell you, Inspector? I'm not sure I've been any help, but I hope you find Matthew's boy and get him home quickly."

"So do we, Marion. Just remind me, though, about the other kids who were there on the day Danny died. Do you know what happened to any of them?"

Marion Simpson cast her mind back.

"It's been an awfully long time, Inspector. You're asking about people, families, some of whom I haven't seen for twenty or thirty years. Paul Cherry's mother passed away about a year ago and I saw him at her funeral. I think he's an accountant down in Kent somewhere. The only other one I can recall was Tim Swain, who I'm pretty sure went on to become a teacher. I don't know any more than that, I'm afraid."

Jack stood, handed Derek his cup and brushed cookie crumbs from the front of his trousers, holding out his hand to shake Marion's.

"Please don't get up, we'll see ourselves out. I'm sorry if we upset you in any way, but you've been most helpful."

"Just get the boy back to his family. Please. I don't want Matthew to go through what Danny's parents had to go through."

Jack smiled and nodded and held the door open for Harry as they left the elderly couple to their newly stirred-up memories.

CHAPTER FORTY-EIGHT

"SO, DON'T KEEP me in suspense."

Jenny Jacobs wondered why she had a delegation of three crowded into her office. Jack Munday had helped himself to a seat without waiting to be asked; Frank Salazar was resting his bulky frame against a dark metal filing cabinet in the corner of the room, whilst Harry Duggan had his back against the glass office door, barring entry for anyone else who may have tried to come in.

Jack slurped water from a plastic bottle he had brought with him into the office. Jenny had already remarked that it looked an unusually healthy option for him.

"We've got a trace on Irina's mobile phone."

Jenny sat forward, put her hands together, fingers interlocked, and rested them on the desk almost in prayer.

"Well, Inspector, you know how to get a woman's interest. Tell me more."

"We've been badgering the mobile phone company all the way through for information about Irina's phone. It's fair to say they've not been quite as co-operative as we would have liked but, that aside, we've now found out that her phone was switched on around eight thirty this morning. Not for very long and, as far as we can tell, no calls were made, but long enough for the signal to be picked up."

"So we know where it was used?"

Jack nodded and smiled. Salazar had a self-satisfied smirk on his face, though Duggan couldn't understand why. He hadn't been involved with tracing the phone at all. Perhaps he was basking in reflected glory.

"It was used in a building in Lincoln's Inn, just round the back of Holborn station."

"That's legal territory?"

Jack nodded again.

"It's packed full of chambers and law firms."

"And you're sure that the person who switched the phone on is our man, Sinclair?"

"I am."

"Are you telling me Christopher Sinclair is a lawyer?"

"I'm telling you he's a barrister and quite a prominent one at that. I'm also telling you he's not called Christopher Sinclair."

"That much I had worked out for myself, Einstein. You know who he is?"

Jack opened the brown paper folder that had been

resting on his lap, and removed a piece of white A4 paper, which he passed across the desk to the Superintendent. She put her glasses on, which immediately slipped down from the bridge of her nose to rest a centimetre or so up from her nostrils. She studied the paper carefully in silence, before laying it face down on the table and removing her glasses.

"Presumably there are more people who work in these chambers than just this Edward Shepherd." She turned the paper back over and glanced down just to check she'd got the name right. "How can you be so certain he's our man?"

"We ran a quick search for him. Twice previously he's made representations on behalf of East European women from outside of the European Union who've wanted to stay in the UK and on a separate occasion he was involved in a licence application for the hotel in which Irina was found dead. I'd say that's reasonably compelling, and get this as well, in his professional life he's carved out something of a niche in representing people charged with sexual offences against young women. We've also checked out his picture on the Chambers' web site. He matches the descriptions we were given for Christopher Sinclair."

Jacobs stood in an effort to pace around a room in which there was no longer any space. She took two steps forward and two steps back before acknowledging defeat and sitting down again.

"If he *is* Christopher Sinclair and he *is* responsible for

Irina's death – and they are still 'ifs' – why do you think he kept the phone? He's a bright guy to be doing what he does; presumably he's hung around with criminals. He must know it's a bit of a basic error?"

Salazar coughed. At first nobody was sure if he wanted to speak or simply clear his throat.

"Could be arrogance, boss; could be a trophy."

Jack's disdain wouldn't let him even turn and face his colleague.

"Why would you want to keep a trophy from an encounter that went so badly wrong… unless you're suggesting that he set out to murder Irina?"

Salazar blustered a reply. "Well, no, but…"

"Because throughout all of this I've thought of Sinclair as a bit of a perv who took things too far, and things went south in the heat of the moment. If you're saying otherwise, then you think it was pre-meditated murder, in which case we could have a psycho on our hands."

Jacobs slapped her hand down on the desk, causing both Munday and Salazar to stop and turn towards her, like children chastised; exactly the effect she had been trying to create.

"Gents, for the love of God stop bickering. We can work out the why once we've nicked him. At the precise moment, the rest doesn't matter. So what's your plan, Jack? Bring him in for questioning?"

"No, boss, not immediately. He doesn't know we've clocked him, and we already have the date with Lesley set up. If we catch him there, in the act, so to speak, I think we're on much firmer ground than if we just lift him today. Bring him in and he can deny everything, pretend he found the phone or some other bullshit. I don't want to give him a second chance."

Jacobs reflected. This was the moment, in front of his colleagues, when she knew she needed to give him her support.

"Okay, let's do it."

She ignored Salazar's sigh of displeasure, in part because of the knowing smile that had emerged across Jack's face, despite his best efforts to stifle it.

"While we're here with you, boss, we also wanted to talk about the missing boy."

Her upward glance was enough to tell him to continue. Never one to miss an opportunity Jack turned over his shoulder.

"You don't need to stay for this, Frank. It doesn't really concern you."

Salazar straightened, turned and, like a reprimanded child, made for the door, Duggan stepping out of his way as got closer.

"So, the missing boy," Jacobs started. "Time's moving on; tell me you have a lead."

"I'm more and more certain it's connected with the boy's father and somehow to his friend's accidental drowning back in seventy-five. I'm convinced it's all linked to those messages everyone's been getting, purporting to come from the dead boy. I can't seem to shake off the idea that the rumours back then that Leo's dad, Matthew, had somehow been responsible for the drowning is weirdly behind somebody's desire for revenge."

"The brothers?"

"Well, maybe one of them. The older brother, Mark, has never really come to terms with what happened and may have made it his life's work to get justice for Danny. Rob and Paul have found him and are bringing him in for a chat. Despite all the house to house stuff, there have been no recent sightings, but enough people have now come forward to say they saw Leo being bundled into a car outside the school and driven off to make me sure he's been taken rather than run away. We're still trying to trace a couple of the others who were there that day, but I just sense we're getting closer."

"Make sure you are, Inspector. I don't want to be the one going in front of the television cameras to talk about a dead schoolboy."

CHAPTER FORTY-NINE

"YOU SERIOUSLY THINK I've taken that boy?"

Mark Carter was twitching and scratching furiously at a patch of eczema on his hand.

"It's just a line of enquiry. Prove us wrong."

"Isn't the onus on you to prove it?"

Jack drained the dregs of a cup of cold, black coffee and began to pace the room. Scum from the hardness of the water had begun to float on the liquid's surface.

"Don't piss around with me, Mark. I have two parents, one of whom was once a friend of yours, frantic with worry. I have a young boy who must be beyond scared and you have a Detective Inspector in front of you who's going to get really fucking frustrated unless you start to talk to me."

Mark Carter put his elbows on the table in Interview Room Two and placed his hands on either side of his face, making marks on his week-old stubble. Jack could see the depth of the dirt beneath his fingernails and the yellowing on his skin from too much nicotine.

"I haven't got him. I didn't take him. I've never even seen him."

"Simon and Esther were concerned about you. They said you'd been acting strangely."

"They're entitled to their opinion, I suppose."

"Why do you think they said that?"

"Probably because I don't fit in with their view of what I should be doing with my life."

"What do you mean by that?"

"I think you know exactly what I mean."

Jack smiled and sniggered a little to himself. If time hadn't been of the essence he might have been prepared to indulge Mark Carter a little more. But neither of them, let alone Leo Baines, had been afforded that luxury.

"Tell me anyway," Jack replied, leaning down towards the table until his face was no more than centimetres from Mark's.

"They want me to forget about Danny and get on with my life, or at least that's the way I see it."

"And you don't want to do that?"

"I *can't* do that."

"Why not?"

"Inspector, when you were fourteen years old, did anyone kill your brother?"

Jack shook his head. "No, they didn't. But from everything I've read and everyone I've spoken to, nobody killed yours either."

"Well, pardon me for forgetting that you're the expert."

"Okay, Mark, let me try this a different way. As far as I can gather, you think Matthew Baines was somehow responsible for the accident that caused your brother to drown. Correct?"

Mark Carter's facial expression didn't change.

"And you've spent the last God knows how many years telling anyone who would listen that you want revenge or justice or whatever you want to call it for Danny's death. You want to get Matthew back for it, show him what it feels like to be hurt, make him suffer. Isn't that right?"

Mark stared straight ahead.

"So, in your warped and twisted mind, you decided to freak him and all of the others out by sending all those messages supposedly from your brother. Am I getting warmer? And when he didn't rise to the bait, you couldn't help yourself, so you started watching his kids and then something inside you snapped, and you took Leo."

Mark laughed. "Is that right?"

"I don't know, Mark, you tell me. *Is* that right? I don't know whether it was planned or whether it was a spur of the moment thing, but it's time to end it now. Where's the kid, Mark? What have you done with him?"

"Inspector, if this really is your main line of enquiry, then I really do feel sorry for Matthew and his kid. I haven't done anything."

Duggan tapped Jack on the shoulder. He knew his colleague well enough to step in when his frustrations were building to a point where his questioning was becoming counter-productive.

"Mark, can I get you a coffee, a tea perhaps?"

Carter shook his head.

"Okay. We don't want to upset you any more by dwelling on Danny..."

"Why does everybody think that talking about Danny would upset me?"

"Look, I'm sure you understand we need to try and find Leo as quickly as possible."

"Well, you've probably got internal targets to hit."

Jack slammed his clenched fist down hard on the table, causing a plastic cup of water to topple, creating a small lake on the tabletop and a stream flowing over the edge and into a small puddle on the floor. Mark laughed again, shaking his head at the detective losing his composure.

"This isn't about fucking targets, it's about getting a young boy back to his family."

"Mark, do you own a computer?" asked Duggan, in an effort to retrieve control of the interview.

"No."

"Do you have an email account, or use social media, Facebook and the like?"

"I have an email address but rarely use it. I don't use social media. I don't want people seeing everything I do and I sure as hell don't want to look at pictures of them."

"So if you don't have a computer, when do you use your email address?"

"Like I said, rarely."

"And where do you go if you need to?"

"The library, sometimes one of those Internet cafes. When I was working, I'd sometimes log on during lunch."

Jack closed his notebook and sat back on his chair.

"So what you're telling us is you may be a bit of a freak but you're not a kidnapper?"

"If that's the way you want to put it."

Jack stood and moved towards the door.

"Thank you for your help, Mr Carter. I'll have somebody drive you home."

The abrupt end to the interview surprised and, in a strange way, disappointed Mark. The young, unformed officer closed the door behind the two detectives. For a moment, Mark imagined what it would feel like to have a cell door close on him. He looked around the empty room, confused.

Outside, Jack tapped Harry on the shoulder.

"Thoughts?"

"I think he's telling the truth."

"I was afraid you were going to say that."

"Back to square one?"

"Maybe. Get him taken home and have somebody follow him for the next twenty-four hours. I want to know everywhere he goes. Also, chase up how the guys are getting on tracing the last couple who were there that day. If we draw a blank, we might have to put the parents in front of the TV cameras."

Duggan nodded. They turned and walked in opposite directions down the long, dark corridor.

CHAPTER FIFTY

NOT KNOWING HOW the man would react frightened Leo Baines most of all. From all that he'd experienced so far, he didn't think that the man intended to hurt him. Although, keeping him shackled, blindfolded and imprisoned, away from his family and with no indication of how long this would last or how he intended it to finish, hardly counted as a sign of friendship either.

But now, Leo had reason to be afraid. It's not easy to control your bodily functions when you are bent double, tied up and only allowed to move when somebody else says so. It was inevitable that, at some point, there would be an accident. He had tried so hard to control himself but the cramps had got worse until mind over matter didn't matter anymore. He didn't know how long he'd sat in his own mess, damp and uncomfortable, trying to ignore the stench but by the time he heard the man's footsteps, he unexpectedly found himself more elated than fearful.

Leo sensed the man's closeness before a single word

was spoken. These seconds of silence, which seemed like hours, made his heart beat faster and his imagination reach into its darkest corners. He realised he was shaking, unable to control his breathing, and trying to stifle tears. The man was close enough now that he could feel his breathing against his own skin, jumping a little when the man's hand wrapped itself around his knee.

"Calm down, Leo," the man whispered. "You're getting yourself worked up."

"I'm sorry. I tried to hold it."

The man made a tutting noise with his tongue against the back of his teeth, the way his grandmother used to when she wanted to signal her disapproval or disappointment. He didn't want to be a source of either, not for his grandmother and, right now, certainly not for the man.

"Well, I suppose it's only to be expected. We'd better get you cleaned up."

The man lifted Leo from his seated position, keeping his arm under the boy's and walking him, shuffling step by shuffling step, away from where he had been seated like a Guantanamo Bay inmate. It was further than Leo had walked in nearly forty-eight hours, since first being bundled into the back of the car. His knees were painful and his muscles tight but just to be moving, even for these reasons, felt good. He was guided down a small step and then almost immediately up another and into a new environment.

"I'm going to untie you in a minute. You'll be able to shower, and I'll fetch you some dry clothes. Your blindfold will stay on. Try and take it off or run and I'll be really unhappy and you don't want that, not now we seem to be getting on so well. Do I make myself clear?"

Leo nodded.

"Good."

He was led forward a little further and heard the sound of water pouring from a tap.

"It's only cold, I'm afraid. The hot's been switched off but then all the more incentive for you to get clean and dressed again quickly."

He felt his hands being released from behind his back and his ankles able to move independently of each other. His initial instinct was to try and punch or kick his way out, but he felt weak and tired, frightened and unsure of what he'd be able to do even if he did land a blow. The man would be stronger and know where they were, so instead Leo chose to do as he'd been told, removing his clothes and stepping forward under the icy water. Initially the cold shocked him but shortly it began to invigorate and refresh in the way that only feeling clean sometimes does. As he rubbed his skin with the water, he felt as if he was scrubbing away some of his shock and anxiety. He longed for some of that expensive shower gel that his mother kept at home and didn't realise – or didn't acknowledge – that he sometimes used for himself.

"You must have cleaned yourself by now," called the

man.

There was a distance to his voice that made Leo realise, in that moment, that the man was not alongside him. He lifted the blindfold millimetres from his eyes and looked around. He was in a shower block, under one of the three or four showers in a line, standing on chipped, dirty tiles. The chrome fittings looked rusty.

"I'm pretty much done," he called back.

"If you reach behind you, you'll feel two towels on a wall. You can wrap yourself in those. Call me once you're done and I'll help you out. I've got clean clothes waiting for you."

THE MAN HELPED him dress before tying his hands and ankles again, albeit a little more loosely than before. He led Leo back the way they'd come before placing his hands on the boy's shoulders and pushing him down onto a chair.

"I figured after all these hours on the floor, you could probably do with somewhere better to sit for a while."

"Thanks."

"And I've got you some food."

The man placed a plastic plate onto Leo's lap, released his hands and guided them towards a sandwich and some crisps. Leo wanted to talk.

"Can I ask you a question?"

"You can ask, I suppose."

"What are you going to do with me?"

The man inhaled deeply and let out a long, deep sigh.

"The truth is Leo, I don't know."

"So why did you take me?"

"To teach somebody a lesson."

"My Dad?"

There was no response. Leo ate his sandwich in silence.

CHAPTER FIFTY-ONE

"YOU HAVE TO try and eat something," Matthew sat down on the stairs in the hallway alongside Susie, holding a plate with some cheese, some crackers and some black grapes. She had been sitting in the same spot for nearly an hour, seemingly oblivious to the comings and goings around her, wrapped up in her own thoughts and what the darkest corners of her imagination were telling her. "Not eating isn't going to help anyone."

"I don't have an appetite. You eat if you want to. I'm more concerned about getting our son back."

"And you think I'm not?"

"I don't know what to think."

Ever since the last police visit, Susie had been unable to settle. Wherever she looked all she could see was evidence of where Leo used to be: discarded clothes, scattered video games boxes with the discs themselves removed. She paced around the house, finding one place for a short while before her anxiety rose up and almost propelled her to another. The only constant was the small teddy bear that Leo had had since he was a baby, which she had refused to let go of since almost the moment she had first returned home.

She went over and over the events of *that* morning, trying to remember anything she might have missed, anything she could or should have done differently, anything that could be a clue to who might have taken Leo and where he might be now. Sometimes she closed her eyes and tried to silently talk to him. She would cling to the hope that somehow, he might be able to connect with her and hear her thoughts. She would tell him how much she loved him, how she would cook him his favourite macaroni cheese for dinner when he came home, how she wouldn't complain or restrict his time on the Xbox and how they would finally plan that family holiday to Florida they had always talked about. She would tell him how much Millie and Crisp were missing him; how Crisp, with that sixth sense that dogs have when they know that something is wrong, had been sitting on his bed and pining. Most of all she would tell him how much she wanted him home.

Matthew pushed the plate a little further forward and she picked herself a single black grape. It was easier than refusing again. Only once she experienced the grape's sweetness awaken her taste buds did she realise that her mouth felt as if it had begun to shut down to conserve energy, a little like the rest of her. She sighed and Matthew placed his hand on her knee. To her surprise she welcomed the physical connection, or at least she didn't instantly feel the need to pull away. She could hear the murmurings of family and friends emanating from the kitchen, even though nobody had anything new to murmur about.

"It feels odd, you know."

"What does?"

"In the last twenty-four hours more people have probably come in and out of this house than at any other time since we moved here."

Matthew nodded.

"So with all these people here, why does the house feel so empty?"

He didn't have an answer and he knew that to try and come up with one would only sound crass. She was right, though; almost since the moment they had realised that Leo had been taken, they had been surrounded by other people. Their warmth, their love and their concern was wonderful and, however things turned out, he knew they would always be grateful. But it hadn't given Susie or him the chance to process what was going on privately with each other. They were living this very personal nightmare in the full glare of the world.

"Do you remember when we first brought him home from the hospital?"

Matthew wanted to talk about Leo; somehow it made him seem present and it felt like it would show Susie that he cared. She looked up. For the first time Matthew could see no anger in her eyes, replaced now by a wistful smile.

"I remember how tiny he was."

"I remember being amazed at how something that small could make a noise that loud."

"Or produce so much to fill so many nappies so regularly."

"He certainly had his father's appetite."

"He still has."

Talking about him in the present tense only reinforced Leo's absence. As Matthew spoke, Susie fell silent.

"Have you spoken to Millie? I'm not sure she understands, but it's important she does without us scaring her."

"I had a chat. I just explained that Leo had gone away and we were waiting to find out when he was coming back. It seemed to be enough for her for now."

"And what if that changes?"

"It won't. We *are* going to get him back."

"But what if it does?"

Matthew felt the unbearable weight of an outcome they all feared but some were slowly beginning to anticipate, if not expect. He felt the mobile phone in his pocket vibrate. He was reticent to look at it in case Susie felt that checking for messages was something that shouldn't even be on his radar.

"Are you going to check that?"

He looked at his wife. She was tired, beaten down and

almost broken by events, but still beautiful. He wished she believed how much he loved her; he wished she felt the same. Matthew pulled the phone from his pocket and opened the Facebook notification. Perhaps it was another message of support and sympathy from some acquaintance or friend of a friend beginning "I really don't know what to say to you but…" or perhaps a humorous picture from somebody else who hadn't heard. His heart almost stopped when he looked down at his screen. Sudden pain threatened to cripple his chest.

"Matthew, what's wrong? You've gone white."

He said nothing; he couldn't speak.

"Matthew," Susie's voice rose and trembled, loud enough that her mother opened the kitchen door to check what might be wrong. "What is it? You're scaring me."

He looked up towards her, his eyes beginning to water. He turned the phone to face her. The message was from Danny Carter. It was a picture of a boy, tied up and blindfolded, but unmistakably Leo. The message read simply "your boy's okay for now".

CHAPTER FIFTY-TWO

EDWARD SHEPHERD HAD been struggling to concentrate. Since lunchtime he had cocooned himself in his dark, serious, mahogany-laden office in the Chambers in Lincoln's Inn Field, his door closed to both colleagues and clients. Part of him hoped they all thought he'd gone home, because as the afternoon wore on, he felt he needed to focus, to push Edward Shepherd to the back of his mind and bring Christopher Sinclair forward to the present. He needed to stay calm. Although excited about the evening that lay ahead, he couldn't allow it to be spoiled by the memory of the Ukrainian girl. He didn't want hers to be the face he saw in that moment of unbridled pleasure he knew awaited him. After all, he was paying enough for it; surely he had a right to enjoy it unimpeded.

When he worked alone it was his preference to keep Radio 4 on in the background, not to particularly listen to in any detail but for the comforting low hum of noise. But now he needed to get rid of the distraction of other human voices and to relax instead. The PM programme had just begun, which would only be conveying depressing news of the disintegrating economy. Today of all days he had no time for negativity. He switched the radio off and stood for a moment immersed in the perfect silence. His contemporaries may have embraced The Who and Led Zeppelin but Edward Shepherd had always been more inclined towards Haydn and Wagner. In the unlikely event of ever being asked onto Desert Island Discs, The Ride of the Valkyries from the Ring cycle would unquestionably have been his choice, though not today. Today he needed something more calming. He poured himself a small, single malt, enjoying the sound of the liquid hitting the bottom of the crystal glass. He immersed himself in the deep burgundy leather of the armchair and let the smoky liquor warm his lips. His head tilted back as his closed and he settled into the tranquillity of Satie's Gymnopedies.

He couldn't have been asleep for long because it was still before six when he woke in the chair, at first concerned in case anyone had entered the room and found him looking so unprofessional. As he regained his composure and opened the window to breathe in some fresh air, he thought about making a coffee but then considered the caffeine would only undo Satie's good work. Gymnopedies played on, though Edward turned down the volume and returned to his desk.

He sat in front of his laptop, logged out of his work

email and shut the machine down. He closed the lid, sat back and checked his watch.

It was uncommon, though not unheard of, for Edward to leave Chambers as early as this and so it didn't arouse the suspicion he feared it might. Of course, he could have been making his way anywhere: out for dinner, to the theatre, to visit his elderly mother. Nobody would have jumped to the conclusion that he was on his way to pay for sex.

To his irritation, the taxi driver wanted to talk.

"You look like a clever guy," he started, steering his cab onto Kingsway and down towards Aldwych. "What d'you really make of this credit crunch? D'you think we're ever going to recover?"

"Of course there will be a recovery," he mumbled, looking down at his mobile to give the impression of being otherwise occupied. "The economy can't be in free-fall forever. It has to recover at some point."

"From your mouth to God's ears, mate, though I hope it happens quickly. Deader than a corpse out here at the moment."

Edward chose not to reply. The cabbie drove on, out towards Knightsbridge. The late afternoon sun made it difficult to focus on that morning's Telegraph. The only thing he could concentrate on was where he was heading and his reason for going there.

It was only a little over three miles as the crow flies from his Chambers in Lincoln's Inn to the hotel he had booked and yet, given the rush hour traffic, the journey would take over half an hour, perhaps closer to three quarters. He gave up on trying to read, folded the paper, returned it to his briefcase and gazed out of the window as the taxi made its way along The Mall. On a day like this, he thought to himself, there couldn't be many cities more beautiful than London. The taxi skirted around Buckingham Palace to take Constitution Hill and the Brompton Road towards Knightsbridge. In the distance he thought he could make out the domed roof of the Royal Albert Hall. Apparently even Wagner himself had played there 1877. What a night that must have been! The taxi swung left along Sloane Street before Edward called it to a premature halt around halfway down, close to the entrance to Hans Place. He paid the driver in cash, adding a full five pounds tip. He needed some fresh air and, having checked his watch, knew ample time remained before his lady for the evening would arrive.

The hotel itself, a red brick building with a white columned arch, had only a small plaque on the right hand column and a few window stickers to give away its business. He inhaled deeply to boost his sense of confidence and calm, and climbed the few, low steps up to the varnished wooden door. He smiled at the young, dark-haired man on reception. His cheap, black waistcoat over an unironed white shirt carried a gold name badge that said 'Danny'. The young man was pleasant enough; he tried to be welcoming and engage in conversation, though

Edward did think it a little strange to find a native English speaker working in a hotel like this. In his experience almost every hotel in London seemed to only employ non-British staff. He thought how those who came in search of a better life were so often exploited until the irony struck him. He kept his answers short and smiled politely, took the key to the room and made his way towards the creaking elevator.

CHAPTER FIFTY-THREE

JACK SAT IN his office; a black coffee newly made but as yet undrunk in front of him. His phone twirled in his hands as he waited for a call or text to let him know that Lesley was okay, and that Christopher Sinclair was in custody.

He'd tried to call her earlier, but her phone had diverted to voicemail. He left her a message, told her he loved her and reminded her to be careful. Jack wondered now if she had listened to it, whether his voice had reassured her or whether her phone had remained off as a way of avoiding distractions and maintaining focus. One thing was certain: the strength of his emotion bolstered his resolve to come clean with Elaine, make the relationship with Lesley public and face whatever implications there may be as a result. He sent a text to Elaine and suggested they meet for dinner. The speed of her reply, the fact that she said yes and, even more so, the fact that she said that she had been thinking the same thing all struck him as a little unexpected.

CHAPTER FIFTY-FOUR

EDWARD SHEPHERD, NOW almost fully immersed in his Christopher Sinclair persona, looked around the hotel bedroom. It was comfortable without being plush, smart without being truly elegant. He pressed down on the duvet of the King Sized bed to test the softness, then took off his jacket, removed his tie and threw both onto an uncomfortable looking brown leather chair, whose fascia was beginning to crack, in the corner of the room.

Yes, he thought to himself, *this will be fine.*

An ice bucket sat on the low table near the chair, from which emerged a bottle of Louis Roederer 2009 Cristal champagne as ordered, sitting next to a silver platter of plump strawberries dipped in chocolate. He lifted one of the champagne flutes, which he thought a little cheap for such a prestigious drink, and poured himself a glass. He held it up to the light and watched as the bubbles dispersed to the sides of the glass and then lowered it to his lips and sipped slowly.

Lesley Hilton's chest tightened when she received the text from Danny Thorne telling her that Christopher Sinclair had arrived. She inhaled deeply. *It's just a job*, she told herself; except, of course, it wasn't. She wanted to send her colleagues a message reminding them not to leave her with him a second longer than was necessary, but to do so would have revealed her nerves. Although she knew that when she needed them most, her colleagues would have her back, neither did she want to give them any ammunition for future ribbing.

She arrived at the hotel a little more than half an hour after Danny's text, walking in the footsteps of the man, the murderer, with whom she would shortly be alone. A thousand and one thoughts were running through her mind: would he be a monster, would she be able to hold her nerve and, most important, would the technology do its job so that her colleagues could get her out of the bedroom and away from Christopher Sinclair's grip before it tightened around her neck in the same way it had Irina's? She glanced at Danny Thorne on reception as she entered the hotel, taking care not to give any sign of recognition to either him or Paul Price, who she caught out of the corner of her eye leaning on his elbows behind the hotel bar. Danny would follow her a few seconds later, then peel away to the room next door where Salazar and Rob Shaw were already waiting. Price, bolstered by a couple of uniformed officers, would wait downstairs to block any potential escape route.

"What could possibly go wrong?" she asked herself as the elevator door opened. She chose not to answer the question.

Frank Salazar and Rob Shaw noticeably sat upright as they listened to Lesley enter the room next door. Christopher Sinclair greeted her warmly, offering his hand for her to shake, taking her jacket and pouring them both a glass of champagne.

"Creep," muttered Shaw. Salazar, earphone in one ear, nodded.

Sinclair was attempting to make small talk.

"So tell me…"

He was scrambling to remember Lesley's name. Salazar was unsure whether he'd genuinely forgotten or whether he suspected something might be awry and wanted to ensure consistency in her story. Lesley was sure Sinclair could probably see her heart pounding in her chest.

"LAUREN."

"Ah, yes, Lauren. Tell me, do you do this much?"

"Only when I've got bills to pay and need money quickly."

Sure this wasn't the answer he was looking for, she knew much of his fantasy was predicated on the notion that the girls he met were in some way in love with him; the psychologist had told her that much. She could see a hint of disappointment etched across his face and recognised the need to get him back on side.

"It doesn't mean I don't enjoy it, though. I wouldn't do it if I didn't enjoy it no matter how good the money."

A smile played across his face. It made her feel nauseous and a little angry; anger that calmed her nerves and strengthened her resolve.

"Of course you do." He replenished her champagne. "It's good to know you enjoy it though. I want to know my partners are getting something from our time together. I'm not a selfish person, you know."

NEXT DOOR, DANNY Thorne had arrived from his reception duties. He sat behind Salazar and Thorne, leaning forward in his chair, his hands locked together. The joking, the banter, the camaraderie, had stopped. This was about getting the job done.

Salazar turned towards him.

"Don't get too comfortable. The minute he makes a move and Lesley calls out, I want you in there and on him before he knows what's going on."

Danny nodded.

"SO, LAUREN, I hope you're ready. Why don't you slip that top off and come and lay on the bed with me?"

Sinclair allowed his right hand to run gently down the outside of Lesley's left cheek, lingering at the first button on her white shirt. In his mind he was trying to be tender. She wanted to gag as she slowly removed the shirt.

"Before I join you there, I need to see the money and I need to know how far you want to go."

Sinclair laughed a little to himself.

"Did I say something funny?" Lesley asked.

"No, you're quite right."

Sinclair stood up from the bed, his shirt undone to reveal a slender white chest with a smattering of greying hair; certainly not in peak physical condition. He crossed the room to the chair, removing a brown leather wallet from his jacket that looked like it had been in there for years. He counted five hundred pounds out, one note at a time, and placed them on the table next to the ice bucket and the strawberries.

"It's the two hundred and fifty we talked about and an extra two hundred and fifty to go a bit further."

Lesley sat down on the bed and gestured for him to join her. She could feel the warmth of his breath against the skin on her neck and had to force herself not to recoil as he began to gently kiss her.

NEXT DOOR THE atmosphere could be cut with a knife. Thorne and Shaw had moved closer to the door, watching intently for Salazar to give them the nod to go in.

"She's stringing this out a bit, isn't she?" Shaw volunteered.

"She knows what she's doing. She wants him to talk about the strangulation. The minute he does, we go."

SINCLAIR FINISHED KISSING Lesley's neck, her fingers in his hair in an attempt at fake affection. He sat up and looked at her and smiled.

"You're beautiful," he whispered.

"I bet you say that to all the girls."

"Not all, no."

"Then I guess I'm flattered."

He stood and began to unbuckle and remove his trousers. Lesley needed to get something out of him soon to enable the boys next door to make their move.

"Let's get naked, Lauren."

Lesley smiled and ran her fingers through the hair on his chest down to the waistband of his boxer shorts.

"You still haven't told me what the extra money's for."

Sinclair smiled again. This one had him in raptures. He liked the way she was standing her ground, though what was amusing could quickly become an irritation. For now, it made her more interesting, more of a challenge than some of the others had been and would, he thought, make the ultimate destination of their night together that much more of an achievement. If so, she would certainly be worth the investment.

"Do you like taking things a little to the extremes?"

Lesley smiled, sensing she'd hooked him.

"Sometimes. I mean, isn't everybody always looking to make things more intense? What do you have in mind?"

He leant in close to whisper in her ear.

"Wouldn't you like to experience the most intense

orgasm you possibly could?"

She laughed playfully.

"So, Lauren, if we restrict a little, just a little, the oxygen, it will make you go all light-headed and giddy. A bit like taking poppers. It takes you to a place where every sensation feels *amazing*."

Lesley knew she had to stop the whispering and get him to speak out loud to ensure the guys next door could hear.

"Tell me more."

"So when we're in the moment, I just press down a little on the arteries in your neck and the sensations you feel will be incredible."

"Isn't it dangerous?"

Sinclair sighed and sat up a little, resting his back on the headboard. His muscles tensed. He was the client, after all. He who pays the piper calls the tune. Didn't she understand that?

"I'm not sure. It sounds a bit like you want to strangle me."

"No, nothing like that. I'll apply just enough pressure for both of us and then you can try it on me, if you want. It's going to be fun. I'm here to look after you. I wouldn't let anything bad happen. I promise."

Lesley's heart raced. She thought she saw a tear forming in the corner of Christopher Sinclair's eye. His smile made her flesh crawl. She needed to bring this to an end.

"You can strangle me if you want. Let's do it."

Sinclair smiled wider.

"I promise you won't regret it."

The noise and the speed with which Thorne and Shaw and three uniformed officers burst into the room had Sinclair looking sharply from one to the other as if trying to grapple with a truth he couldn't understand. Before he could process what was happening, he had been turned over and pushed face down into the mattress, his hands pulled tightly behind him and locked into cuffs. Lesley jumped off the bed, grabbed her shirt from the chair and allowed one of the uniformed boys to escort her rapidly next door. She passed Salazar on his way in to see Sinclair. They exchanged a smile and he held her briefly by the arm.

"Great job Lesley. I'll be back in a minute."

As he entered the room, he could see Thorne holding Sinclair down with his hand locked onto the side of the man's head. Sinclair's initial wriggling had stopped and he was now quietly sobbing to himself. Salazar gestured for Thorne to turn the man round and stand him up. Salazar wanted to look directly at him. Sinclair looked so disappointingly ordinary; not at all like the monster they believed him to be. But then Salazar had been around long enough to know they rarely did. The distraught Sinclair was shaking and crying as realisation dawned, though Salazar thought he also detected just a hint of relief. It was all over at last.

"You may have promised her she wouldn't regret it. I'm here to promise you that you will."

Sinclair turned his face away. Thorne forced it back towards his senior officer.

"Christopher Sinclair – or should I say, Edward Shepherd – I'm arresting you in connection with the death of Irina Kostyshyn. You do not have to say anything; but it may harm your defence if you do not mention when questioned, something which you later rely on in court. Anything you do say may be given in evidence. But then given you're also a hot shot lawyer, you probably know all of that."

Sinclair remained silent. Salazar nodded to two of the uniformed officers.

"Get him out of here."

CHAPTER FIFTY-FIVE

THE KNOCK ON his office door startled Jack Munday. For the first time he could ever remember, Mike Sheridan entered without waiting to be asked. Jack knew immediately the reason for the knock and still couldn't wait for the news to be imparted.

"Danny Thorne just called. It's all done. Sinclair's in custody. Lesley's all okay. He's going to get her to call you in a few minutes. DS Salazar is on his way back to brief you."

Jack hadn't been prepared for quite how sweeping the wave of relief that overcame him would be. He couldn't marry the elation of knowing that Lesley was safe with having to stifle an emotional overload that had him on the brink of tears. The fact that Christopher Sinclair was in custody seemed almost incidental. Now all he wanted in the world was to hear Lesley's voice. He passed his mobile from hand to hand as though it'd become too hot to handle.

The young officer hadn't left the room, but Jack certainly wanted him gone before Lesley called. He didn't need to be seen as a quivering, loved-up wreck.

"Thank you, Mike. That's great."

Sheridan stood his ground. Jack threw him a quizzical look.

"There was something else, guv."

"About Lesley?"

"No, sir. About the missing boy."

Jack waited, fearing something dreadful.

"You asked us to look into everyone present on the day that Danny Carter drowned?"

Jack nodded.

"So, I've just had some information that may or may not be useful."

"Mike, unless you tell me what it is, I'll never be able to decide."

Sheridan swallowed nervously. "One of the kids there that day, Timothy Swain, went on to become a primary school teacher himself."

"And?"

"And two months ago, one of the children in a class he'd taken to a swimming lesson drowned accidentally. There was no question of him being responsible but apparently he struggled badly to come to terms with what happened."

Munday's adrenaline surged.

"Where is he now?"

"That's just the point. He vanished a few weeks ago. Nobody has seen him or heard from him since. Just packed a bag, jumped in his car and left."

"His car?"

Sheridan nodded. "A small dark blue Ford Fiesta."

"Fuck me, Mike. I think we might get this kid back after all. Call DS Duggan and get everybody who's available into the office now. We need to find this guy. No time off until we bring this kid home."

CHAPTER FIFTY-SIX

HE HAD OPTIONS; of course he had. Not all of them were palatable, perhaps, but they were options, nonetheless. He could leave immediately and once he was a good distance away, he could send Matthew Baines another Facebook message from the Danny Carter account telling him where his son was. That way, they could quickly find him and get him back and that would be the end of it. Except, of course, it wouldn't be. The police would look for him. He'd still be a hunted man, forever on the run, always looking over his shoulder and wondering if every apparently innocent question was a loaded one, was the one that would hand him over. He hadn't meant any harm though he doubted anyone would believe him. How could he explain it to people? How could he cope with the look of revulsion and disappointment on the faces of those who were the centre of his world only a few weeks ago? Running might be the slightly more attractive option out of a batch of unattractive choices, but where could he go?

It had begun as an ordinary day, like the thousand before it. Some of his colleagues regarded swimming as something of a lesser lesson, a bit of light relief from the constant drive on literacy and numeracy. But ever since that day as an eleven year old when he had watched his school friend drown, swimming, for Tim Swain, had been every bit as important a life skill as reading, writing and being able to count. Without telling colleagues or parents why, he had been almost evangelical in his determination to help their children swim.

It had no real bearing, of course, on what had happened all those years ago. Danny Carter could swim. He couldn't put right what had happened to Danny, the best he could probably do was to make sure the children in his charge were well equipped to be safe in the water.

He'd sat by the side of the pool and listened to the joyous sounds of the children playing in the water before the lesson started. The echoing hall made their laughter feel as if it was bouncing off the walls and booming around the room, three times louder than it actually was. Some of the children slapped their hands palms down on the water to splash their friends, ignoring calls from the side for them to stop. Others played with polystyrene floats whilst two or three practised their breaststroke, trying to get the rhythm of arms and legs moving like a frog's, working perfectly together. Some were successful, others less so.

Tim wished he was able to say what Jordan had been doing at that point but the young lad with the mop of blond hair and the cheeky smile had been one of thirty and, at that moment, Tim had no more reason to focus on him than any other child in the group. He wished he had, of course, because twelve hours later, when he found himself sitting with Jordan's devastated parents, their world turned on its head, their future forever changed and their son's stolen away, his tears flowing as freely as their own, he would have given anything to be able to tell them every tiny detail of Jordan's last hour on earth. But he couldn't and it haunted him.

From the moment that Jordan's body had been spotted, Tim had rushed from his seat to get the other children out of the water and back into the changing room. He couldn't bear the thought of them watching from the side as he had been left to all those years ago. With the class secure and being comforted by colleagues, he took it upon himself to accompany Jordan to the hospital. Suddenly, the boy who had been so alive and so vibrant an hour earlier looked so small, so vulnerable and almost violated as the paramedics, in their bottle green uniforms, moved around him with composed urgency. Tim sat frozen. As he looked at Jordan, all he could see was Danny. The pain of 1975 began to overwhelm him. It rose up from deep inside, with a power he'd never previously experienced. He started to shake, so violently that one of the paramedics started to work on him rather than on Jordan. He implored her to stop, pushing her away, urging her to leave him alone and return to the young boy prone on the gurney behind her. She crouched down onto her haunches, clasped her hand around Tim's knees and looked up into his eyes.

"He's gone, I'm so sorry. There's nothing more we can do for him, but we can do something for you. So let me help you."

Somehow, in that instant, the horrifying realisation of history repeating made him instinctively know he had to get away. Not immediately, perhaps, but get as far away as he could as soon as he could.

The moment he left Jordan's parents, he took a taxi back to the school and climbed into his car. It felt so claustrophobic that he struggled to calm himself enough to breathe. In the darkness he sobbed. For all these years he had carried with him the pain of the day that Danny died. But now it had well and truly broken free and its liberation frightened him. He turned the key in the ignition, rubbed his eyes, inhaled deeply in an effort to stabilise his breathing and pulled the small hatchback away from the school and towards the flow of evening traffic. And then the pain, the memories and the anger took control.

Tim approached the junction at which, every night for more years than he cared to remember, he had turned left towards the town centre and his home. Except tonight he didn't. Swerving erratically across the road, he cut in front of a silver Mercedes, causing the driver to stamp heavily on his brakes and swear at him out of the window, pushing through the lights and off to the right just at the moment when amber gave way to red. He had no idea where he was going, but rather had an overpowering sense that he had to make things right for Danny and, yes, for Jordan.

He drove all night and when he became frustrated by the missed calls and the tones alerting him to incoming text messages from friends and colleagues anxious to know where he was, he pressed the button to lower the passenger side window and threw his mobile phone out onto the grass verge that he was speeding past. They may report him missing but, whilst they would no doubt be sympathetic, the police were unlikely to do too much. He was a grown man who had chosen to go away. There was nothing really for them to investigate. He hadn't committed a crime. Yet.

It was time to bring everything out into the open. It was time to open Pandora's Box and right now he didn't care much for what the consequences might be. For the first time he could ever remember, Tim Swain felt as if he was dictating events. For the first time he could ever remember, Tim Swain was in control.

CHAPTER FIFTY-SEVEN

SINCE SPEAKING TO Lesley, Jack had been reminding himself to play it cool if others in the station saw them together. When the moment came, all such caution went out of the window as she fell exhausted into his arms. He clutched her tightly and kissed the top of her head, trying to stifle his own tears of relief that all had gone as well as anybody could have hoped. Just because they were professionals didn't mean they weren't allowed to worry. It wouldn't have been the first time that something had gone tragically wrong. Just the thought of it, and the sense of being powerless to affect events, added to the anxiety that now flowed freely from their bodies.

Jenny Jacobs stood beside Harry Duggan and smiled at the sight of them further down the corridor. A ripple of applause built from among the team, though neither Jack nor Lesley appeared aware. To his slight alarm, Harry realised that his Superintendent had clutched his arm. He stiffened his posture and straightened his back almost as a default reaction.

"For never was a story of more woe
Than this of Juliet and her Romeo."

Harry turned towards her, perplexed. Jenny just smiled in reply.

"Take them home, DS Duggan. I think they've earned a few hours off together. We can call him if anything happens with the boy."

CHAPTER FIFTY-EIGHT

THE FOLLOWING MORNING, as he stood in the bagging area, piling the newly-purchased food and drinks into a blue and white Tesco carrier, Tim Swain tried to conduct himself as normally as possible in an effort not to arouse suspicion. The reality, though, was that nobody was paying him particular attention, except for Paul Price, who stood in the queue some places behind him, clutching a boxed cheese and tomato sandwich and a bottle of sparkling water. Jack Munday had resisted calls to circulate a photograph of Timothy Swain to the media, at least in the short term, for fear that it might spook him into running. Instead, he remained convinced that Leo was being held comparatively locally and, with Jenny Jacobs' approval, had swamped the streets with as many plain clothes officers as he was able to muster to try and see if they could spot him. The officers were everywhere: in stations, on buses, in shopping malls and supermarkets. It was Tim Swain's shuffling, hunched demeanour –

walking as though consciously avoiding showing anyone his face – that first interested Paul Price. The man seemed agitated, glancing around nervously, wearing a heavy coat and a woolly hat pulled down on what was by no means a cold day. Price had got up from the bench and had begun to follow the man who seemed strangely intent on making himself appear anonymous. He needed to get a clearer view to work out if this was Timothy Swain or just another of the growing number of people in the town centre that it seemed that life had forgotten.

Price went into the same shops, even had a coffee at the far end of the same cafe. When the man removed the hat to scratch a patch in his unwashed hair, Price took a surreptitious picture on his mobile phone that he shared with Munday. Together they decided that this looked too much like Tim Swain to be a coincidence but, together, they also decided not to move in with reinforcements just yet. Price wanted to stay close and follow him further to see where the journey led.

As Swain paid in the supermarket, Price ditched his sandwich and drink to the tutting displeasure of other shoppers in the queue and followed him out at a distance. Swain walked at an unnatural pace and with a curious lopsided gait. The handles of the carrier bag were wrapped tightly around his hand almost like a dog's lead out on a long walk. It seemed to be an aimless, directionless journey, walking for the sake of walking, and Price began to wonder whether the surveillance would lead anywhere at all. *Perhaps*, he even thought, *it would be better just to pick him up and see what information they could get out of him.* Munday feared that if they did and he refused to speak they would be no nearer to finding Leo Baines. Not once did Swain turn and look over his shoulder; not once did he speed up in an effort to break free and get away, and not once did Paul Price have to take evasive action to avoid being seen. As agitated as he seemed, Tim Swain appeared to be wrapped in his own world, preoccupied with his thoughts rather than what was happening immediately around him.

Keeping a distance, Price gave Munday a running commentary of his pursuit over the phone. He was assured that back-up was nearby and could be with him in minutes as soon as he felt the time was right to move in. Price valued the responsibility; his relationship with Munday had always been professional but slightly distant, but he liked the feeling now of being the one to decide how events should play out.

Swain crossed the road, weaving between cars travelling in both directions caught stationary at red traffic lights, incurring the wrath of one BMW driver for having the temerity to touch the bonnet of his car as he did so. Swain looked at the driver as if he had seen a ghost, held two hands up in apology and continued his disjointed journey.

Price followed, continuing along a parade of shops, past a newsagent, a convenience store, a Turkish barber and a boutique that seemed completely out of keeping with the rest of the area. At the end of the street, for the first time, Swain stopped and looked over his shoulder. Paul Price turned his body away and examined the watches in a jeweller's window. He could only dream of one day earning enough to own one. As Swain continued, so Price began to follow again, speeding up a little as Swain turned right and began to walk up a gentle hill.

After fifty yards Swain stopped beside a wall of corrugated iron. Price spoke into his mobile to update the listening Munday as Swain pulled one part of the iron sheet forward and stepped through the gap.

Price followed, in front of him lay a disused car park and up ahead a boarded-up 1970s style two-storey building of light brick and peeling white paintwork.

"It's an old leisure centre," Price informed. "He's only been holding him at a fucking swimming pool."

"We'll be with you in five."

"Make it discreet, though. Hold back a bit. Let me go in. We don't want to freak him out so he runs."

"Paul, wait until we're there. He might be armed."

"He's got a Tesco's carrier bag, boss. What's he going to do, hit me round the head with a box of Coco Pops? No, I'm going in now. You just back me up when you get here."

Munday heard the phone click silent. As much as he hated not being in control, he also knew that in the same situation, he would have made exactly the same decision.

Price ran towards the door through which he had seen

Tim Swain enter a few minutes earlier. He held his breath in case the door creaked when he opened it as if, bizarrely, that would have made any difference.

The reception area gave the impression of having been evacuated suddenly; clipboards with paper attached littered the desk, posters on notice boards were torn but still hanging at untidy angles where drawing pins had fallen or been removed. An empty vending machine, the glass cracked but not broken, stood isolated in the corner. He had no idea how long it had been since the place had been in regular use, but he was sure he could still detect the smell of chlorine lingering in the air. But where in this yawning space could Tim Swain be holding Leo Baines?

As quietly as possible he followed the signs towards the swimming pool, passing an open door, the notice on which indicated it had once been a gym. All equipment had been removed, save for one blue crash mat that had been torn savagely from one corner to the opposite. To his left as he walked down a bare brick passageway where a series of windows that acted as a viewing gallery of sorts over the empty pit that had once been the pool, littered with broken tiles and dirt from who knew where. In the farthest corner where, presumably, swimmers would once have entered from the changing area, he caught a fleeting glimpse of a man moving.

He checked his mobile to make sure it was switched to silent and began to type a text message to Munday.

"Pretty sure he has him in the changing rooms. I'm creeping my way down."

"We're two minutes out, Paul. Wait."

Price looked at the message, smiled to himself and ignored it. At the far end of the passageway a door led to a staircase signposted down to the changing rooms. His heart beat so fast he thought it might be him needing medical attention once this all played out, rather than the boy. The muscles in his legs had tightened, making it harder to walk down the stairs than it should have been. He told himself to pull things together. He could see another door at the foot of the stairs. Maybe Munday was right; maybe he should have waited for backup. The inquest could wait for later. He was committed now.

He tiptoed down the stairs in an exaggerated fashion to avoid making any kind of noise, extending the length of his legs with each step and ensuring he placed his feet flat, firmly but softly on the surface of each step. The last thing he wanted was to alert Tim Swain to his presence until ready to do so. Price was armed with nothing more than his instinct. How useful that would be, only the next few minutes would tell. Removing the element of surprise could throw the onus back to Swain and place Price in a particularly vulnerable position. His mobile vibrated as he reached the foot of the stairs. Munday had arrived with reinforcements. He replied with all that he knew and much that he didn't and told him what he was going to do next. The Superintendent would have called it 'joined up thinking'.

Price returned the mobile to his inside jacket pocket and, with both hands gripped tightly around the large, dark blue plastic handle, pulled the door an inch or two open towards him. It made a similar sound to air being released from a vacuum. He stopped absolutely still just in case it alerted anyone inside. It didn't appear to. He leaned in, craned his ear towards the opening and tried to make out the muffled sound of voices… or was it just one voice… coming from the all-tiled echo chamber that once had been the men's changing room. He stepped forward, opening the door just wide enough to squeeze his frame through. He turned and closed the door behind himself as softly as he could, crouching a little as he inched forward towards the main body of the room. He looked down – why oh why hadn't he thought to wear a black shirt this morning rather than a gleaming white one? Anything that would have made him fade into the shadows would have been welcome now.

The voice was becoming a little clearer. Paul Price strained to make out the conversation.

"You have to eat. You can't not eat. That's not right. If you don't eat, Leo, you'll get sick."

Price reached into his pocket to retrieve his mobile and tap out a message to Munday.

> *Confirmed. Leo here. Listening to Swain telling him he has 2 eat. Am going to try and get closer. Where are u?*
>
> *Fire exit from changing rooms 2 car park. We are outside waiting to kick the door in. How do u want to do this?*

Am going to get closer, try and approach from behind. When I call his name, I'll do it loud. When you hear it, you come in?

Agreed.

Just don't leave me standing on my own with him like a twat.

As if.

Price crept forward, leaning against a tiled wall that signalled the barrier to what had once been a shower area. He looked around the corner and could clearly see Tim Swain's back, his hat now removed, crouching, laying food out in front of a boy who was seated on the floor, his eyes covered with a cloth and hands tied behind him. At one point, Swain tried to force the corner of a sandwich to the boy's mouth, Leo turned his head sharply to his right.

"Leo, this isn't going to work. You can't refuse to eat. You have to eat. I *want* you to eat. I don't want you to get sick."

The boy spoke.

"What do you care? I want to go home. I want to go home." As Leo repeated the line, Paul Price was certain the boy had started to cry.

"You *are* going to go home. I promise you."

The boy turned his head back towards Swain's voice.

"When?"

"Soon, I promise. I just need to work a few things out first."

Paul Price had heard enough. He kept his body tight to the tiled wall and moved himself around so that he stood around ten metres behind Timothy Swain, ready to step out into the open to confront him. Across the far side of the room, he could see double doors with a Fire Exit sign, behind which he expected that Jack Munday and other colleagues were waiting. He just hoped they'd be able to hear him. He inhaled once to steady his nerves and stepped forward from the wall.

"Tim Swain, stay exactly where you are."

Swain turned, a look of disbelief and confusion on his face, glancing first one way and then the next as if his brain was trying and failing to process what was happening or what his next move should be. The indecision kept him rooted to the spot. Much to Price's relief, the double doors were kicked open and a dozen uniformed officers, lead by Duggan and Sheridan, now filled the room. Munday casually strolled in behind them.

Duggan crouched down by Leo Baines, who was visibly shaking, and lifted the cloth from his eyes, watching as he adjusted as much to the light as he did to the scene in front of him. He looked at Duggan with suspicion and then glanced around the room.

"Leo, my name's Harry," Duggan whispered, his arm around the boy's shoulder, "we're here to take you home."

Three uniformed officers had Tim Swain in a hold, his hands cuffed behind his back, his rights read to him and ready to be taken away. He looked directly at Leo and mouthed that he was sorry. Leo knew he should have hated him but he felt nothing. The largest of the uniformed officers noticed the attempt at communication and clasped the back of Tim Swain's head with the palm of his hand and pushed him forward.

"Shut the fuck up, arsewipe. Save your talking for the interview room."

Munday walked across the room towards Paul Price, who was sitting on a low, tiled wall. The adrenalin had left him exhausted.

"That was a brilliant piece of work." He offered his hand for Price to shake. "Go get yourself a coffee, write me a report of what happened for the record and then sod off home and get some rest."

Price smiled. He wanted something more.

"If it's okay with you, I'd rather hang around. I'd like to be in the room when you interview him."

There was nothing Munday admired more than ambition.

"Square the circle?"

"Kind of."

Munday smiled at him.

"Okay, take the boy back with Harry and get him checked out by the doctors. I'll go with Mike and tell the parents we've found him and we'll bring them down to the station. We can make a start with Mr Swain in the morning."

"Thanks boss."

CHAPTER FIFTY-NINE

"It's not Matthew's fault, you know. You can't keep blaming him forever."

"Is that so?"

Susie was not in the mood for one of her mother's lectures, but she had a horrible feeling she was going to get one regardless. The anxiety of the past couple of days had given way to exhaustion and, despite her best efforts to retain a positive outlook; she was starting to believe she would never see her child again. It wasn't the time for a sermon from Cynthia.

"I know things between you and Matthew haven't been great, but *he's* not the person who has taken Leo. *That's* the person you need to focus your anger on. Believe me, Matthew's hurting every bit as much as you are, maybe even more so because you seem hell bent on making him feel responsible for what's happened."

"And how do you know so much about how Matthew's feeling?"

"Well," Cynthia replied, pulling a chair away from the kitchen table and sitting down next to her daughter, "I've actually taken the time to ask him."

She picked a small photograph from a pile spread out on the table in front of them, pushed it in front of her daughter and began to smile. It depicted a small boy in swimming trunks, his skins splattered with white sun cream, standing on a sandy beach in the sunshine.

"Broadstairs, I think. That was a lovely day."

Susie took the picture and started to cry.

"I just want him back. I want to hold him, to make him his favourite dinner, to watch a stupid DVD with him or let him beat me at a video game I don't care about. He's my child and I just want to protect him."

"And you're mine and that's all I want to do as well. Let me tell you, age is irrelevant when it comes to a parent's instinct to protect their child."

Holding the photograph close to her chest, Susie fell back against her mother and began to sob. Cynthia wrapped her arms around her daughter and kissed her on the forehead. The phone hadn't rung for a while and, in the absence of knowing what to say, some of their friends had started to stay away. They pretended it was to give Susie and Matt some privacy, some space but, in truth, for some it was more to avoid drowning in the prevailing sadness that had enveloped the house.

When the knock on the door came, it startled them both, not so much breaking the silence as shattering it completely. Susie jumped and Matt returned from the garden where he was alone with a black coffee and his own disturbing thoughts. He placed his mug on the table and made eye contact with his wife. It was the possibilities of extremes – the best news or the worst – that made them most anxious.

Susie pushed open the wooden kitchen door as widely as it would go and watched Matt walk down the hallway towards the silhouettes of two men behind the stained-glass panes set into the doorframe. She hadn't noticed it previously, but Leo's scooter was propped up at an angle against the right-hand wall, its handle bar lodged against the top of a radiator.

Matt opened the door. She could see the Inspector who had been before and a younger, less familiar officer. Matt stood back and ushered them into the house. Susie joined them. The tension that gripped her meant she didn't notice the smile on Jack Munday's face.

"We've found him."

Susie folded in on herself, collapsing in a heap on the floor. Her crying was so intense she barely had time or room to breathe. Cynthia bent down to hold her and to persuade her to sit back on the chair. Matt, tears pouring down his cheeks, stood in the hall, his head leaning against the wall. Munday gripped him by the upper arm and guided him to a seat as well.

"And is he alive?"

"He's alive. He probably needs a good meal, a proper

bed and because he's been sitting down for so long, he might have a bit of trouble walking for a little while but, yes, he's basically okay. We've taken him to the station where we have a doctor waiting to check him out."

"Can we see him?"

"Of course. We'll take you there soon."

Matthew turned to Susie and held her close. He tried as hard as he could to control himself. He didn't want her to see him cry, but that was really all she wanted to see.

"Where has he been?" Matthew asked. "Was it connected to the messages?"

Munday nodded. Susie pushed back away from her husband. Munday watched as Susie's mother escorted her away to wash and change and prepare to see her son again.

"He's been held inside a disused leisure centre on the other side of town. In the changing rooms of the…"

"…swimming pool?" Matthew made the connection instantly.

"The swimming pool," Munday confirmed.

"And the person who took him? Do you have him?"

Jack nodded, but didn't provide a name. He wanted their focus to be on Leo and, to be honest, to be on each other and to leave dealing with everything else to him.

"We're still confirming exactly who he is. We have him in custody and we'll be sitting down to question him later. The important thing is that Leo is safe."

"But you have an idea of who he is?"

"We do."

"I'd like to know. Was it somebody who was there the day Danny died?"

Munday nodded.

"Tell me, Inspector. I'm not going to go to the press about it. I just need to know."

Munday sucked some air in through his teeth as he considered Matthew's request. "If I tell you, you breathe a word to nobody until I tell you that you can; not even your closest friends and family?"

Matthew nodded.

"We believe his name is Timothy Swain."

"Tim Swain," Matthew repeated. He said the name again and again as if to mask his disbelief. "Tim Swain was a nothing."

"Well, that was thirty-odd years ago and maybe now he thinks he's a something."

"Has he said why?"

Munday shook his head.

"That's what we'll be talking to him about, but we know he's had a traumatic few weeks himself. He's a primary school teacher and he recently lost a pupil to drowning during a swimming lesson. It seems as if it brought it all back to him and maybe caused some kind of breakdown."

"But that doesn't explain the kidnapping and it doesn't explain why Leo."

"No, it doesn't and, as I said, we will try and get to the bottom of that. Your focus now should be on Leo and on

Susie. Leave Tim Swain to us."

Matthew locked his hands behind his head, stretched his torso wide and then ran his hands through his hair as if to shake some demons out.

"I want to see him."

"Leo? You will. As soon as Susie comes down, Mike and I will take you both to the station so you can see him."

"No, not Leo. I mean, obviously Leo. But, I mean Tim Swain. I want to see Tim Swain. I want to look him in the eyes and ask him why. I haven't seen him for God knows how many years, so what have I ever done to him that made him want to do this?"

"That's not happening, Matthew. I'm not letting you near him. I will tell you as much as I can as soon as I can, but you need to leave Tim Swain to me and you need to concentrate on Leo, on your family."

Matthew slumped into one of the wooden chairs next to the kitchen table, as if forced down by the enormity of everything that had been imparted in the ten minutes since Munday and Sheridan had knocked on their door. In some ways the relief exhausted him as much as the uncertainty of what would come next.

"Matthew, it's over. It's time to let it go. Why don't you start texting whoever you need to text to let them know that Leo is safe? Spread a little happiness and focus on that rather than worry about Swain." Jack paused for a moment. "There's just one other thing I need to talk to you about."

Matt looked up inquisitively.

"My Millionaire Boyfriend."

"What of it?"

"You never told us it was your business, when we were talking."

"It's not really. It belongs to a guy called Anderson James."

"But you're listed as a director."

"Yes, but I mainly do the marketing and the design. Anderson runs the business."

"Where can we find Mr James?"

"I can give you his mobile number, but I think he's out of the country at the moment. What's all this about?"

Jack sighed. There was only so much excitement he could take at any one time.

"It's in connection with a different case we're working on. We'll need to have a chat with you both in the next week or two."

It didn't register as anything serious with Matt but then, given the news about Leo, nothing would. Matt nodded. He pulled his mobile out of his pocket and began scrolling through his list of contacts to circulate the good news.

SUSIE AND MATT sat in the back of the car on the way to the station. They barely spoke and sat at arm's length, watching the world speed by out of opposite windows. Once, Matthew reached out to try and hold his wife's hand. Their fingers briefly interlocked before she pulled her hand away and laid it, isolated, on her lap. From time to time during the fifteen-minute drive, Munday would try to fill the interminable silence with words of encouragement and support, to try and prepare them for what to expect when they came face to face with Leo again, but even he gave up when they gave him nothing in return.

Munday was used to being with people during some of their lowest moments, had watched as they had clung to each other for encouragement, for support and sometimes for the physical and psychological strength simply to survive the unimaginable. Rarely had he seen a couple so distant at a moment of such emotional intensity and, he had to remind himself, this case had ended in success. How much worse would they have been had the unimaginable come to pass?

Sheridan parked the car and helped them out of the backseat. Munday could see Jenny Jacobs looking from a window, a smile fully stretched across her face. They made eye contact. He nodded in her direction; she returned the greeting and, he was almost certain, winked towards him.

Susie and Matthew Baines seemed leaden-footed, walking as two individuals rather than a couple to be reunited with their son. Munday guided them up a short flight of half a dozen concrete steps and through the police station's back entrance. Susie had started to shake. Matthew tried to place his arm around her shoulder only for her to wrestle herself free almost immediately. They walked along a featureless corridor until Munday turned as they closed on a light wooden door, the same as the previous twenty or thirty they had passed.

"Can I get you a coffee or some water?"

Both Susie and Matthew shook their heads. Matthew offered an appreciative smile. Susie, her gaze resolutely fixed downwards towards the floor, said simply that she only wanted to see her son. Munday nodded, knocked twice on the door, and then reached behind him to grasp the handle. As the door swung back, Susie and Matthew got their first glimpse of Leo, sitting on a blue, bucket-shaped armchair that appeared as if it is was meant to be more uncomfortable than it seemed. In that split second first glance, he looked clean, wearing a white T-shirt, grey tracksuit bottoms and white socks with no trainers. He looked up as he heard the door open and tried to process the sight of the parents he'd begun to believe he would never see again. The initial, unforced smile of excitement quickly gave way to tears of reprieve.

"I'm sorry," he mouthed.

Susie ran forward, pushing past Munday into the room and all but fell on top of her son, clutching at the back of his head and pulling him tightly towards her in a manner that suggested she was never going to let him go again. Matthew watched the scene unfold before him from his position on the threshold. Jack gestured for him to enter, reaching out to grip his shoulder.

"He's your son too," he whispered, leaning in. "You're not responsible for this. Only the guy who took him is responsible and we'll deal with him."

Tears flowed down Matthew's face. Susie helped Leo stand tentatively, encouraging him to grip tightly onto the sides of the chair. Matthew stepped closer still, his body convulsing with a toxic mix of guilt, relief and euphoria. They held each other tight. In that moment, they were a unit again and, for now, only that moment mattered.

"I thought I wouldn't see you again," was the first thing Leo said.

"We never stopped looking," said Matthew. "We weren't going to stop until we brought you home."

"He said he was a friend of yours."

Susie clutched Leo closer as she threw the iciest of stares towards her husband.

"He knew me once," said Matt, "but he's no friend of mine."

The doctor, a late middle aged man in a misshapen pinstripe suit, had finished his examination and was packing his case away when they'd entered. He explained that Leo was exhausted and hungry, but otherwise seemed fine. He had demolished a McDonald's meal and could probably demolish another, but also needed to keep up his fluid intake and get some proper rest. Other than that, he saw no serious issues and so, if all was okay with the police, they could take him home.

Munday gestured to the uniformed officer who stood

in the corner to give them all the time and space they needed and to let him know when they were ready to go home. He captured the image of this family reunited in his mind's eye to remind him one day that this was why he did the job. And then he turned, softly closed the door behind him and restored their privacy to them.

CHAPTER SIXTY

WHEN MUNDAY DROPPED the Baines family back at home, a small welcome party of friends, family and neighbours had hastily erected banners and inflated balloons as a sign of everyone's relief and joy that Leo had been safely returned. A couple of television news crews were present, calling out questions to Matthew and Susie, who simply smiled and gave a thumbs-up to the camera. Once they were inside, Jack had given a brief impromptu interview to confirm nothing more at this stage than they had a man in custody, to commend his fellow officers for their determination to see a happy ending to this distressing story and to thank the public and the media for their support. And with that, he climbed back into the car and let Sheridan drive him back to the station.

Jacobs was waiting for him when he returned and smiled as they moved towards each other for a hug. After what had happened to both Leo and Lesley, Jacobs knew that Jack would likely be emotionally spent. She had poured two small glasses of malt whiskey, one of which she handed to Jack. They clinked glasses.

"Listen to me, mister. You're my knight in shining armour. Don't you forget it."

"Boss?"

"Katharine Hepburn says it to Henry Fonda in *On Golden Pond*. You should see it."

Jack smiled.

"I'll buy the DVD."

"I'm serious Jack, you did good."

"We all did good, boss; all of us. *We* did good."

"How're you going to celebrate? You going to take Lesley out for dinner? I'm sure you could both do with it."

It still seemed odd for him to accept that his relationship with Lesley was now out in the open, though it reminded him even more pertinently that he still needed to tell Elaine. That box needed to be ticked before he could move on with any other plans.

"I'm meeting my wife for dinner. We have things to talk about."

"I can imagine. Well, go easy on yourself and I'll see you tomorrow morning, Detective Inspector."

Munday smiled. She giveth with one hand, she taketh away with another.

"You will, boss."

"Bright and early, Jack. We'll have work to do."

CHAPTER SIXTY-ONE

ELAINE WAS ALREADY waiting at the small corner table when Jack arrived at the restaurant. As he walked through the crowded room, weaving his way past tables of other diners, she placed her glass of sparkling water back on the table and got up to welcome him. In that moment he stopped to think how he should greet her: a handshake seemed too cold, too formal for a woman he had spent half his life with and with whom he had been in bed only weeks earlier, and yet a kiss seemed inappropriate given the information he was going to deliver. He opted instead for the compromise hug, opening his arms wide and welcoming Elaine into his embrace. He couldn't deny that it felt good to be holding her again, not just for the familiarity but because it just felt right. It had always felt right. But thoughts like those had no place in his head and he forced himself to remember that, although part of him would always love her, his future lay with Lesley. He would have to explain that to her as gently and as kindly as he could.

"Been waiting long?"

"Just arrived."

"You look well."

"Why, thank you. You don't look so bad yourself. Good result with the kidnapping. You must be happy?"

Jack poured himself some water but was desperate for something stronger. He looked around for a waiter, trying to make eye contact rather than call out.

"Relieved rather than happy. It's nice when it all works out the way it should. And when it's a kid like that, it seems a bit more personal. I couldn't stop thinking of Connor all the way through."

The waiter, a tall man in his late thirties, arrived unheralded at the table. He had the air of somebody bored with his job and frustrated with having to serve yet another couple. He laid menus before them and offered the wine list, which was politely declined. After summoning him in the first place, Jack now wished he would just go away. If he told Elaine about Lesley straight away, there was the possibility she would fold her napkin and just get up and leave. The last thing he wanted was to create a scene. He ordered a Peroni and another bottle of San Pellegrino for Elaine, which seemed to be enough to send the waiter temporarily scuttling back towards the bar.

"Connor seems to think you could get him some work experience at the station," Elaine began.

"Oh, does he? Well, I think the last thing we need is

another copper in the family."

"I don't think there's much danger of that. There's not enough money in it for him."

"What do you think he'll end up doing?"

"No idea. I think *he* thinks he could be the next Mark Zuckerberg or something. I don't want to shatter his illusions but I'm not sure he's realised that that kind of stuff only happens to one in a million."

"Why shouldn't he be the one? Then he can keep us in the manner in which I intend to become accustomed."

Elaine laughed but it was a nervous laugh. Jack suspected she knew what he wanted to say but he needed more time – and courage – to psych himself up to tell her. She picked up her glass of sparking water, sat back in her chair and looked at Jack almost as though studying him. He returned her smile a little uneasily but hoped she wouldn't notice.

"What?" he asked after a few moments of silence.

"Do you remember what it was like when Connor was born? Do you remember how it felt?"

"Exciting, terrifying, exhilarating, and grown-up all at the same time."

"You forgot exhausting."

"How could I forget exhausting? I don't ever remember feeling so tired, before or since."

"Do you remember when you actually fell asleep in a bowl of cornflakes?"

"Now you're making that up."

"I swear I'm not. Connor had colic or something and was up all night and you took him downstairs so I could get some sleep. You managed to get him off eventually and laid him in his carrycot and obviously decided you had the munchies. I staggered down about seven to find you asleep, face side on in the bowl. I had to gently try and pick drying cornflakes off of your cheek without waking you."

"I honestly don't remember that."

"We were happy then."

Jack smiled, but the last thing he needed was an emotional trip down memory lane. "We were both different people then."

"If we knew then what we know now then maybe…"

They both laughed. The waiter had returned to take their order. Jack's appetite had all but evaporated but, as much for appearance's sake as anything else, he ordered a plate of pasta vongholi. Elaine asked for a salad niçoise. Apparently disappointed that their order wasn't more imaginative and, presumably, more expensive the waiter retreated to the kitchen with a huff that made them smile to each other.

"Have you had any more luck finding a DCI's job?"

Jack shook his head.

"Nothing so far but that's mainly because I don't want to move away. We have a new Superintendent; she's indicated she may not be around for long, so there may be an opportunity when she goes. I'm settled where I am. I'm happy to bide my time a bit longer."

"Don't bide it too long otherwise there'll be other young go-getters coming up behind you."

"You make me sound old. I'm not ready to be pensioned off just yet. How about you?"

Sometimes, Jack thought to himself, small talk can be excruciating between two people who know each other far too well to be indulging in it. When the food arrived the waiter placed it unceremoniously in front of them. The act of eating seemed to stifle conversation for a while until Jack resolved that he needed to bring their discussion around to the matter in hand. Elaine spoke first.

"I know there's something you want to discuss but before we do there's actually something I need to talk to you about."

For no reason he could put his finger on, Jack sensed himself beginning to shake. His chest had started to pound. He smiled as best he could and gestured for Elaine to go on. She sipped from her glass of water and swallowed hard.

"Remember a few months ago when we went out for the night, got a bit drunk and ended up back at mine?"

Oh no, thought Jack, *she's about to profess her undying love just as I'm about to tell her it's already dead.*

"The night we ended up having sex and you threw me out the next morning?"

He tried to keep his voice down. Talking sex in a crowded Italian restaurant rarely went down well with fellow diners.

"I prefer to think of it as making love."

"Given that you threw me out I prefer to think of it as having sex but let's not argue the point."

"Okay, so," she took another sip of water. "There's no easy way to tell you this. It turns out that I'm pregnant."

Jack burst out laughing. Elaine stared back at him with a combined look of anger and hurt.

"That's good, I'll give you that," Jack uttered between laughs, other diners beginning to turn towards them to see what the commotion was all about. "I almost believed you for a second."

Elaine's countenance hadn't changed.

"It's true. I'm pregnant. I'm sorry if it wasn't what you wanted to hear but it's true. I thought you had a right to know."

"Yes… ahem no… I mean, yes, obviously. Fuck, I wasn't expecting that. I mean, how did that happen?"

"You mean you really want me to explain it to you? It looked like you knew the way it worked on the night."

Jack shook his head in disbelief. The waiter, approaching with dessert menus, picked up on the tension and moved away.

"Aren't you on the… you know, on the… pill?

"Yes, but stranger things have happened. Nobody ever said it was a hundred per cent."

"How many weeks?"

"Twelve. I have the first scan next week. I thought you might want to come with?"

"So you're going to keep it?"

"Of course I'm going to keep it. What kind of question is that? And it's not an 'it', this is our second child we're talking about."

"Does Connor know?"

"Of course not. I wouldn't tell him before I'd told you."

Jack shook his head again. And then he remembered Lesley; Lesley, the whole reason for him arranging the dinner with Elaine in the first place. How the hell was he going to explain this to her?

"You never know," Elaine continued, "you may just get what you've been angling for after all."

Jack looked at her quizzically.

"Well, you've been the one saying we should get back together. Maybe this is the time."

He saw the irony in the role reversal that was about to take place.

"I'm not sure getting back together simply because of the baby is the best idea."

They sat in silence a moment longer and then both began to speak at the same time.

"I don't want to bring the baby up alone," Elaine said, at the same time as Jack blurted out – without thinking either long or hard about it, it has to be said – "if you're determined to have the baby then obviously I'll support you."

Jack ran his left hand over his stubble and took a swig

from the Peroni bottle. He hoped that offering support wouldn't be interpreted as anything more.

"Thank you," Elaine whispered, dabbing the corner of one eye with her napkin, reaching out across the table to put her hands in Jack's. His first instinct was to pull back but instead, he found himself leaving his hands where they were.

"Now," Elaine began, energised by what she believed was Jack coming back to her, "I've rather ambushed the evening. You wanted to tell me something. What was it?"

Jack felt cornered. He was sure he was beginning to sweat and, if he'd been prone to hypochondria, he would have been concerned by his racing heartbeat.

At home was the woman to whom he had committed himself, the woman he loved, the woman he knew – or at least he thought he knew – he wanted to be his life partner. He owed it to Lesley to be honest with Elaine but then he would also have to tell Lesley he had slept with Elaine whilst they were together. But then didn't he owe Elaine something too? The reason they were no longer together was because he had treated her badly, had hit her in a moment of madness and now she not only needed him, she wanted him too. Didn't he owe her that? He felt nauseous.

"Come on Jack, don't be shy. What was it you wanted to talk about?"

"It's nothing important. It'll keep. Let's order some coffee."

Dear Reader

Thank you for reading *Know Your Own Darkness*. If you enjoyed this book (or even if you didn't) please consider leaving a star rating or review online. Your feedback is important, and will help other readers to find the book and decide whether to read it, too.

Acknowledgements

I am always grateful for the support of many friends and family for their continued encouragement and enthusiasm, as well as my publishing team, whose constructive criticism during editing makes the finished product far better than it would be without them.

Writing is a very solitary process and handing over a manuscript for people to read for the first time is nerve-wracking so I am thankful to have people around me who will read and give feedback with honest, practical suggestions that only ever enhance the work.

I hope you enjoyed reading it as much as I enjoy writing it.

About the Author

Howard is a part-time author, full time marketer. In his writing, he enjoys taking ordinary people and placing them in extraordinary situations and playing around with the way they would respond. He says it brings out the megalomaniac in him.

His first novel, "The Bitterest Pill", is available in paperback and for ebook formats. Other novels, "Micah Seven Five" and "The Sixth Republic" are also available. Short stories, including "A Time To Mourn & A Time To Dance," "After Twenty Thousand Nights" and "The Conversation" are also available.

He is married, has two grown up children and lives in London.

Find the author via their website:
www.howard-robinson.com

Or tweet at them:
@howardprobinson

More From This Author

Micah Seven Five

"Trust ye not in a friend, put ye not confidence in a guide."

– Micah, Verse 7 Chapter 5

When a sunny morning presents an unnamed corpse stuffed into a black carrier bag and dumped outside a local charity shop, Detective Inspector Jack Munday and his team scramble to piece together the man's identity.

The trail leads them into the excesses of London's highly paid bankers, where a lifestyle of drugs, sex, risk-taking and flamboyant living come easily.

Doing his best to keep his messy personal life from affecting his job, Munday works to uncover the surprising past of a now-powerful cohort, whose present mission is to keep the Detective away from uncovering the uncomfortable truth behind the uncharitable murder.

Available from all major online and offline outlets.

Lightning Source UK Ltd.
Milton Keynes UK
UKHW041205301120
374347UK00002B/93